Elizabeth Gill

The Foundling School for Girls

Quercus

First published in Great Britain in 2019
This edition published in 2019 by

Quercus Editions Ltd
Carmelite House
50 Victoria Embankment
London EC4Y 0DZ

An Hachette UK company

A CIP catalogue record for this book is available
from the British Library

PB ISBN 978 1 78747 338 6
EBOOK ISBN 978 1 78747 336 2

10 9 8 7 6 5 4 3 2 1

Typeset by CC Book Production

Printed and bound in Great Britain by Clays Ltd, Elcograf S.p.A.

Papers used by Quercus are from well-managed forests and other responsible sources.

We hope you enjoy this book. Please return or renew it by the due date.

You can renew it at www.norfolk.gov.uk/libraries or by using our free library app.

Otherwise you can phone 0344 800 8020 - please have your library card and PIN ready.

You can sign up for email reminders too.

NORFOLK COUNTY LIBRARY
WITHDRAWN FOR SALE

NORFOLK ITEM

30129 083 537 614

Elizabeth Gill was born in Newcastle upon Tyne and as a child lived in Tow Law, a small mining town on the Durham fells. She has been a published author for more than thirty years and has written more than forty books. She lives in Durham City, likes the awful weather in the northeast and writes best when rain is lashing the windows.

Also by Elizabeth Gill

Available in paperback and ebook

Miss Appleby's Academy
The Fall and Rise of Lucy Charlton
Far From My Father's House
Doctor of the High Fells
Nobody's Child
Snow Angels
The Guardian Angel
The Quarryman's Wife

Available in ebook only

Shelter from the Storm
The Pit Girl
The Foundryman's Daughter
A Daughter's Wish
A Wartime Wish
The Hat Shop Girl
The Landlord's Daughter

. . . and many more!

For Sylvia Betty, beautiful, generous and kind.

Prologue

Her mother called out to her from the door.

'I'm going now, Ruth.'

Ruth would have said goodbye and even held her mother, though her mother would not want to hold her. Her mother never wanted to hold anything or anybody; when Ruth reached the outside door of the house, her mother had already set off down the path towards Stanhope.

She had said earlier that she was going to the village, but she was always saying that and never going. Ruth's father did not like either of them to go out, other than to bring in milk from the cow, vegetables from the garden or to feed the hens.

Ruth watched her mother's skinny form until she could see it no more. She worried, because if her mother did not get back before her father came home from the quarry at the end of the day, he would shout and swear. She comforted herself that tomorrow was Christmas Day, even though he would have been paid and he would probably go to the Grey Bull. It was the pub at the bottom of the hill, and there he would spend as much of his wages as he could drink while still being able to climb up Crawleyside and fall in at the front door; it was not something to be looked forward to.

Ruth stood at the door after her slight, grey mother was out of sight. She knew that her mother had been stealing from his pockets for months. She told Ruth it was so that they could have a decent Christmas, because otherwise they would have as little as they always had. They always had to make do because he gave her mother so little to keep them and yet he complained. But Ruth was not convinced. Her mother often took money from him and so far there were no signs that this Christmas Day would be better than any other.

She let go of her breath. She decided that she would make everything right for her mother coming home. She cleaned and swept, she saw to the animals, she kept the fire going and the kettle on the boil and she kept herself busy. Yet her mother was gone such a long time.

She had gone off shortly after her father had left in the morning and she was not back by mid-afternoon. Ruth thought that perhaps she was enjoying this rare freedom and had stayed in Stanhope. Ruth could not remember the last time they had been to chapel though her mother assured her that they had gone at one time. Now her father did not want them to go, but her mother probably remembered people in the village and maybe had even spent time with them. Ruth never did. She tried not to begrudge her mother the contact just because she had no contact herself. Her mother deserved a little time, so she made sure that when her mother came home she would have nothing to do.

As the sun set very early, she locked up the hens, saw to the fire and made sure everything was right so that her mother could come home to tea. Ruth had even made a cake; she sat and waited.

The sun went down, it set, the darkness came on soon as it

always did at that time of the year. Ruth hated how the darkness covered the land as though it was suffocating it. By four it was pitch-black, and she did not like to use candles or the oil in the lamp because there was so little left.

She did build up the fire, thinking that both her parents might come back together. That they had never done so before did not deter her. They might and she would be there, and it would be Christmas and the Christ child would be born. She thought it was such a lovely idea that she dozed but when she awoke the fire was almost out and she was still alone.

She was worried now that her mother did not return. She listened and listened and nothing happened. She couldn't eat, she couldn't drink. She went into the tiny room which was hers but she didn't sleep. She had no idea what time it was, just that she should let the fire down. Had something happened to her mother? Had something happened so that her father did not come back?

She lay there awake and longed for the light of the next day. The night seemed endless. She was convinced that her mother had died.

Ruth had never liked her parents. She knew that it was sinful not to love the people who had given you life. She knew enough of the Bible to be aware that you must honour your father and mother, but she didn't know what more she could do. Her parents were unhappy. She felt as though she had caused it. Daily her mother told her that they would have had a much better time of it had she never been born. As though there was something she could do about that. Maybe she should have been able to. Maybe she should have walked out and put herself into the river if they disliked her that much.

Her mother called her hair 'that devil'. Ruth knew that her hair was a very strange colour, so red that it looked like the fire. Her mother brushed it and combed it and Ruth cursed it because it was always full of knots. Every time her mother brushed her hair, it hurt, so she hated her hair too.

There were no mirrors in the house, no looking glass, so she had no idea what she looked like, but her mother convinced her that she was the plainest girl in the world and would never get a husband. Ruth thought her chances of marrying were few since she never saw a man or a boy. Besides, if marriage was like that her parents had, who on earth would want it? Though she had no idea what else life could hold. Were things worse in other places? She couldn't imagine it somehow.

Ruth thought her mother plain so if she looked like her mother she must be awful. Her mother was skinny, with sunken cheeks, and she wore the kind of pinny which came up over her shoulders and fastened at the back of her waist so that it covered her dress completely. She never took it off, except presumably when she went to bed.

Her mother cooked and baked and cleaned and knitted and did crochet work and embroidery and she taught Ruth to do all these things. The only book they had in the house was the Bible and Ruth was not allowed to read. Her mother didn't read and didn't see why women should. Her father did not approve of such things. In the evenings on Sundays he read the Bible to them, but haltingly because he didn't know many of the words. Ruth suspected he made it up from the garish pictures which illustrated the book.

They lived on what was called The Velvet Path because of the heather that covered it so smoothly in August, above Stanhope near Crawleyside. Her father worked at the quarry there. Sometimes he would bring home his pay. More often he went into Stanhope and drank it. Her mother would wait fretfully by the door until he came back and fell in and then she would extract any copper that was left from his pockets.

Her parents shouted at one another. She found things to do when they did this. She went outside or started sewing or knitting. She liked best the piece of land which was as sheltered as anything got up there near their tiny cottage. It stood below the house and she grew vegetables there. She couldn't remember a time when she didn't grow things. It was the only pleasurable thing in her life. Life was duty and nothing to do with pleasure, her father said very often, so why it was that he drank she did not know. She and her mother got no pleasure from that and there was often nothing to eat so she presumed he did it for his own pleasure.

The house was built of stone and her father said proudly that his ancestors had lived there for hundreds of years. She thought he was wrong. The house was owned by Mr Forster who owned a great number of small farms in the area, but she didn't think any of them could be that old. Perhaps it was true, stone wellbuilt there lasted.

She didn't know why her father would be pleased about that. She had thought they should try and get away to better places, but it was a disgrace to do that, so her father said. You were stuck in one place because God had allowed your ancestors to build here. You would be accepted nowhere else, her father said, because you did not belong. This was their home and they must cling to it and look after it.

Everything seemed to fail up there. A fox killed the chickens. Sheep suffocated in the snow. Their only cow ate something which blew up its stomach and it died with its legs in the air. Ruth felt as though they were doomed never to have anything go right, and in time, she thought, you got used to that.

So her mother went down to the village, ignoring what her husband had said about not going, that he would bring back what he could. She would go down and make sure they had something to eat for their Christmas dinner.

Ruth lay in bed in the half-light with the fire almost out since the wood was low, and waited, worrying that her mother would come back to the darkness. Perhaps something might happen to her on the way. Nothing happened until her father came back, drunk and singing as ever, and then he fell in at the door.

Shutting it, she left him there. That was what her mother had always done. In the morning he would wake up and know where he was and be amazed that he had yet again climbed that hill to get back to his house. He always said the same thing. How he had got there he would never know. Ruth was so tired of hearing this.

In the mid-morning she could hear him yelling her mother's name and then he came out of the bedroom; it was the only bedroom of any size. Her room was tiny and had nothing in it but a narrow bed. He had no doubt made his way there some-time in the night. He came out shouting for her and calling for her and then he said, 'Where is she?'

'I don't know. She went out yesterday and didn't come back.'

He so obviously didn't believe her, as though her mother was under the bed or had gone outside into the frosty morning.

'Is she collecting the eggs?'

'I said, she didn't come back from Stanhope.'

'What was she doing in Stanhope?' he said, as though the place were a hellhole.

'She said she was getting some things for today.'

'What things?'

'For Christmas Day.'

'You didn't tell me.'

She wouldn't contradict him. There was no point. He would have knocked her across the room. She said nothing. He gazed all around, then he went outside and she could hear him shouting.

'May! May!' He went on shouting from time to time all the rest of the day and then he fell back into bed and slept.

The following morning, he went to the village, and presumably to the pub. When he came back in the middle of the night he shouted his wife's name over and over again and when he didn't find her he came into his daughter's room. She sat up suddenly at the intrusion, but he came over to the bed and pushed her down. She shrieked and cried and said that she was not May, she was Ruth, but he didn't hear her. She didn't think he could hear anything.

She screamed and fought but he was a big man and she was very slight. This could not be happening to her. He had never done such a thing before and she was almost fourteen. In all those years, he had never touched her except to knock her down when he was angry and drunk, and that didn't happen so very often. He pushed open her legs and put himself into her. Her body recoiled at the pain and the intrusion and it got worse, and hurt more and more as he went on, despite her screams. Ruth thought she had died and gone to hell. She screamed and wept and tried with all her might to push him away. She was horrified but he took no notice and held her down.

Whatever he was doing to her, it was disgusting and awful, and went on and on until she thought that it would never stop. Then he grunted and shoved and shoved and then stopped suddenly and after a few seconds – though it felt like forever – he took his disgusting thing out of her, did more grunting and then left her as suddenly as he had come to her.

Ruth could not believe it. She went on disbelieving it, trying to convince herself that she had had the most awful dream of her life, but the bed was bloody and she was in a lot of pain. The pain did not go away, inside and outside, and she could do nothing more than lie there, fearing he might come back and in his drunken state maybe do it to her again. But as she lay there in the darkness, waiting and not daring to move, she could hear him snoring. He went on snoring. When daylight eventually arrived in a thick snowstorm which blotted everything out, she got up as usual and lit the fire. When she had sufficient hot water, she put a hot cloth between her legs and washed herself. It stung and she was in a lot of pain, but it did help. Then she stripped her bed and got rid of the bloody sheet.

One

Ten Years Earlier

Jay Gilbraith remembered nothing before the streets. He did not know who had given him his name. There must have been a mother at some time. Maybe she had died. Maybe she had weaned him, and taught him not to piss or crap in his pants, because he didn't, and he ate food and drank water, but that was all. No matter how often he struck at his memory, he could find nothing.

Nobody had taken him in. Why would they when he was just a ragged child and there were so many? They slept where they could, ate what they could find on the ground or steal. Often he had to fight for bread and he learned to sleep anywhere, no matter what the weather. You had to learn to look after yourself. He stole a knife from an ironmonger and learned to use it.

There were men who had you, literally, and used you badly, so you had to learn to hide; he had become very good at such things. He was quick, and though he was tall, he was light and could use his fists and dodge and weave. He could outwit other heavier or stupider boys or men and they were almost all these things. And some of them drank and others sat about too much. As he learned to own the streets, they did not better him.

He didn't remember when he first met Wesley Hallam. It seemed to him as if they had been together always. They were about the same age, he thought, and Hallam too was a street child. It was good to have a friend. There were lots of people about, but nobody knew you and nobody stopped to help you. The crowd was always moving on, always had somewhere to go, but you had nowhere to go, you were stuck here because you had not the strength, the maturity or the money to go anywhere. The rain came down and soaked you, the road came up and chilled you, but there was sunshine, which dried out your clothes and your body, and there was always a wind off the river. He didn't know whether to love or hate the wind that came off the Tyne, just that it was always there like a faithful though poor friend.

It would softly touch his shoulders while he slept, on long summer nights when darkness barely arrived, in May and June and July. It whispered to him that the snow would not fall too hard upon him because there was too much salt where the river flowed to the sea, and it was not that far away. It was somehow too far away for him to move nearer. When it was cold, he slept under the bridge near the water so that the rain and wind were tempered.

Hallam was always around and he needed a friend too, so although they didn't talk much, they stayed close. Jay soon saw why Hallam was a good friend to have because two men jumped him down a dark alley. They put a rope around his neck and tried to throttle him and he was gagging, falling to the ground, and all of a sudden one was taken away and then the other.

By the time he had loosened and got rid of the rope and could breathe, the two men were lying on the ground, one of them moaning, the other turning over and over, clutching at his stomach.

Hallam turned around and walked away. Jay followed him. Hallam had a big gash on his face where somebody had knifed him. It hadn't improved his looks.

At first they stole anything they could reach, anything they could manage, and the more they stole the quicker they were to run away. They never got caught no matter what it was; they knew the streets around them so well and could outrun any shopkeeper. It made them laugh to outwit folk. In the end, Jay found a broken-down house which was empty, and he gave people who had nothing a place to shelter, and he went out and found food for them. There they lived, sheltered from the rain.

Most of them were very old and ready to lie down and die, or very young and could not steal well. Jay became so adept at it that he taught them to steal. Then he went into a church and stole a Bible and began to teach himself to read with help from an old woman, Morag McInver, who slept in the house he had provided. Hallam told him he was mad but went along with it, being helpful although he would have denied it.

Jay gave Mrs McInver clothes and blankets and all the food she could take, bread sopped in milk when her few teeth gave out. She helped both of them to read and write. She died in the winter, as so many people did.

'Now what?' Hallam said.

'I want to buy a house so that I can let other people come inside.'

'Bloody hell, are you Jesus?' Hallam said and then they laughed.

'Have you got any money?' Jay asked him.

'You want it?'

'Aye, give it up.' Hallam did.

By then Morag had given them both a basic education. Lads like them were born knowing how to add up. They knew how important it was and learned before they could speak. So with the money in their pockets, and bartering what they had, they began to steal anything that was worth money. They were able to feed the people in the house. They grew better and more wily and started to prosper. It was strange how suddenly they were able to buy new clothes and decent food. Eventually they bought a tumbledown house in a backstreet and put it right and put tenants into it who could pay. Then they bought another and they began to put money into buying and selling and building.

Jay liked the building best of all. He could then attract people who would pay because he employed good workmen to do what he could not do himself. Specialists were the way forward, he felt sure.

They went to the best tailor in the area and began mixing with men of business in Newcastle. Hallam hated it and did not care to get involved but Jay thought it was a good idea. Either they liked him or they admired how he was making money. He lived in a respectable house and was soon seen as a man who was on the way up.

Hallam jibed at him and stayed away from these gatherings. He didn't like people and most especially he didn't like rich men. He always spat when he said this, but it only made Jay smile and say nothing. In particular Jay admired the architect, Henry Charlton. He wished he had been this man's son. He wanted to be with him all the time, to be of his set, because he thought Henry Charlton was a genius.

He was building churches and large houses and a hospital. Jay discovered that Henry Charlton lived in a broken-down house by the river and he saw also that this man was so modest and caring that he kept nothing back for himself. He was astonished at this but also aghast when he saw Charlton's daughter at a distance;

the man's only child was beautiful. How could he keep her in such awful circumstances?

'Oh God,' Hallam said when Jay talked of her. 'You want to rescue her, don't you?'

There came an evening when Henry Charlton took him back to the house in the muddy lane by the river. There he introduced Jay to Madeline and Jay fell in love. He couldn't believe it. He thought the whole idea of love, especially falling in love, was nonsense, and so unguarded and costly that he would never have ventured there, but he did. He tried not to call it that, he would have named it dangerous and a thousand other things, but he would never have called it love before he met Madeline Charlton.

She was so beautiful that he thought he might have died happily just for having met her. She was all silver and black. Her hair was black and her eyes were silver-black and her skin was pale. Her clothes were grey-white and also silver somehow.

He knew it was an illusion, but he could not help it. He thought about her day and night. He conjured for himself a world in which she was his wife. She was the first real lady he had met, and he knew that he had to have her for keeps. He loved her voice and her smile and how kind she was and how she read and knew all manner of things that he didn't know.

He imagined them teaching one another because they had so much and so little in common, and yet everything. He was astonished that he could love a woman and yet glad; he felt like a bird soaring high. If he could have this woman, he could do anything with her by his side.

The next time he saw her was at a dance and he knew then that he did not want to be without her.

He did not know what to do to gain her. He had the feeling that if he spoke to Mr Charlton, he would never be in company with the man again because Henry Charlton knew who he was and where he had come from. Ought he just to creep away and hide his feelings and not acknowledge even to himself that he loved her? He had no right to love her – no chance of touching her ever in his whole life, he was sure – but since he had always tried to better everything, he went to her and told her how he felt.

He had never forgotten that day. It was winter in Newcastle and the snow was falling fast, despite the damned river which usually held it fairly well at bay. The tide with salt helped to turn the snow to sleet or even hail or rain.

He knew that he should not have gone and yet he did. She was by herself in the dark, cold house. He had hoped so, that her father would have gone to his club as he so often did in the middle of the evening. Jay knew because occasionally Henry Charlton took him along. It was the proudest evening of his life when Henry asked him to go there and introduced him to other influential men.

Henry went there to think things over with like-minded people, to mull over the day's doings, so he said, and occasionally he invited Jay to dine and drink among his friends. He discussed how things could be better on the morrow than they had been today.

So Jay went to the house and there she received him in the drawing room. He could have smiled at the idea. It was a ghastly little sitting room, cold and dark and damp and drear, and he wished he could have taken her out of it. As they entered, he thought he heard the scurry of mice, or was it rats? A lot of old buildings held vermin, but he had become unused to it. The curtains and furniture were shadowed and there were few books.

The fire in the grate was tiny as though she did not stay in there for very long, and why would she, he thought. She looked very surprised to see him and he was worried about that because he was rather hoping that she liked him. It was the best he could ask at this point.

Draughts howled down the hallway and in the room, where they met the wind sweeping down the chimney until the whole room smoked. He had been very surprised when he first learned that they lived there, but was not now that he knew Henry better. But even so he ached to marry and take her to some lovely dwelling that he would build for her. He would buy her jewels and gorgeous dresses and take her to Europe and be proud of the fact that she was his. He would do anything to get her to accept him, but he didn't hold out much hope.

It was then that he saw this girl was almost always alone here. And though she was beautiful, her dress was shabby and old and had been mended several times by the look of it. There was no smell of a decent dinner. He wanted to ask whether her father was out every night and managed, 'I thought perhaps Mr Charlton would be here.'

'Oh no,' she said, 'he rarely comes home in the evenings.' She said it simply, without pity, but he longed even more after that to give her everything he could, to make her happy.

'Miss Charlton, I know we have only met twice and I'm sure this seems very forward, but I wondered whether you might let me see you sometimes.'

She looked mystified and then understood and the colour came up in her cheeks like a winter sunrise.

'Oh,' she said.

'If you dislike the idea completely, I will go away. I don't mean to intrude.'

'No, I – it's just that I don't know you very well.'

'Perhaps we might get to know one another a little better. Might you allow that?'

'I don't know. I'm not sure. I haven't really thought about it.'

'It's just that I have spent a lot of time thinking about you and I like you very much. Would you allow me to speak to your father so that I could come here from time to time? If you don't wish for this, please say so.'

She didn't. Her gaze turned from surprised to rather pleased.

'I did like you when we danced together,' she said.

'You did?' he said, hopeful. He remembered her then in a worn white frock, looking the nearest thing to an angel he might ever hope to meet. Ethereal and fragile, yet not.

'Yes, I – I have the feeling it had something to do with how tall you are. That's silly, I know, but I liked dancing with you.'

'You did?' he said again, unable to utter anything sensible. He couldn't help but smile and then felt stupid, having said the same thing twice. He had had a number of dancing lessons at a place in Pink Lane so that he would survive in society. Hallam had mocked him for it and then laughed at his enthusiasm. Jay thought he could go on looking at her for years.

'I felt safe there,' she said.

He wasn't sure that was the impression he wanted to make but it was certainly a start. He did want to look after her, he did want to shield her from hot sun and cold rain and poverty and loss and whatever else he could.

'Then if your father gives permission, I may visit you.'

She agreed and smiled and nodded and then he went off to her father's club very worried about what he would say and what Henry Charlton might think. But there was no other way; he could hardly address her without asking her father. So he braved the man.

Charlton had dined and had a few drinks, he could see, and he slapped Jay on the back and told him to sit down. He had ordered brandy and cigars for himself and several other men.

Jay thought of the girl alone at home, but for a maid, as far as he could judge. He had heard noise from the kitchen. In this club, men dined on the best food and wine, the most expensive brandy and cigars. That evening they had been drinking champagne. He tried not to think badly of Henry Charlton, but the picture of Madeline poorly dressed, and alone with a low fire which she was evidently letting go out – and only two candles to see by – came to his mind and he had to stop himself from becoming angry.

This club was of Georgian build and had every luxury. The long wide windows, the huge fires, the silk curtains which stretched from floor to ceiling, the smell of good food and wine, the men who wore evening dress and enjoyed what seemed to Jay the best of everything. He hated it.

He half thought he should tackle the man in the morning but when he said he had something to say, Charlton took him aside, insisting on giving him a cigar, though Jay loathed tobacco and had never been able to afford drink. He tried to explain that he had seen Miss Charlton, that he would like to get to know her. That was all he said, but Charlton's brow darkened.

'You went to my house?'

'I thought I should ask her whether I might approach her—'

'You didn't think to ask me?'

'That's what I'm doing now. But that would have been foolish if she had disliked me.'

'How could she possibly like you? She doesn't know you.'

'We've met twice and we've danced and I liked her the moment I saw her.'

'Well, of course you did. Half of Newcastle wishes to marry her. You think I'd let her go to an upstart like you?'

Jay told himself that he had no right to be offended by this, but he was.

'I can't help my background; I can't do anything about that. But if you would allow me to address her, I am doing very well and I do care for her.'

Henry Charlton laughed and that was when Jay saw him for what he was: a very clever man, but fat, red-faced, middle-aged. He drank too much, smoked too much and he was self-indulgent. Yet he wanted his daughter at home, waiting for him in that appalling, damp house by the river, as though she was some kind of plaything to be put down and taken up at his bidding. It was not much of a prospect for her if no one was allowed to court her.

'She is a prize you will never win.'

'Will any man ever win her?' Jay said, angered and affronted.

Henry Charlton frowned.

'She is all I have. No man is good enough for her.'

'Except you as her father. What about her future? What about when you aren't here anymore? What will happen when you die?'

Henry Charlton laughed.

'I will never die,' he said, 'and you will never address her.'

Overnight Jay tried to imagine Henry Charlton in the nasty throes of death. The trouble was that those you wanted dead lived forever and Charlton couldn't be more than fifty.

Two

Jay turned up at the house quite early the following morning. Madeline was having breakfast and she had not expected him, or that the maid – who was new and understood nothing; they were always new for everybody – would let him come in without asking. It was cool in the dining room and all she had was a pot of tea growing cold and a crumbling piece of toast – so her first thought, that she should offer him something to eat, was no use at all. Her second thought followed on so swiftly that she forgot about the first.

'You saw my father?'

'Is he here?'

'I presume he went early to work.'

This was a lie. Very often he did not come home. There were rumours she had heard that he kept a woman and very often went home to her, but Maddy didn't know whether this was true and could not even stand the idea of it. The fire smoked. She saw Jay looking around with disdain, as though he had expected better, but since he had been there once, she misread his face, she knew.

'Did he give you permission to address me?'

'No.' Jay said the word, and then again, as though he needed to make sure he was accurate. She saw that his face was all disappointment. 'No, he didn't want me to.'

'My mother died when I was very small and he isn't well,' was her explanation, though only the first half of this sentence was true.

'I want to marry you.' He was looking at her so earnestly that Madeline found it difficult to meet his gaze. 'I haven't ever wanted to marry anybody before, so I'm not quite sure how to go about this. I am doing very well and making money. I'm building houses and plan to do all kinds of other things. I can offer you marriage, and I will build you a house anywhere you like, and I would love you and look after you and see the future through with you. Will you marry me?'

'Oh,' was all she could manage.

'I didn't put it very well,' he allowed.

'No, you – you did put it very well. It's just that – I don't feel as if I can leave my father.'

'I can understand that but he – he has a great deal in his life, and forgive me, you seem to have little. He says he doesn't want you to marry anybody.'

'I think he has the idea that he will approve the man I marry.'

'I see. Well, he said I wasn't good enough for you, which I'm sure is true, but also that nobody would be good enough for you. That can't be true, I think. Presumably if you cared for me, you would leave him and come with me and be my wife, despite what he says.'

'There's only been the two of us for as long as I can remember.' This was not quite true, but her father had never brought another woman back here. He was not here much but still, he had been true to his wife's memory in essential terms, having not re-married. She had dreaded him marrying in case he chose badly, as she knew men sometimes did, and she did not feel as if she could leave him now. It would be some kind of betrayal.

'Is there anyone he approves of?'

She had to think, and of course saw that there was not. He rarely brought his business colleagues here, and when he did, they spent hours shut up in the library where the fire smoked. Somehow she felt responsible for the fire smoking and was never easy about it. He would say to her that it was annoying, but he never said anything should be done about it. If she provided food, he would complain about it: the beef was tough, the soup was thin, the pudding was thick, the custard was lumpy and the wine was sour.

He would take the other men away with him. They would go to his club and she would be left with a smoking fire and dirty dishes and a sense of failure that she could not rid herself of, however much she said to herself that it was not her fault. It was her mother's fault, in a way, that she had not been here. She wanted to make up for her mother not being there and she failed. She wanted to shout at him that she had no money, that the house was his, and the failings were his too, but she could not. He had been widowed so long ago and with a small child and he was due all her love and devotion.

'I cannot leave him. I cannot marry you.'

'I suppose you would if you loved me.'

She did not tell him of the times when she had been small and her father had read stories to her. She could not tell him of her small self, skipping to church by her father's side, and how he had held her hand. She could not tell him how her father had cried quietly in the night for years, before he stopped spending the nights at home.

Her father had come to terms with so many hard things in

his life, and she could not leave him to come back here to the silence. He counted on having her there, like a wayward young man who loved to stray from home because he thought that somehow it completed the balance. Here he could imagine that his wife was still waiting. If Maddy left, his wife would never be waiting for him. He could never come home again. She could not do that to him even though he had condemned her to that silence.

Jay wanted to tell her that if she changed her mind, she could go to the three-storied black and white house on the quayside which he had recently bought, despite Hallam telling him he was an idiot and it would fall down around his ears. He went back there and began to work and he tried not to think about her anymore.

He could not believe that he missed Henry Charlton as much as he missed Madeline, that was the stupid part about it. For all he now disliked the man intensely, he could see that he wanted to be Henry Charlton; he wanted to build, to go forward, to put something new where there had been nothing. He was not Henry Charlton's equal – the man was a superb architect, whereas Jay was not even a builder. He knew that, but he could put his ideas into place and get other people to work for him and create something worthwhile, and house people who could not afford housing otherwise, and he liked that.

He and Hallam went on building houses and putting people in them, buying and selling, but it was not enough.

'I want to do something special,' he kept on saying and Hallam kept on ignoring him. In the end, he said,

'We have everything.'

'No, we don't.'

'Well, if it's respectability you're hankering after – though I don't know why – we are making friends with people who own things and can think for themselves.'

Jay said nothing to that. He had not talked to Hallam much about Madeline and yet Hallam said to him,

'You wanted to get married and you're fed up about it. There are plenty of women in the world.'

'Not like that.'

Afterwards nobody said anything, but that was when Jay decided what he would like to do.

'I want to build something bigger. I want to build a town.'

Jay had gone up to the top of the Durham fells where he had chosen to build his town several times before he did anything about it. He knew it was the right place. It had pits which gave up good coking coal for making iron and there were a number of limestone quarries nearby that he could easily buy. There was no town here, but the land could be bought. He went there and stayed at the Bay Horse, an inn at the bottom of the bank in Wolsingham, and there he pulled his plans together.

He put in motion searches to find the pit that would be right by his town. He called it The Hope Pit, and there he paid and temporarily housed pit sinkers in tents to find what he needed. He bought a quarry so he had the iron ore, too. It was exactly the right place.

At first Hallam had made all kinds of objections. The quarry wouldn't work, the town was in the wrong place, the men were idle. He didn't like the pits, especially the one in the town that was Jay's favourite because it had been the first one he had sunk.

The only thing Hallam said, and Jay took it for a token gesture, was, 'Thin seams, eh?'

West Durham was notorious for its eighteen-inch seams, where men sweated and laboured more than most. But the coal was of the finest, which was needed to make coke. And he had built high up from beyond the seams – to the wagonways, as best he could – so that the men could do their jobs and not worry.

Jay acknowledged it and Hallam clicked his tongue. The coal was costly to get out.

'We have everything we need here to make iron and we have the railway.'

Hallam still said nothing.

'Oh, come on, Wes—' Hallam's mother had been a whore, but obviously a clever one because she had named her boy for the preacher. He had never had any father, but he was better off than Jay, who had known neither parent. He had no idea about his name but had stuck to it. 'You must think it's a good idea.'

'I think it's a very good idea, if you had nothing else to do, but you have huge business interests in Newcastle. You don't need this. We have good lives. We have lovely houses. People even talk to us.'

Jay wanted to say the things he always said, but there was no point; they knew one another so well. He didn't want to talk to people in Newcastle. He didn't want to go on doing what they had been doing the past few years, reaching into the small society that existed there and pretending to be a gentleman because he had money. Hallam knew all this but continued to bait him. It was a form of humour, teasing.

Hallam half-wanted to be a gentleman, though he knew he never would be. He had no voice, he had no background, he had

had little parenting. He had no history and seemingly no future. Jay had learned to live with this. Hallam had not.

'I've spoken for it all,' Jay said now.

'I know you have,' Hallam said in even tones. 'I tried talking you out of it over and over again, but you wouldn't listen.'

'I said, you don't need to be involved.'

Hallam mooched about. It was freezing and they went and looked at the fell and how open it was. The wind was howling with a sideways snowstorm behind it, but they stood.

'Don't you just love it?' Jay said and Hallam laughed.

'Oh, come on, man,' Jay said, 'help me. I'll make the farmhouse really nice.'

'It's already pretty good,' Hallam allowed, having seen it that morning. He dismissed it as he always did.

Three

Nobody said anything, just as though nothing had happened. From then on, each night Ruth was terrified, and lay there waiting for her father to come into her room. She wondered if it was something she would die from, but she didn't. She thought that her mother would come back. After all, she had nowhere else to go. But after a week she had to accept that her mother must have taken a great deal of money with her when she had left. Perhaps she had been saving for a very long time and it was just that Ruth didn't know about it.

Her father worked and when he could, he got drunk, but he did not come into her bedroom again. She had no money and nowhere to go. He would bring things back from Stanhope as he had always done, flour and yeast and sugar; sometimes meat, because all they had were chickens. She grew vegetables in her garden. Their diet was monotonous except the cakes. She was good at making cakes.

Things were easier with her mother out of the way. It was a horrible thing to think, but her father seemed to drink less and come home earlier. They never spoke of what had happened; she wasn't even sure that he remembered it. She tried telling herself he had thought she was her mother, that all he remembered was the act itself and perhaps not even that. He often forgot things when he was drunk.

He was a lot less quarrelsome, and with them both out of the way, Ruth could do more or less what she chose. She was a better cook, baker and housekeeper than her mother, and the place was cleaner than ever because she worked so hard. It was a strange kind of contentment.

Ruth soon began to think again that she was dying, but in a way it was worse than this. Her body began to swell. She hid it as best she could but one night in the late spring, her father went down to the village and got drunk. When he came back, he realised that she was having a child, called her a dirty slut and demanded to know who the lad was who had done this. How had it happened? When she told him how it had happened, he said she was a liar and said that he was her father, he would never have done such a thing. She was sinful and ungodly, and she was filthy and a whore. He tried to come at her, to hit her because of what she had done. Punishment was always due, according to him. Whereupon she bolted herself into her bedroom. After that, she kept a knife under her pillow.

He stopped drinking again but his silence was as difficult to bear as anything else had been in her life. He did not question her again. Ruth was horrified at the way that her body had reacted. She was getting bigger and bigger and there was nothing she could do about it. Her mother had told her in intimate detail how awful her birth had been so she tried not to imagine what would happen, but there was no help for it. The baby was there and would be born.

She became more and more tired as the baby grew bigger, until the late summer when she was convinced it would be born and there would be nobody to help. She was finding everything she had to do hard work and kept falling asleep in the afternoons. She and her father no longer spoke. The little happiness she had gained after the awful act he had perpetuated on her vanished like early-morning mist and a horrible tension settled over the house.

He did not accuse her again, but he went to the pub more and more often and came home less and less. He did not give her a single penny, so she could go nowhere, and all he brought back were the bare essentials. Often she was hungry, and the hunger made her more tired.

The baby began to take over her entire existence. It got in the way, it moved around at night; she could not get comfortable no matter how she laid in bed, and the tiredness was all day now. Her back ached and her body went on swelling until she started to think that it would never stop. By late summer she was huge, and so scared as to how the baby would get outside her, though there was nothing she could do to stop it.

Somehow she knew that her father would attack her again. She didn't know how she knew; perhaps the baby was fine-honing her instincts. He was losing control over himself in all kinds of different ways. He had gone mad, she felt sure – because of her mother leaving, because of what he had done to her. Whatever it was, had she had somewhere to go, she would have left. But she had not a penny and nowhere to go to. She knew no one who would take her in. She had to stay there and endure whatever might happen now.

First of all, he forgot to go to work, and then they had no money. He forgot to feed the few animals they had left. He didn't light the fires; he didn't do anything to help. She used what stores she had and fed the animals they had, and she cooked and cleaned and lit the fires. He had begun spending more and more time in bed.

And then from somewhere he found money, and quickly he put on his clothes and disappeared out of the door. Ruth wanted to cry because she needed food. As the child got bigger so she got smaller, until she thought she would disappear, that the child would somehow eat her up as its needs became greater.

So it was by early autumn, she was huge in front and she could not get comfortable. That night, when her father left, she lit the one candle she had. It didn't matter which way she turned, her stomach was still too heavy and too uncomfortable, and she needed the chamberpot all the time in what light there was.

So she heard his footsteps as he came in. She lay quiet as she had done before and hoped that he would remember who he was and who she was and that he would just fall into bed and sleep. It was almost morning, but he had sobered sufficiently to throw open her bedroom door and after that she knew what he would do next.

He staggered to the bed and tried to get hold of her. When she resisted, he pleaded in his wife's name again and again, and when that did no good, he hit her and hit her until she felt sure that he would kill her and the baby. He would not blame himself if he did such a thing. He would convince himself either that someone else had done it, or that she had been so sinful with some man that she did not deserve to live. He would have cleansed the world of his shameful daughter.

That was when she drew the knife from under the pillow and stabbed him.

It was not a big knife. Had it been big, it would have been useless in her thin hands. In fact, it was her favourite kitchen knife, that she used to peel vegetables. It had a lovely sharp edge to it and the blade was short. This she now stuck into her father's shoulder, the nearest part of him she could reach while trying to free herself from his hands.

He howled in pain and grabbed at her again, whereupon she took the knife back out – it took more doing than she had thought it might – and she struck again. He didn't stop. In the end she didn't know how many times she put the knife into his body and drew it back out again, only that she became deft at it and began to admire her own dexterity because he was not assaulting her, just trying to ward her off. The whole thing took on a rhythm and it became easier and easier, long past when he had stopped trying to grab her.

Finally she registered that he was not fighting back, that he stopped trying to grab her and she breathed very carefully. She had not known the effort involved and how it took the strength from her. She was hurt; she ached everywhere – especially in the region of the baby where his knees had found contact. She was smarting from the blows and she was breathing carefully, exhausted. She was in pain: whether from the blows or the baby or the horror, she didn't know. She was hurt seemingly everywhere, and couldn't move.

All she was aware of was that he didn't come at her anymore. She managed to disentangle herself from him, crawl out of bed, and then in fear that he would come around and begin again, hurting her even more, she put on as many clothes as she could find in the darkness. The candle had long since given up. Her shoes were too tight and pinched her toes and blistered her heels. She donned her coat. She had a big shawl which was full of holes – she thought it must have been her mother's – and then she took the last slice of bread from the kitchen table. She drank until her thirst was quenched, stuffed the bread into her pocket and let herself out of the door.

It was early autumn, but early autumn here could be as cold as November. The summer had been hot. The summer was well over, she thought, as the rain came down like needles on her head; it soon drenched her clothes and her body and made her shoes squelch. The road was somewhat up and down but she knew her way.

After the rain stopped it was a brilliantly clear night and there were many stars. She didn't want to go down into the valley, even though it would be warmer there out of the wind – her toes would be strained at the front of her shoes and that would make the walking harder. It was already hard enough with the baby so big and so low; it was like carrying a huge heavy bundle, almost weighing her down.

The dawn broke not long afterwards with the kind of beauty that hurts your eyes. Why were the sunrises and sunsets so beautiful when everything was going wrong for people? It was bright red orange, and as she walked she began to make out the odd house up there on the tops, but she did not linger.

She could not think what she would say to anybody if she happened to meet them, big with child as she was and desperate. She did not know where she was going, just that she would eventually get to Frosterley and Wolsingham. She knew that she had to get as far away as she could before her father came after her.

Once the drink and her inadequate attempts to hurt him wore off, he would follow her and she was unsure what might happen then so she kept on walking, eating her bread as she went until it grew dark again. She met nobody. She drank from a stream and then she went on again. She was not afraid of the dark, it was a friend to her such as she had never had in person, but she grew very tired and wanted to sleep.

She was afraid that if she fell asleep in such places the burden she was carrying might be too much for her small young body, so she didn't stop until she could not go on any longer. When she did sit down – not on the road, but carefully to one side, for what reason she felt unsure – she was grateful for the respite and glad when she fell into unconsciousness.

Four

The Daughters of Charity, Newcastle upon Tyne

It was raining in Newcastle but then it rained so often in Newcastle that Madeline Charlton, who had always lived there, was used to it. She was now Sister Madeline. She loved how the rain battered against the windows of the convent while she was warm and snug inside. She shivered even now, thinking of how she had been left without a home or family. Her father had dropped dead in the street; it was his heart, the doctor said, but to her it was a terrible shock, and she was still grateful to the sisters for taking her in.

There was a buzz about the convent this morning as there had not been in a long while, and she knew it meant that something was afoot. Sister Bee had gone to Reverend Mother's office early and not been seen since. It was raining and since Maddy could not get outside to do the garden, which was her special province, she went into the kitchen to help Sister Hilary, who was washing up the breakfast dishes and would be preparing vegetables for dinner at one o'clock.

They were both very happy at this time of year because the garden was at its best. The summer for once had been long and dry and Maddy was pleased at the downpour; it would be bliss for the fruit and veg. In time it would plump out the fruit that was growing on the apple and pear trees, which had been there for a long time – possibly since the convent had first been lived in so long ago. Nuns had come back to it in the past few years when they were allowed to practise their religion once again. She initially did not like gardening, but it had to be done and she was the one chosen to do it; but the more she did it, the more she liked it.

Hilary was singing. Hilary was always singing. Mother was given to saying that Hilary must have been born singing and it was a good job she had not gone into a silent order. Hilary had an exquisite voice and led them in chant, and when she was asked, in prayer. They had prayers four times a day, the daily offices: morning prayer, eucharist at noon, evening prayer and compline, for completion. Maddy had come to love these times best of all, the convent and its chapel, and to remember the idea that happiness was to be found in prayer.

Teresa of Ávila once said of prayer that it wasn't about spending time with God, it was an opportunity to take off your mask and be who you were in front of God and expose your deepest concerns and fears. Maddy thought this was a wonderful idea. She also thought that Hilary had no mask and she loved her for that – but also for her voice, her many talents and the downright loveliness that she gave to everyone she came into contact with.

Hilary had finished the washing up and was eyeing her with pretend disdain.

'Exquisite timing, Sister,' she said, 'all done, and since there is nothing here for lunch, you must get yourself out there. I need a great deal of lettuce, a huge amount of tomatoes and some cucumbers.'

Hilary was desperately polite, frightfully, Maddy thought, with a smile. She was what Maddy's father had called 'snowing, blowing and going', and she called the meal in the middle of the day 'lunch'. Everybody else Maddy knew called it dinner.

'I'll get wet,' she objected.

'What a city girl,' Hilary said with a smile, but until the downpour stopped they worked in the kitchen. There were always shelves to clean and floors to scrub and Hilary was a big soup maker. There was almost always soup for the first course and it was never less than superb.

'So what's going on?' Maddy asked her.

Hilary always knew everything; being in the kitchen she had to know who would be at meals, and outsiders were always interesting.

'Old Father Time is gracing us with his presence at lunch.' Old Father Time was the way they referred between themselves to Father Samuel; he was so old that nobody knew how old he was.

He reminded Maddy of pictures of Saint Nicholas, for he was very red-faced, had white hair and was more jolly than other people might have thought a priest could be. Maddy had no doubt that Father Samuel had got more men to go into the priesthood than Jesus could ever have hoped a follower might. His love of God shone from him with a kind of radiance, so that she thought he should have been called Gabriel. He was learned and kind and encouraging and every time she saw him she liked him more.

When the rain stopped, which it did soon afterwards, she trod outside in big boots, taking with her secateurs and a wicker basket that had formerly belonged to some lady who liked to gather roses, she had been told. It was boat-shaped with a narrow sweeping handle and dipped like a fishing vessel in the middle.

Under instruction from Hilary, she gathered lettuce. Not that she made much impression; there was so much of it, they had been making it into soup that week. Hilary said that Potage du Père Tranquille – which was mainly lettuce, stock and nutmeg – was aptly named, as it soothed the soul. None of them ever tired of its taste.

Maddy got the impression that Hilary's father had sent his daughters away to some ghastly boarding school where they learned French, because Hilary seemed to know words in a different language. Or perhaps it was just that she had been brought up as the right kind of Catholic. Maddy had the impression that her mother had been French and her grandmother Eastern European, because Hilary knew some very odd recipes, but since they always worked nobody could complain.

Today Hilary was giving the Father tomato soup, which was nothing much more than tomatoes stewed in good butter with salt and pepper, hot water and herbs fresh from the garden, cooked until it was mush. But the simplicity of such things was their bliss. And she would make herb bread and there would be fresh butter and cheese, and good red wine because Father Samuel loved his wine.

Maddy therefore picked a great number of ripe tomatoes from the greenhouse, several cucumbers, and rosemary, thyme and bay leaf. Then she went into the other garden and picked flowers so that Father Samuel would comment on how beautiful her displays were. She was proud of them, though she would never have said so, but she liked hearing him. He always remembered each nun by name.

When she had reached the convent five years before, she didn't know a rose from a dog daisy and had spent a long time repairing the greenhouses, having begged glass and putty from various workmen she knew in the city. There was something so satisfying about puttying the glass back into the sturdy frames that made her late for meals and prayers. She was always running back inside, trying to make herself look tidy, as though she had not spent the last two hours doing repairs.

Mother smiled on her, for she loved industry and also, up to a point, initiative, so when Maddy first got there and deplored the state of the greenhouses, Mother had picked up on the idea and said would she see what she could do.

Maddy's father had been an architect and had built a good many of the best buildings in Newcastle, and it was one of the reasons she had been taken in by the convent when she was left alone. She knew all there was to know about buildings, and a greenhouse was an opportunity for her to help.

Now, four years later, she liked how the downpours could not reach the precious vegetables like tomatoes and cucumbers, which were nurtured there all summer by the sisters; they provided them – and very often the houses beyond the convent where the sisters helped the poor – with plenty of food. They put outside great buckets of fruit and vegetables for people to take. Maddy loved July best because the sun was hot and everything grew and ripened, but July had gone, and the downpours of September had just begun.

She had already started to think about autumn and how she would help Hilary, who was an expert in such things, preserve the fruit from the orchard, box the pears and apples in sand, and store the potatoes separately so that they did not touch one another and rot. The soft fruit would be made into jams and chutneys. She thought it was her favourite time of year. The harvest. She liked best that the Brussels sprouts could be left outside and picked even in the snow. Turnips would do the same and sometimes even cabbages and cauliflowers lasted, though they hated wet weather.

Father Samuel was late as ever, and then he spoke to each nun he met so that he was even more delayed, but none of them minded. He told Maddy how wonderful her garden was and her flower displays throughout the convent. By the time he had finished talking over the roses in the hallway, Sister Hilary was almost apoplectic.

The soup was ready and the lentils which went with the lettuce for the main course would be past their best if Father wasn't hurried towards the dining room. This wasn't true. She wouldn't even put the lentils on until the diners were well into the first course, because they had been boiling already and were just to heat, but Hilary loved drama and nobody begrudged her.

Eventually, having beamed at and spoken to everyone, he was seated and given wine. Then they sat down to Hilary's wonderful tomato soup with fresh bread and newly churned butter. Father Samuel gave every sign of relish, sighing over the taste and saying he never got anything this good in his monastery. They knew this was untrue; he lived very well, it was said – his scarlet nose gave evidence of it – but it was good to hear.

They had hot lentils on top of lettuce with a mix of a tiny amount of vinegar, melted butter and various herbs and seasonings. The first time she had seen this, Maddy was horrified, but it cost little and was excellent eating.

Then they had raspberries from the garden, picked after the rain so that Maddy worried they would disintegrate, but they had survived. Hilary had made meringues, gluey inside and crisp outside, a lovely golden honey colour, and there was cream.

After they had eaten, Father got up and addressed the nuns. Maddy liked how there were no secrets; it was open and if anything interesting happened, you got to hear about it. You didn't get to give your opinion or even indicate that you were not pleased. That was not the point. You made your vows each year and this included what Sister Abigail called 'keeping your trap shut'. So Maddy tried to appear sanguine when inside her a little worm of doubt and panic grew like, well, like a wriggling worm, she thought.

'I have come to ask for your help,' he said, 'and I know you will give it to me willingly. There is a new town being built on the fells up in Durham and the priest I have there, Father Timothy, is alone. I sent him to find out what was going on and I was right in thinking that there are poor children coming into the area who have neither parents nor families. Some of them are from Ireland. I pray, and I'm sure you all do, to keep them safe.

'There are stories of folk dying of hunger on the docks when they reach Liverpool. Some have managed to make their way across country and they are scattering even as far as this little new town so they need our help. Mother has promised that we shall have four nuns; it's all she can spare.' He turned to Mother and beamed down on her so that Maddy half expected Mother's head to burst into glorious flame. 'And we have decided that Sister Bee' (Bee was called Deborah and Maddy had no idea why she was Bee, even to Mother, but she was), 'should take Sister Abigail and Sister Hilary and Sister Madeline with her to assist. I know that you will all do your best – not only those who are going forth to do our work, but also those of you who are left. You must pull together as well as you might, since there will be more work to do; the chasm left by the four sisters will fall on everybody.'

He must have said other things, Maddy thought afterwards, but she didn't hear them. All she heard was a horrible clanging in her ears. She had to leave the convent? She had to leave Newcastle, which was the only place that she had ever known?

She was inexperienced compared to many of the others but she soon understood. Mother was sending one older nun and three young ones because there was no telling how much work must be done. She needed young bodies and minds, full of enthusiasm, and the older nun for experience and good sense.

She tried not to look at Mother, but to bow her head and do God's will as she had been taught, but she was not very surprised to get a summons to Mother's office in the middle of the afternoon, when she was hoeing weeds so hard that many of the plants would be lucky to survive.

She went as quickly as she could, considering she was not meant to run. If she had tried to run, she would have run away. Tears misted her eyes when she got there, for this woman was the only Mother she had known, her own having died so early that Maddy did not remember her.

Mother got up and took Maddy's hands when the girl would have knelt before her.

'I know you are upset,' she said and Maddy shook her head and fought back the tears. She knew that she had no right to be upset and it was too good of Mother to say such things to her. 'Come and sit down.'

She gave Maddy several moments to gather herself together in some semblance of what passed for an obedient nun, and then sit down at the front of Mother's desk. Mother said:

'You have done good work here. When you came I knew you would, for your father was a great man and he loved God, and he gave so much to this city that his name will be revered here for a very long time after we are all gone. You have many talents. It isn't just that I am sending you for your youth and your usefulness; I think you need an adventure. We do not want you falling into boredom inside these walls when you have so much to offer.'

Maddy raised her head at the wild idea and then smiled as Mother had meant her to.

'You and Sister Hilary and Sister Abigail all have different skills,' Mother said, and then they both smiled because Abigail had come in from the streets, having been alone for a very long time and starving; she knew many things which ordinarily young women did not know. She could pick a lock or take a purse without anyone noticing.

When she had first been there, she had to be discouraged from trying to sell the altar candlesticks, which were gold and valuable. She had only been trying to help, Mother asserted. Gold could be turned into money and money could be turned into food, that was how Abigail had looked at it. She had been astonished to think that the sisters had not seen earlier that gold could feed many mouths. Somehow, Maddy thought, the idea lingered with them all.

Hilary was a farmer's daughter from Northumberland, from a devout Catholic family. Her father had despaired and been somewhat relieved when his younger daughter expressed a desire to go into a convent, but he must have been sorry too, Maddy always thought, for Hilary was a joy to be around and a very skilled woman.

Her parents must miss her. She spoke of them with such joy and longing, and of how much they loved her and how much she loved them, so that her calling from God must have been huge, Maddy thought. Hilary had so much to give and she gave it all so freely, so honestly.

She went home of course, now and then. Their convent was

not a prison. Maddy had noticed when Hilary's father left her at the convent, how he held her and how his face worked so that he would not cry, while her mother staggered back to the carriage out of the way; they loved her so much. It reminded Maddy of what an orphan she was.

'I know that you will achieve great things in the new town and Sister Bee is so very capable that she will keep you all right,' Mother said, 'and you will see Christmas in the countryside.' Here, Mother sighed, for she too had come from the country and knew how exquisite the landscape would be then, white with snow and icy with frost.

Maddy worried about Sister Bee. She had spent several years in France with Mother before coming here a few years ago. She was quiet, reserved. Maddy knew that she was the right person for the job, she just got on with things, but she had not the kind of personality that inspired people. Inspiration, she knew, was needed here, but perhaps when Sister Bee got away from the convent where Mother reigned she would feel differently.

Their order was quite different from others. In the first place, they made their vows each year, and if they did not want to renew, they could leave without question for whatever they thought life had in store. But also Mother was proud of her nuns, because they were so very different from anything before. They were there to pray, yes, but everything they did was to aid other people. Faith, hope and charity, but the best of these was charity.

There was no vow of silence, there was no picking of faults. They were poor and obedient and chaste, but they went out into the community and they did all kinds of other things which some nuns would have thought unsound. Mother stuck with the word 'unusual'. She ruled there by kindness and understanding and she often said that it was better to use a carrot than a stick. It was very rare that anyone left and she was keen that they should use their talents, instead of asking for things which were impossible, as a lot of orders did. Nobody was moved around to do anything for which they had no talent. There was no hiding your light under a bushel. Here, under Mother's guidance, you let that light shine, and you held it to enable people, families, everyone you came into contact with, to lead happier and more fruitful lives.

Privately, Maddy thought that all four of them had had difficult lives, and had not come to the convent because they felt their lives should be dedicated to God; it had been more of a cry for help, a need for safety for various reasons, and Mother had been good enough to take them in. Now she was setting them a task which was meant for unusual women, and she thought they might be just right for it.

Five

Ruth became adept at hiding. Why she did it she was not certain. She knew nobody and she thought that nobody knew her, yet every time she heard the hooves of a horse – or imagined that it was a horse and cart – she scurried from the road and hid behind a wall. If she was within sight of a house of any kind, she hovered behind anything she could find: an old gate, a dip in the road. Whatever, nobody saw her, or if they did, they did not recognise or acknowledge her, and therefore passed by.

She did not feel well after the first day. She had nothing to eat and had to drink only water. Usually that wouldn't have bothered her, but the child inside her devoured everything. She came to hate its appetite and to hate that it was her father's offspring; it would be her brother or sister, and her child, too. It was too awful even to consider. She had to put off again and again talking to herself about it, but soon there would be nowhere to go.

She would have drowned herself had she had opportunity, but here the water tumbled downhill and was nothing much more than five inches wide and an inch deep; it flowed so fast and shallow. You could not have drowned a field mouse in it had you desired to do such an awful thing. To deprive life, she thought, was the worst, but then she thought of the life inside her and wished to be rid of it even to an early grave. In fact, she wished for both of them that it would end so.

On the third day, she was so dizzy for lack of food that she could barely walk. Her shoes were full of blood where her toes and heels had no space; she pulled them off and it was easier without them. Her feet and ankles seemed to have blown up. Was that because she had not eaten? Was the child inside her taking revenge? That was ludicrous, she knew, but as she did not eat and could not sleep, the wild thoughts ate away at her mind – and perhaps even at her belly. As she went into what she thought of as the fourth day, the pains began to bite at her stomach so that she feared the child would come and she would die there all alone. She wished that anybody would venture past who would help but it was such a lonely road. In the end she lay down because she could not go on.

Her stomach was empty and her mouth was dry and the pains came and went at regular intervals. She did not know what it was like giving birth by yourself, but from what her mother said, even with help it was truly awful. She was not going to have help and she was too young and it was all wrong, but she could not do any more. She lay down and hoped for nothing,

After a sleep she was able to get up and walk on. She was too terrified to ask for help, though she knew that she would need help soon, and that if none was forthcoming she would die. She knew no one and was afraid that they would not aid her. People here were wary of strangers, and she was a stranger to them and they would be to her. She dithered between being afraid of having the child by herself, and asking others, because she thought she might die. Then she thought, would dying be so awful?

She had had no life. Perhaps God had decided that she was

not worthy of any kind of life and she should not try to go on anymore. But dying in childbirth and alone would be so painful. It was not the dying that mattered, it was the pain that came first that took her in such fear.

She kept stopping and drinking water from the streams that started up there and then became a good body of water when they reached the bottom of the hill. The water was clean and cool. She also found several apples which must have fallen out of somebody's bag. They were sour and did not make the aching in her any less, but they were at least food and it would help her to survive. Best of all was when she was so tired that she slept. This was all she could be pleased for, grateful about. She had given to crying when she woke, because it meant that she was still alive, that she was required to go on and do what she could to live.

She came across a deserted house. Many houses in the dale had been left by people thinking they could do better in another place, Canada or Australia. That was what her father had said. She was trying not to think about her father and what he had said and what he had done and how she had effected her escape.

She was worried and kept thinking that she should go back. What if he was badly hurt? What if she had wounded him so that he could not get up and go for help or get better? It was nonsense, she thought; she was so small, she could not have damaged such a big man. But she remembered how he had stopped hurting her, how she had pushed him back with the knife and the way that she had kept sticking the blade anywhere she could in order to get him to stop. No, he would get up and come after her; she had to keep moving. But now was she far enough away that she might rest?

The house was set back among trees and though it looked as if there was nobody about, there could be. She went very carefully towards it. It didn't look as if anybody lived there, but if they did, they would send her away, maybe throw stones or shout. It was unlikely they would be kind. She needed to stop for a day or two. The pains for now had gone, even the pain in her back from walking. Her feet hurt and she dared not take off her shoes again for fear they would not go back on because her ankles were so swollen.

Her legs felt like large tree stumps. Her body felt enormous and terrifying. But she made her way very carefully down the track towards the house. She thought about calling out to attract the attention of whoever might be there, but she was sure there was nobody. She ventured nearer. There were torn net curtains up at the windows, but when she got around to the side and then to the back, it became obvious that it had been a long time since anybody had lived here.

The back door was lying outside and many of the windows were broken. The grass grew up around the door and was so tall that she could see nobody had been there in a long time and the house felt lonely.

Inside, glass littered the floor as though someone had deliberately smashed the windows from outside. There were several broken chairs and a table still intact. All the downstairs rooms were empty. She did not venture up the stairs; the staircase was rotten and had given way in places.

She went into the back garden and there she found several trees which had almost ripe fruit on them. There were still vegetables in the garden. She might stay here for the time being, she thought, she might rest. She felt well; the baby must not be due. The rest would help, so she gathered what vegetables she could and ate, and then she fell asleep on an old chair with her legs up on another close by.

She was so grateful there was nobody to bother her. She could sleep here, perhaps for as long as she needed to, until she was not so tired and could go on. She lay down and slept.

For several days she was almost happy there alone. She ate and rested and there was fresh water. Then on the fifth day, the pain came back and it kept coming and going. She told herself that it would go away again, but it didn't, and each time it came back it was worse, until she could not breathe, she could not speak. She wanted to scream but hadn't sufficient breath and then she knew that if she couldn't find anybody to help her, she would have to have her baby here alone. That was not a concept she could deal with.

She had to get some help. She tried to get away. She was in pain and couldn't but then she tried more and more to get to the road. It had not seemed like such a long way. Now the path leading to it seemed endless. Worst of all, rain began to fall. She slipped and fell and then the pain stopped. Everything stopped, everything faded away.

Six

The nuns set off from Newcastle in a howling gale that tried to whip their heavy grey skirts up past their knees. The rain was coming sideways at them so there was no chance of getting away from it. They started off by train but had to change twice and all the luggage they had brought to help set up had to be changed too. It took time and Maddy was very aware of how people stared, as though they had never seen a nun before. Maybe they hadn't.

Maddy thought that Sister Bee was very quiet, even more so than usual. She was probably thinking of the responsibility she would have; although she was organised and capable, she had never had to do such a thing before. Perhaps it was worrying her, because she had said very little as they went along. She looked tired too; her patient face was pale.

The nuns and their luggage changed at Durham and then they changed at Bishop Auckland. They finally came to a full stop in the middle of nowhere. The wind cut across your legs, your arms, your face and any other part of you which might be exposed, and although in summer Maddy sometimes hated how hot her habit was, she was glad of it now.

Their belongings, furniture, books and foodstuffs were put on to a cart. They had to walk. They carried the candlesticks and other valuable items for the altar, which they would use to set up the chapel they would eventually have. It was not far, but it felt like a very long way from the mother house in Newcastle. When they came to a stop there was so little to see because the wind and rain sheared across the tops. She could not see any of the new town very well, but the man who was helping them unloaded everything in front of a building, which – though not visible beyond shadow – was substantial; even big, she thought. Then he went off, not waiting to give them any more help.

Everything had to be carried inside but the door swung back and forth in the cold wind until they pushed a table against it. Once inside, she was astonished. She wished her father could be there. It was a very old house; sixteenth century, she surmised.

It was a butterfly house, the most beautifully shaped building that had ever existed. The way that the rooms billowed on either side at two angles with a door in the middle gave it the shape of a butterfly. This was a particularly good version because it had three floors and probably twelve rooms, though she could not tell from the ground floor.

She wanted to tell someone, but knew that she should not boast of her knowledge. It would mean little to the other nuns and had nothing to do with why they were there. The building was large because they needed space.

Sister Bee was concerned with practical things. She told Maddy to look upstairs and see if there were beds, if the furniture that they needed had been delivered. Maddy hurried upstairs and looked at the rooms on both floors. They were empty. The downstairs was the same.

The nuns had brought with them a large dining table and several chairs, linens, bedding, kitchen utensils, crockery and cutlery and some food to see them through until they were established.

Sister Bee was unhappy, Maddy could see, and said to her, 'Find Mr Gilbraith and ask him where the beds and the other furniture and the supplies are that he was meant to send, so that we would have these things upon our arrival.'

'Yes, Sister.'

Maddy had no idea what the man was like. Gilbraith was a common enough Scottish and border name. There were many of them in Newcastle. But she was glad to be let out, to leave Sister Bee and Sister Hilary to do the boring things like sorting out the house. Earlier she and Sister Abigail had gone into the backyard, where there were several buildings, all locked.

'What on earth can we do?' Maddy asked.

Sister Abigail merely took a hairpin from her pocket, fiddled about with a lock for a few seconds, and then it yielded. Maddy shouldn't have been surprised, there were few things which fazed Abigail.

'Maybe we should wait to be given permission,' Maddy said.

Abigail looked scornfully at her.

'We need a fire making now,' she said.

She opened the doors and there was a huge house full of coal, with logs and sticks. 'Just don't say owt to Sister Bee, she'll never think to notice,' Abigail said, and began piling sticks into her arms, heading back into the kitchen where there was an enormous stove.

Maddy was eager to see what the new town looked like; she had not been able to pay attention before, being tired and unsure. Now she saw exactly what had been done so far. There was a big sea of tents, but along the top where the butterfly house stood, various buildings had been erected. And not hastily – they were stone or brick built, made to last.

The winds came clear and clean across the fell, with a sharp, cutting edge. A street had been built on two sides and it was for necessity, she could see, to keep off the weather and establish a core to the place.

There was a grocery store and a blacksmith's shop and they were now building houses. They too must know that in a bad autumn, their tents would blow down, and so the street went on for quite a long stretch. There were other shops that she could not make out from where she stood, and houses in between them and no doubt behind them on both sides, and it was beginning to look like a substantial town.

There was a pit head at the top of the village, and further down on the right, some kind of quarry. Further down she could see more houses being built. The road went further and further but she stopped there because she could see the man she was looking for. It could only be Gilbraith. Nobody who stood that tall, sweeping one hand to demonstrate direction, did not run the place.

He was talking to another man, just as tall. Gilbraith had his back to her so she picked her steps carefully across the rubble road. The wind had dried up the roads as soon as the rain fell. One must always be glad of small mercies, she felt.

The men who were building stopped and looked up when she enquired of them, just to make sure that she had chosen the right person. The two she spoke to took off their caps, which she was rather pleased about. It showed respect and more, somehow. Perhaps that they might even like her, because they smiled, be she nun or no, she felt, as they would have smiled at any comely young woman. She wasn't sure it felt right, and she wasn't used to regarding herself as young or comely, but it was very kind and warm and not negative in any sense. And moreover, they knew where Mr Gilbraith was; she had been right.

'Aye, Sister, ower there talking to Hallam, the under manager.'

Maddy thanked them and moved away. Both men wore hats, as they did up here for practical purposes, no doubt since the weather would be fierce very often. Mr Gilbraith still had his back turned to her. He was tall and lean, but then, they were all thin; it was the nature of the work they did.

He was gesturing with one hand. He wasn't old, she thought, by his stance, but when she arrested his attention by greeting him, he turned around. She stared and he stared back at her.

The other man went off almost immediately and they were left. She recognised him immediately, even though it had been ten years and he must be nearly forty. He was not much different, his face brown and a few lines around his eyes, but he had changed in other ways, which she could not at present work out. She wished she could run away.

She couldn't think of a single word to say to him. She had thought she would never see this man again. He was thinner than he had been, and on his face were several days of black stubble. The last time she had seen him, he was wearing a beautiful suit and asking her to marry him.

His eyes, which she had thought cool blue, were now like frost, his face pale under the general brown of being outdoors all the time. She could not meet those glacial eyes or the closed look which flitted over his features.

He looked down at her for what felt like a long time, as though trying to get used to how he hadn't seen her before. Then he said haltingly, and to her chagrin, surprisingly quickly, 'Miss Charlton,' and then stared.

She looked away for something to do. She was astonished.

'A heathen,' her father had said. 'As though I would give my most precious girl to a man like that, common, vulgar, uneducated, out of a gutter. He was mad to think so.'

Strangely the words which upset her most were 'my most precious girl', like she was a vase. Did she not have a will of her own? She excused herself that she had been very young, and yet known she would have to choose one or the other. If she had chosen Gilbraith, her father would never have forgiven her. So she had chosen him, but it had not been an easy decision.

She had liked Jay from the first moment they met. He seemed so much more sensible than the other men she knew, as though he had needed to be an adult before his time. She had not known that for an attractive quality, but men who were willing to take responsibility must always be so to women, she knew. That was, if a woman wished to marry, and some of them had very little else to hope for.

A lot of men were only interested in gambling, drinking and spending money. They thought and talked about nothing but themselves – but a man with money and a future was husband material. Jay had been very good-looking with his cool blue eyes, dark hair, tall slender figure and elegant stance.

She had been twenty. She tried not to blush at the memories and so turned her face from him. How difficult. How awful this was. How on earth could this have happened? How unlikely was it?

His accent was thick Tyneside, which her father would have deplored. But she liked the sing-song cadence of it, and she had liked his lack of arrogance and the way that he had smiled on her. Also, she thought now, he had an ear for language; he could change his accent and his way of speaking at will so that he was at home with his company.

She had had no idea that he would want to build his own town.

'The furniture and such that we were expecting – it hasn't arrived.'

'Oh,' he said, suddenly very friendly. He had recovered himself, she thought. 'I'll sort it out. I'm glad you came, we need help. We have several orphans here already.'

'You asked for us?' She finally managed to look at him.

He smiled at her and it was a good smile, it made her feel important and wanted.

'It seemed like a good idea.'

'What are you doing here?'

'I'm making iron for the ships and this seemed an obvious place; it has such good resources. And there are lots of people who need work, and some children who have come here without any parents, and we need shelter for them. I'm determined that all the children here shall have an education, so I asked for help from Newcastle. If you need to ask anything else, I'm living at the farmhouse at the bottom of the valley with my friend, Wesley Hallam.'

Seven

Eve Gray had lived in Wolsingham all her life and could not have hated it any more than she did. She longed to be away. She longed for excitement and beautiful dresses and musical concerts and fashionable people and there was nothing of that here. She had been born into the middle of nowhere and nothing happened, nothing changed. She thought she might die of boredom.

It was, other people thought, a lovely little town in the valley of the Wear, the beginning of Weardale, awash with farms and small towns – and with all those prejudices that such places have.

It didn't like people it didn't know. It didn't like people who thought differently. And she was already so different that she thought she had no place here. Her father was a doctor so that set her aside. He wasn't nearly as important as the vicar, but he was above the shopkeepers and below the wealthy farmers. He did not shoot or fish or ride to hounds so fitted in nowhere.

He had come from Berwick, and to these people, Berwick could have been the far ends of the earth, instead of just another small town between Scotland and England. Her father said it had a very fine bridge.

His accent was strange to them, and so was his wife, since they knew she had gone off her head, and so was Eve, because she did not go to school. Her father found her a governess; he knew that to go to school here among the ordinary people would be beyond her, considering her circumstances.

Also he was not convinced that the ordinary schooling would suit her. He wanted her to learn to love literature and languages – and even science, if she could manage it – because his wife had loved the arts and he loved science.

Her mother was from the area and her grandparents had been well off at some time. All that was left was the house where they had lived. It was, to be fair, a most beautiful house. It lay beside the river, had extensive grounds and gardens. It had been built in the eighteenth century and had three stories, high wide rooms which opened out on to land all around it. There were three acres for horses, stables and hay lofts, and a number of outside buildings, including a wash house, close beside the back kitchen door, and a hen house. It was big and her father had to keep it going because her mother had no money. Her mother had lost her mind, everybody agreed, though not within Eve's presence.

It was common knowledge that for years her mother had not been outside. Having a mother who had no social contact was very hard for Eve. With a father as a doctor, and a mother who fitted nowhere, she too fitted nowhere and it was hard. She had a good father, she had everything she wanted, except the one thing she craved. To be somewhere, to do something, to go away and have things be new and interesting and exciting.

It didn't happen. There was nobody for her to marry. To be fair, the local curate had asked her to marry him, and it had taken all her ability not to laugh in his face. He was little and shrunken; she could see the top of his almost-bald head, his hair growing around the edges like a hairy halo, and he talked to her of the Bible. He smelled of damp pages and cheap sherry, and he had thin lips, and breath which reeked of three-day-old onions. His clothes smelled too, as though he was thinking of God too much to wash. She imagined getting into bed with the curate and almost choked.

She had nobody to disparage him to, so when he had gone, when she had told him as respectfully as she could that she could not marry him, she laughed only to herself. Mrs Florence, when told, said that she thought Miss Evie might have taken a fancy to the young man, and her father looked dismayed. She could not say what she really thought, that she would rather die an old maid than marry him.

There was nobody for her to befriend, so when the fell-top village began, she thought little of it, until her father had to go up there when there was an accident and came back and said to her, 'Mr Gilbraith has asked me to go and work there two days a week and I have asked him to dine with us.'

Her father never asked anybody 'to dine' with them, so she said that she would ask Mrs Florence, the housekeeper, to order a good dinner, and her father smiled on her.

She had never thought that Gilbraith would be eligible. She had imagined him middle-aged with many children, a fat wife, no conversation and little hair except upon his chin, which might hold yesterday's egg. So when he turned up and she liked him very much, she was amazed.

He didn't stay long; he had to go back to the new village before darkness fell completely. When he had gone, she began to think about what it would be like to be his wife. He was rich – her father had unwittingly, in a sense, let her know this, so that she suspected him of manoeuvring things, except that her father was naïve in such matters, or why would he have married her mother?

She had long since been told that her mother's madness was only for her, and not to be passed on, but Eve lay awake at night and wondered what her life would be when she was shut up like her mother. Not that her mother was shut up, but she thought that she was and often battered against invisible walls and cried for she knew not what. Eve thought her father did not want to frighten her by telling her that such a thing could be inherited, so he held her gaze while he told her that she would never be like that.

Eve could remember being very small when her mother still came downstairs, but she could not venture outside; she wouldn't even go near the windows or doors. She didn't know who Eve was, or her husband, and didn't ask. Eve thought there had been a time when her mother did know who she was, and she thought she could remember her calling her father by his first name, which was Iain.

That was a very long time ago and sometimes Eve didn't know whether these things had actually happened or if she only remembered her father telling her.

Her mother ate little and was skinny and shrunken, but did no one any harm, so they didn't mind when she wandered about, which was always during the day.

She had to be bathed and have her hair washed and her clothes changed, or she would never have noticed how dirty and unkempt she became, but since she had been ill for so long, Eve's father had always employed a nurse to take care of her. Mrs Florence, who could calm her down like no one else could, was treated like her mother's mother, though never her grandmother.

Mrs Florence was trusted and relied on by the doctor's wife to make everything work well. Eve's father was always saying that she gave her mother the confidence to go on. To go on to where, Eve did not know, and it made her feel bitter. She knew that lots of other girls had no mother or no father, or were even orphaned and lived with family or people they didn't like, but she resented how her father went on and on about her mother, how she trusted the nurse and Mrs Florence. The nurses came and went, so her mother could not be that easy to deal with. Sometimes they were there only a few weeks. Maybe her father didn't pay them sufficiently, maybe they hated the quietness of the dale, or maybe they just didn't want to have to deal with a woman who lived in a dream – or was it a nightmare?

Sometimes Eve could hear her father talking to her mother so softly and so gently that it made her cry, thinking of how it might have been. Her father could have had her mother put away into a place where maniacs were shackled and ill-treated, he said, and Eve had been sure that he meant it. She must accept that her mother was at home with them, and that however hard it was, it could be nothing compared to her mother's short future if she was ill-treated physically and left to die. There were better places than he knew of, but the truth was that he could not let her go. Did he hope for better times, or was it just that although he had lost his wife, he was dedicated to her forever?

Eve longed to suggest to him that perhaps her mother could go to people who would be kind to her, and they would not have to deal with her anymore, but she dared not; it was so mean and selfish. She tried not to hate how dependent her mother was, and how her presence in the house ran their lives and they never seemed to get any further. Eve's world went round and round in circles of tedium.

Eve wished that her father could have helped her mother, but he said that you could not help everybody. It had long since destroyed her peace and made her the more determined to get away.

For the past few years, her mother had not come downstairs. Eve had lost her mother to her madness as it grew worse and confined her more inside her head, upstairs where she could see the garden she had given up attempting to visit.

Jay Gilbraith looked like the person who could help Eve, so she smiled on him. She didn't think she loved him and she wasn't sure that he loved her – it was almost as though he needed to marry to be respectable – but she did like him very much. Perhaps that was a necessity too. She had never loved anyone as she had imagined she might love the man she married. How could she know if this was love; perhaps it was just fancy or desperation? She was desperate – not desperate enough to marry somebody physically disgusting, but certainly to marry a man who had a lot of money and could change her life.

He did not come back to eat with them again, and she longed to see him just for diversion, but she could not ask. She could not go there. She could do nothing to bring him to her.

Eight

Maddy had been so upset about meeting her former lover that she could feel her heart thumping as she made her way back up the hill towards the butterfly house. She tried to pretend that she had not met him, tried to keep her mind on what she was doing, but he had been so normal, so friendly. He had even smiled at her. She had no doubt that he would succeed here, it was what he did.

She had to search for Sister Bee when she got back. She was sitting down while those around her did everything. It was so unlike her that Maddy saw straight away she was not well.

'It's nothing but a summer cold,' she said.

Maddy was beginning to worry. Perhaps the whole thing was just too much for Sister Bee. She was small and stout and looked capable of anything, but Maddy thought that the determination in her face was just that, and there was nothing much behind it. She began to feel rather sorry too, because Sister Bee was not usually this quiet; but since they had left Newcastle, she had not felt good. Maddy was regretting what she regarded as her city too, but she thought that Sister Bee's problem went beyond homesickness.

Maddy told her what Gilbraith had said and she looked grateful. Nobody knew better than nuns that such men were invaluable, as there were so many things to put right, things which nuns could not accomplish. Mostly they went without, but here they had responsibilities to the people, and most especially to the children they would be called upon to look after.

Father Timothy, who had gone there as soon as help had been asked for, had been asked to assess the need and get back to Reverend Mother. He had been looking after the children until they could get there. Maddy was shocked when she saw the building he had the children in.

It was nothing more than a long, low hut, built probably in a great hurry for the original pit sinkers when they needed to be inside a proper building rather than tents. They would have been the first persons employed by Gilbraith, because if there had been no coal in the area, he could not have built the town. It was not suitable for its present use, she thought.

There were five children there, four girls and one boy, and they looked as though they had not eaten in weeks.

'I haven't been able to do much for them, I'm afraid,' he confessed.

Maddy stared. He was not joking. Where was the practicality? She wanted to ask him if he had been to see Mr Gilbraith to get something more done, but he obviously hadn't. Somebody had fobbed him off with dirty blankets. The children wore few clothes and were scrawny from lack of food. They eyed the nun in silence.

Maddy said she would get Sister Abigail to help, and that she thought the children should go straight up to the house where the convent was going to be because the sisters would be able to feed them. He gave her no argument and when they ushered the children out, he seemed relieved.

'I must go back to Newcastle,' he announced.

Maddy stared at him. She had not understood that he would not stay and help. Perhaps she had been at fault, interpreting things in a wrong way.

'I was told only to remain here until you arrived,' he said. 'As you can see, they are all, but one, girls.'

As though they didn't matter, she thought, from his tone. It could not be that important. It wasn't up to her to say anything. She thought he was pathetic for a priest, but then you got useless people in all areas of life, so she merely nodded and ignored him. People who were useless were best getting rid of.

So she and Abigail shepherded the children up to the butterfly house. Maddy offered to carry the little boy, who was very small, and so afraid that he began to cry, but his eldest sister shook her head and she lifted him up into her arms. She didn't look at Maddy so Maddy let her go on. The four little girls were so weary that she was glad it was not far.

Hilary had built up the stove and made porridge. They had no milk so it would have to be nothing more than oats and water, but they had sugar so they were able to give each child a palatable meal.

Sister Bee tightened her lips as she did when she was angry when Maddy told her that Father Timothy was leaving. They distributed cake and biscuits and bread they had brought with them. None of the children fussed; they ate with eager determination and then huddled together, as though afraid of what might happen now.

The furniture which Gilbraith had promised soon arrived. The nuns set up beds with clean linen. They also had hot water now that Abigail had sorted out the fire and put cold water into the boiler alongside it. A big line was set up with the tin bath so that the children could bathe as they wanted to.

Nobody told them what to do, but the eldest girl – who had obviously done these things before – stripped her little brother and put him into the warm water and soaped him and washed his hair. He cried throughout, but it was more tiredness than protest. He did not make much noise and all through it, the eldest child – who couldn't have been more than eight or nine, Maddy thought – talked to him in low sweet tones.

When he was done, she towelled him dry and Maddy helped to dress him. Then his big sister carried him to the nearest bed and sang him to sleep. It didn't take long; he was worn out.

She then came back. Maddy smiled at her.

'What is your little brother called?'

'Patrick. I'm Hannah and my sister is Shannon. Some people brought us here. We left Derry a long time ago and our parents died on the way. We didn't know who the people were but they left us here and that man took us in.'

She meant Father Timothy, Maddy saw, and the look on the girl's face told her a lot.

The other two girls said nothing and Maddy didn't like to ask too much in case they were scared. Once all the children were bathed and clothed, they lay down on the beds and Hannah sang to them. Maddy didn't know whether to be grateful at this maturity, or horrified for what might have caused her to behave like an adult.

Abigail made a fire out the back and burned the clothes they had taken off them, confident that the nuns had brought what would do. More could be made. They were aware that other children would turn up and need help.

Mr Nattrass, a farmer who lived about a mile away, brought vegetables and salad from his garden and fields. He promised them lots of plums and pears and apples when they ripened, which would not be long now. He also brought them two young cats to keep down the mice, and in case there should be any rats, which he assured them was unlikely. Rats tended to go where there was food and they used all their food.

He also brought his two sheepdogs, Dobber and Bonny, who got lots of cuddles from the children.

Maddy was very impressed with Mr Nattrass. The sisters gathered around him, so happy with the great sack of potatoes, carrots, cabbages and turnips he brought, and also tomatoes and cucumbers from his greenhouses, and peas and beans and leeks from his garden. The leeks were enormous. Mr Nattrass said that he used to show his leeks, but if they grew too big they didn't make good eating. He had brought them while they were perfect. He also shot rabbits and pigeons on his land. Maddy felt she could have hugged him for his help. He said he lived by himself, and since he had heard they were arriving, he wanted to do all he could to keep things going and to help feed the orphans.

Later that afternoon, Abigail came in with a large black and white goat.

Earlier Hilary had said, 'If only we had a cow.'

Abigail had stared at her.

'What do you mean?' she said.

'For milk.'

'Can you milk a cow?'

'Of course.'

'Where did that come from?' Maddy asked as they went outside to see it. The children were asleep in what had become their dormitory, a huge long room on the first floor. They were exhausted but now full of food; they needed to rest and then eat again before nightfall.

'It just appeared,' Abigail said, face innocent, 'like visions in the Bible, ye knaa, Sister. The Lord will provide.'

Maddy was dying to ask which field it had appeared from. Sister Hilary got herself down on a small box and milked the goat into the large pot they normally used for baking stews and vegetables in the oven. She let them all taste the milk. It was rather strange in flavour, like nuts, but warm and frothy and there was a goodly amount. They gave milk to the children, and made sure they all had some, keeping just a little back to colour their tea.

The goat seemed quite at home and ate the grass on the roadside, and although it was not tethered because they couldn't find anything to tether it to, the goat didn't get wet; it followed them inside. Hilary assured them that goats hated wet weather.

'And where is it to stay?'

There were outside buildings but they weren't sure whether the goat would stay there by itself. They had sorted out rooms for themselves. Sister Bee had an office on the ground floor with a bed to herself. The other three nuns slept in the same room on the first floor to be near the children. If any of them woke up and were scared, they wanted to be nearby.

Abigail offered to sleep on the ground floor with the goat, and although this produced some laughter, a bed was set up for her, along with a blanket on the floor for the goat since she demanded it should be comfortable.

On Hilary's advice, Abigail found the goat lots of rosebay willowherb, tall with bright pink flowers, and tied up bunches for the goat to eat. Hilary said that there was a superstition that if you picked it there would be a storm.

'But that's always the way in early autumn,' she said.

As autumn took hold, the seed heads became grey wisps and

told of summer ending on the roadside. The goat happily ate all the greens they could supply, and after that, it took to following Abigail around as though they had adopted one another. Maddy expected that any minute some irate goat herder would appear and complain, but nothing happened.

She was glad that at least the storm had blown itself out; a fine evening glowed through the cracked panes of the house. Maddy liked the Irish tones of Hannah and her siblings. They had a sweet sing-song voice, rather like Newcastle, she thought. The other two had yet to speak, so she had no idea where they were from.

The first night they had all slept and it made things easy. The second day, with more to eat and somewhere they were unsure of, they didn't move from the room unless they had to. It was not until the third night that Maddy heard crying. It was not loud but it was getting louder. She did not know how frightening she would seem to a small child, but out of her habit with her cap on and what she hoped was an ordinary nightgown, she crept out of the room, taking a candle, and found the child.

She had thought it would be the little boy, but it was one of the girls who had not spoken. Maddy sat down on the bed and waited for the child to shrink from her, but the crying lessened a little way, so all Maddy did was stroke her hair. It was contact but she hoped not intrusive.

A clear but decisive tone came from Hannah's bed. Very quietly she said, 'Shall I sing to her, Sister?'

'Yes, do, I'm sure she will like that.'

So Hannah sang a lullaby in soft tones; perhaps it was one that her dead mother had sung to her. Maddy was grateful, but for some reason the child's voice made her want to cry as well. She cleared her throat. When the little girl was asleep, she tucked up

Hannah and thanked her. The girl merely nodded and turned over. Maddy went back to bed and couldn't sleep.

She went downstairs to where Abigail was asleep. The goat sat up and greeted her with a happy little bleat and Abigail stirred. Needing comfort herself, Maddy sat down on the floor beside the goat and began to stroke her.

'Are you all right, Maddy?' They were not meant to use first names like that, but Abigail didn't care. They didn't do it in front of Sister Bee because she would have been offended, but when there were just two or three of them, they acted like friends. Maddy relied on the other two and they did on her. They were indeed sisters, she thought gratefully.

Maddy went on stroking the goat and explained about the children. Abigail had not known her parents and she would understand better than anyone, Maddy knew. Abigail said very little but nodded from time to time. All she said at the end was:

'Don't worry. We are here now.'

Maddy remembered that when she went back upstairs, and she fell asleep immediately.

Nine

Eve's father was caught up in his practice and went on going up to the new town and having nothing to do with her. She thought she would die if she had to spend another evening reading by herself, or going into the village for what passed for a social life there – talks with tea, and cake afterwards, church socials where everybody talked about their families and old women bored her with tales of remarkable grandchildren. People even came to her with their ailments, as though she could help. They were not beyond asking her if the doctor would mind calling on them at home.

She longed for real entertainment, music, theatre, somebody to talk to who read.

And as if he had heard her, Jay Gilbraith trotted his horse into the yard one Wednesday afternoon. She felt rather than knew it and was ecstatic. He came to her when her father was on his rounds and then he stayed and had tea with her.

It was not as she had imagined. He could not talk to her about the arts. He knew nothing about such things. He talked to her about the village and what he was doing; he told her how clever her father was. He asked about what she was doing, and there she faltered. She could not think of a single interesting thing that she did, though she was grateful for being asked. No other man that she could remember had asked her about her life.

'You do know about my mother?' she said, testing him.

'Your father told me that she has been ill for years. That must be hard for you both.'

And she began telling him about all the things she wanted to do and he listened.

'Have you ever been anywhere?' she asked him.

'No.'

'Haven't you wanted to?'

'Many times, but I haven't had the chance. I have always had to work. Perhaps when the village is complete, I may leave Hallam in charge and go away and do other things.'

'Like what?'

'New places, new people. Learn languages I don't know and try something else.'

She smiled at this and was encouraged and said that she felt the same.

'Perhaps further,' he said. 'First of all Europe, and then the East, which I know nothing about and I'm sure holds many splendours.'

She liked him more and more. He could get her out of here. He could take her to new places; she could travel in luxury and wear beautiful gowns. They would go to London and Paris, to the opera and the symphony. He could rent houses in places like Florence, where she believed there was a wonderful river. She could look down on it and know that she was rich and beloved, and could have anything she wanted.

'I'm glad you like him,' her father said later. 'I think he will make a fine man in time. He is at the moment rather raw, and understands little about good society, but he has new ideas and is eager to give people jobs and homes. I don't know anybody else with such ambitions. He will go far.'

'He talked to me of Europe.'

'Did he now, or did you talk to him?' Her father was pleased at the idea, she could tell. She knew that he wanted her married but was aware that it would not happen easily. He encouraged Gilbraith to come and eat with them.

She also asked him to dinner and she liked how the two men regarded one another with respect. Her father was fond of saying that he loved his work and that he liked very much going to the new village and establishing the surgery and clinic. Mr Gilbraith suggested that he could do with some help, an assistant. Her father said that he had a friend in London, a Mr Esher, whose son was looking for an apprenticeship, and he was thinking to give the lad some experience of a different place. He might write to his friend and suggest the lad come to them, and Mr Gilbraith said he thought it an excellent idea.

Jay had fallen in love again. Having told himself for years that he never would, and feeling bitter against Maddy and her father and the circumstances, he had given up on the whole idea of finding a woman to marry him. He told himself that he was quite happy with the work, with the ideas driving him forward and the friendship he had with Hallam, and left it at that. Then he met Eve Gray, the local doctor's daughter.

She thought that he would ask her to marry him and he had thought up a wonderful scheme. He would build her such a beautiful house up on the tops above his new town that she would never want to leave this place. The ideas spilled out of his head, and since he was beginning new projects every day, it seemed nothing to think about the kind of place where he wanted to take his bride. He found the perfect spot just beyond the town, with a clear road to the border on one side and a long wide view of the fell on the other.

He put some ideas down on paper and then went to consult the man he would get to build it for him. He lived on the tops above Wolsingham in Weardale, the pretty valley beyond his village where the road plunged down to the bottom in two steep hills.

He enjoyed being there and stayed the night, because they had a lot of ideas to think over, and the builder and his wife were good company. She was a superb cook. They had two small children whom the maid put to bed and then they sat and talked across the table, the three of them, because the builder's wife had ideas as rich as either of the men's thoughts.

Jay loved their enthusiasm. It matched his own. So he had had a good time when he set off in the late afternoon. It would be light for a while yet, it was the beginning of autumn, though the nights would be drawing in in a few days. He hoped the weather wouldn't give out just yet.

When it rained here, it didn't know how to stop, and they had had a very wet time that August. But it wasn't raining now and he was thinking about the house. He didn't dare acknowledge to himself that things were going well because that automatically meant that something awful would happen, but he was thinking about Eve, how beautiful she was and how they would be happy together.

He would be starting with the building the following week, and although it was going to be a big project, the builder was used to large dwellings. He had a team of experts and another of labourers, so it could be done in a matter of weeks, if the weather stayed dry until they put the lid on it. Jay liked that expression – it made the house sound like a teapot – but he knew that this was how it worked. If you could get the structure right, then you could do the inside without being hampered once the bad weather came. If you delayed, then you might get nothing done until the following April.

The stone was already in place; it had to be cut and the walls had to be built after the foundations were put in. He had good stonemasons and good roofers. Rob Slater was his main man; Jay would have asked Rob to do the building if he had a bit more experience, but Rob had agreed to help as much as he could. He would bring his men too, so it would be a joint venture.

Jay loved new ventures as he loved nothing else, and with building, you got a proper result. You got to do something which, if good enough, would last lifetimes, such as the house where the nuns lived.

He had stopped thinking about Maddy. It had been a shock when he saw her, but that was all he felt. He had found the right woman, and by the look of her, Maddy had found her right road too. They could both go forward without regret.

He was hoping that the house would be ready by Christmas, but this was perhaps expecting too much. So certainly by the spring, if the weather was not too bad. Up here on the tops sometimes it snowed for weeks, the wind screamed and the ice held everything in its grasp. He tried to think positively. They might have a mild winter and so the house would be ready soon.

He wasn't thinking particularly about the sights he passed, so he almost missed the bundle of clothes by the side of the road. But his mare, Phyllis, a good friend to him, did see it, hesitated and stopped. When he questioned her, she neighed.

The horse had better instincts than he did. She had cost him a great deal of money and was cleverer than most of the rest of the world put together. When Jay didn't move or say much, the horse made several snorting noises through her nose as though she was disturbed. She wouldn't move. When he had first got her, he had not understood her, but since he was always gentle with her, he thought she must be right. He would get off and investigate.

He slid to the ground, noticed the bundle and saw that it was a very small person. He thought it was dead. He had seen lots of dead people. In Newcastle when he was a child, there were frequently dead people on the streets and in the hovels and alleyways beyond, in gutters in the rain. He always wished he could have made their lives better and it had led him here.

People starved every day. It was one of the reasons he had wanted to build a new town, a good place where people could work and live and have their children and gain some enjoyment from their lives. If he could manage it, none of them would have to live badly again.

It was a young girl. Her hair was as red as a winter fire. Her face was alabaster and her eyes were shut but he noticed the thick black lashes which covered the tops of her cheeks. Her skin was cold when he touched her and when he spoke, she did not awaken, but he felt for her pulse and it was there, fleeting.

'Good lass,' he said, as he lifted her up. She was tiny and for this he thanked God, because he had to get them both on to the horse. It took a bit of doing, even with the horse's help. Phyllis let him draw her to a large stone and stood there while he tried gently to put the girl on her, and then managed to get himself into the saddle, so that he caught the girl safely in his arms. She was in front of him and easy to hold there, as somebody bigger would not have been.

It took him longer to get back than it should have done, and darkness had fallen. At some point he had to let go of the reins to hold her and the horse made slowly for home, knowing that it held precious cargo. He kept up on the tops, not caring to negotiate the hills which led out of the dale to his new town, and by the time he reached the convent, he was tired.

Ten

Ruth was horrified when she came to. She heard a man's voice and wanted to scream but she couldn't. He was talking to her. He was touching her. She tried to scream again but her voice had gone. What was he doing to her? Was he doing what her father had done? She tried to struggle against him but her strength was no better than her voice. When he lifted her, she was lost to it and then she felt the horse under her. She had died. She could not endure any more. She had died and had been lost to life and it was all over. Soon the pain would stop and the horse would stop and she would know nothing anymore.

The horse's hooves took on a rhythm and she kept her eyes closed; the man who had taken her up against him was holding her like she was a bundle, not as though she was a woman, or even a person. He held her up so that she could not fall. He did not smell like her father, of sweat and five-day-old piss on his clothes. He smelled of some kind of soap and she liked it and it reassured her.

How stupid to be reassured by a smell, and yet there against his coat she felt more content than she had felt in a long time; she felt safe. What smell was safe? She couldn't identify it, but this was it and she was happy just to lie there and remember nothing and go neither forward nor back, timelessly.

The movement of the horse went on and on. The pain had stopped again for the moment. She was so glad that she managed to get herself almost to unconsciousness; the horse's gait was steady, not quick and not slow. Ruth kept her eyes closed against the man.

It was a man. A woman could not have put her up on to a horse nor held her like that. She remembered how her father had treated her; he was the only man she knew, but this was different. She felt differently about it. They did not know one another and it did not matter. All that mattered was the horse and its movement; it was lulling her back into sleep, which she had thought so surely she would not come out of. She wouldn't have minded slipping slowly out of life, she wouldn't have minded that at all; just to let go and to have to feel nothing ever again.

Maddy came across with another nun whom Jay had not met. He thought she was called Sister Hilary; she was tall and well-built. They got him to carry the girl into a small side room, where he put her down on a bed. It was obviously some kind of sick bay, but there was nobody else in it, just several empty beds and large cupboards and a table and chairs.

'Bring her straight through here,' Maddy had said, embarrassment gone. That was one of the things he had loved about this woman, he now remembered. She would make a good nun because she was practical and cared about other people and never about herself.

That had prevented her from becoming his wife, he thought. She had cared so much for her father that she did not do what she wanted. And he was not the man to persuade any woman to marry him when he was less than thirty, and she couldn't have been more than twenty. He had been too proud to go any further. He had known that it would do him no good. She was determined, that was the other quality he had seen in her. No doubt that too was useful now.

Maddy had forgotten who he was; it didn't matter but that he had helped, he could see. She looked wildly into his face as Sister Hilary knelt over the girl.

'What happened?' she said.

'I don't know. I just found her up on the tops beyond Wolsingham. She was still breathing then.'

'She is now,' Sister Hilary said.

'Don't worry,' Maddy said, 'we'll take care of her.'

When he had gone, Sister Hilary clicked her tongue against her teeth like somebody much older.

'Oh, Maddy,' she said, in a way that she would never have done had anybody else but Abigail been there, 'she's having a child. She's just a child herself, look at her.'

The girl stirred and tried to say something, so they sat her up with a lot of pillows and a blanket. They put warm tea to her lips and tried to get some toast into her. She was wet through and shivering. They cut off the rags she was wearing and her shoes, which were in tatters. Her feet were blistered and the blisters wept blood and yellow pus; they bathed and dressed them and put ointment on them. They put loose, dry clothes on her, but they tried to be as careful as possible, because her pain became worse and worse.

Abigail came in and said she would attend to getting the children fed and into bed; they must stay with her. Hannah was nothing like a child, but they suspected there was a story from the Irish children who had no parents. The other two girls cried quietly, but they too had some kind of bond, though they were obviously not sisters. Nobody knew where they had come from. The questions would wait, Maddy thought.

All the children needed now was to be full of food and to sleep as much as they wanted to. Then the school could begin. It had been Mother's most important idea. She believed that the best thing of all was the education of women. Something had to be done now, and it would, in time, take women out of poverty and away from the power that evil men might have over them. She didn't actually say this, but they all knew it.

Eleven

Ruth was by now fully awake. She was aware of having been carried down from the horse, just when she was getting used to it. Then the pain began again and this time it was a lot worse, as though a large animal was biting at her stomach and below it. She came to and didn't notice her surroundings.

There was nothing beyond the pain; there never would be anything beyond the pain. She moved and turned over and over as if she could get away from it, but it followed her movements as though it were alive. If only she could have stayed on the horse and against the warmth of the man and slept her way out of this life. But it was not going to be that easy.

The pain made her open her mouth and scream. She would have given anything to make it stop but it didn't. She couldn't understand how anybody could survive such agony. She fastened her arms across her front where the big mound of the baby lay, because it seemed to her now that this was what was causing it, her father's damned bastard. Whatever had she done to deserve such a thing?

It had to stop but it didn't and she thrashed about on whatever bed she was lying on, and everywhere she went the pain followed her. It was all over her, it pricked at her very being, it was unendurable, and yet it must be borne.

*

Once the girl was properly awake, she began to hold her stomach and complain, so when Jay arrived early the next morning, Maddy begged him to go and ask Mr Gray if he could come. But the doctor was away at the limestone quarry in Stanhope, halfway up the dale, where there had been an accident. They had to manage as best they could.

The baby did not arrive. Maddy and Hilary knew little about such things and were terrified as the girl sweated and cried and screamed, until they were convinced that neither she nor the baby would survive. Her pain cost all of them; they were at a loss as to what to do and watching her suffer was awful.

It was a hard birth; anybody could have known that. It went on for three days, during which time all they could do before Mr Gray got there was put wet cloths on her forehead and on her sweaty body, shove as much cowslip wine as she would take into her mouth for the pain and hope for the best. If they prayed they did it separately.

Maddy thought she had never been as glad to see anybody as when Mr Gray walked in late on the day when Jay had gone to him. His face was as pale as his name. It was obvious to her that he had not slept in a long time. His eyes were narrowed and his cheeks were drawn. He gave the girl laudanum to deaden the pain so that she stopped crying. She was very weak, he said privately to them, but at least he could help.

Maddy felt a wave of relief when the girl stopped screaming with pain. Nobody should have to go through such a thing.

When she finally gave birth, the child was dead; they had

imagined nothing different. The doctor was desperate to save her and didn't leave her side for twelve hours. Maddy had assumed the girl would get better after the dead child was out of her body, but apparently not. The afterbirth was hard in coming and she kept losing blood, but at least this slowed.

Maddy had never seen so much blood and was convinced that the girl would not come through. She had never heard such pain. Both she and Hilary wanted to cry; she could see tears in Hilary's eyes. But neither of them allowed those tears to fall. It would not help this poor young thing. It would not do any of them any good. There was no release in such tears at that time.

When the afterbirth was over, she was still alive but only just. She was breathing very weakly. The doctor wrapped the dead baby in cloths and Hilary took it away.

Maddy waited for the girl to die, for her to take her last breaths. They waited and waited, but the doctor kept her alive and out of pain. She went on breathing; her chest went up and down. It went on and on and every second Maddy thought it was over. When the doctor pronounced that he thought she was not going to die, Hilary and Maddy both went outside the room for a few moments and hugged each other and wept, but silently in case the girl or the doctor or anybody else should hear.

Mr Gray went off to see other patients. Maddy felt bereft and deserted when he did, but he assured her that all the girl needed was nursing, a little food and water, and to be kept warm and still. With God's help and their prayers, she might be all right.

One of them always stayed with her. The others helped generally and it was so much easier to do other things. The room where she lay was their new clinic inside the butterfly house. Mr Gray had set up regular times when he came to see the various families who were pouring in now that there was work and the houses were built. When she was well enough, they might move her into the room where the children slept. This was something which had to be discussed, whether she would be better alone or with other people, but for now she was staying where she was.

If more boys came, they would need to rethink the arrangement, but Maddy was just glad of this great big house which would accommodate their needs. She did not like to think of what they would do when they needed more room, but she tried to think of it as Jay Gilbraith's problem. Perhaps like the Lord, he would provide. If he did not, then he had not done what he said he would and she felt certain he hated to fail.

Ruth was certain she had gone to hell. There could not be enough pain in all the world for this. She was not having a child, she was being tortured to death, and those around her didn't notice, didn't care. Her mother had told her that childbirth was like this. No wonder she had not wanted more children. Did other women go through this again and again? How could they? How could they endure this horrible pain? There was nothing left in her life but screaming, and the endless pain and the whole of her existence being in this agony. She screamed so much that she could not scream any more. She had but to endure and the endurance of it took everything she had, and more, so that in the end she had no self and no voice. She was nothing but the hell that she had gone to. She could remember nothing beyond it, nothing at all.

Ruth had not thought that the pain would ever cease and then it began to lessen. And then it lessened some more and she began to breathe among the pain and the pain receded. It only went so far until it was bearable, and after that she knew that she had never been so thirsty in her life. But somebody was there to aid her.

Somebody put water to her lips and then tea. Tea had never tasted so good. She went to sleep. She had never been so tired; she had never wanted to lie down so much. She was lying in the cleanest bed she had ever smelled. She thought of the washing on the line on fine days above the cottage in summer when she was little and her mother had been different. She had helped her mother hang out the washing and the summer breeze would lift it and the washing smelled of soap.

After a week the nuns began to relax. The girl wasn't going to die. She was eating and drinking and sleeping. The doctor said that they must let her go on like this and she would eventually recover. After that, they looked in on her from time to time, giving her soup and then more substantial food. That was when they saw that she was older than they had thought; it was just that she was very small.

She did not ask about the baby, nor did she say anything. Jay went every day to find out how she did. They had not wanted to tell him that she was having a child, but since they needed the doctor's help, they had done so, both together, stuttering since it was a new and difficult territory.

'She is a child,' he said.

Maddy shook her head but she couldn't bring herself to glance at him. Hilary looked as though she would have given a great deal not to be there.

'No, she must be fourteen or even a little more. She is just very slight, which was why she had problems giving birth, so the doctor said.' Maddy's cheeks were roasting. She knew it wasn't the thing to talk about such matters, especially to men, but he had to be told. She told him when the girl began to get better.

He stared but only for a few seconds. He was quick; she was grateful for his good mind.

'So what happened to the baby?' he said briskly.

'We still have it, wrapped up in clean linen. We didn't know what to do.'

'I'll bury it with lots of stone over it,' he said.

'She hasn't spoken yet.'

'Not at all?'

'Nothing.'

During the days which followed, Ruth became aware of what was around her. She had not gone to hell, at least she didn't think so. If she had, then there were a lot of nuns around and that seemed unlikely. The pain got less and less. It was still there but it ceased to be the raging, all-consuming force which had seemed to be killing her. She had not died.

This idea took a lot of getting used to. She had no idea where she was and nobody said anything to her other than general words of comfort as the nuns flitted in and out. They reminded her rather of butterflies, if there were ever butterflies in black and white. Had they been birds, they would have been magpies. They made little sound; if she was sleeping – and that was the easiest place to be right now – they spoke in whispers.

That worried her at first. Was she still going to die? She didn't want to die anymore. That was surprising; after the first few hours of examining the likelihood, and deciding it wasn't going to happen, she started to feel different. It wasn't a good feeling; the confusion became so much that the only thing to do was to sleep.

She replayed over and over the horrible birth. She wasn't sure where the baby was, and she saw herself being attacked by her father and knifing him until he stopped trying to hurt her. After that, she thought that perhaps she might die so that the images would stop.

She began to refuse to eat and the pretty nun with the dark eyes told her that she must eat, it was good for her. But Ruth turned her face away. After she refused to eat for the third time, the pretty nun sat down on the bed and said to her,

'I'm Sister Madeline. What are you called?'

What did it matter? Ruth didn't answer.

'We are only trying to help you. You must try to take something.'

It was only when another nun spoke more roughly to her that it had some effect. Ruth lay looking at the wall and was surprised to see a very small, brisk individual come to the bottom of the bed. They had some form of eye contact and then she said, 'Sister Maddy is cross with you. You are lucky to be here, you good for nowt. Stop behaving like a bairn and eat your breakfast. Plenty of lasses would be pleased at what we've done. Now sit up and do as you're told.'

Ruth tried not to but she could see, even without looking, that this skinny person standing there looked most un-nun-like. Or at least so Ruth thought, having not encountered such a person before. She only knew of nuns generally and had imagined that they came in fairytales. The nun stood there with skinny hands on her hips and when Ruth glanced at her, there was a look of determination in her eyes.

'Howay then, sit up and stop going on like this.'

The nun had eyes like raisins, Ruth thought, but she did what she was told.

The nun fed her; all she had to do was open her mouth and into it went scrambled egg. Ruth thought she would choke; she couldn't remember anybody feeding her before. When the bowl had been scooped out, the sister took it away and gave into Ruth's hands a large pot of very sweet tea and stood over her while she drank it. When the cup was empty, the nun took it from her. Ruth had thought she would go and leave her in peace but she didn't.

'Now then, you are going to get better. Many folks have had worse than you've had. You need to help yourself, lass.'

'What happened to my baby?'

Ruth had been wanting to ask that. At one point it had been the only thing in her head. The only enduring thought.

'It died. I'm sorry for that and you will grieve over it, I feel sure.'

'It died?' For some reason this had not occurred to Ruth, though surely if the baby had been alive, they would have brought it to her and they had not. But now she couldn't bear the idea. She went through all that for nothing? Tears, unasked for, took over her face like a hot army until she could hardly breathe.

The tiny nun sat down and took Ruth into her arms, patting her, holding her as Ruth had never been held before, and she said, 'My poor lass, my poor lass.'

When the tears stopped, the nun actually kissed Ruth on the forehead before she went out. Ruth felt as though there was some kind of imprint there. It was the first time she had been shown affection, and that magicked itself in among all her awful thoughts so that there was something to combat them.

It was like a shield in her head; now she could eat and drink and sit up.

When she got her legs to the floor for the first time, she passed straight into blackness and came to back in bed. But it was a temporary lapse; she was able to get up and walk a little that day, and although it did still hurt where the baby had come from, it was nothing like as bad as it had been.

Twelve

Two days later Jay received a visit from two men he had never seen before. They were policemen. He had known a great many policemen in various ways in Newcastle, but not in the dale where the folk were law-abiding and had too much else to do. So he couldn't think what these two were doing here. One of them introduced himself as Billings. The other said nothing.

He took them down to the farmhouse, away from men's curious stares, because whatever they wanted, it couldn't be good. Billings either didn't care to hide his general disapproval as they walked down the hill or he was just given to having a long face.

When they were in the big room which Jay had chosen for his office, the long room at the back of the house with two huge desks covered and overflowing with papers, he offered them tea. Two women, Mrs Tempest and Mrs Neville, held the place together. He was glad to have given them work as they were widows. They had come here with children, having nowhere to go with nobody to help, and they worked hard. One of them had a small child and she brought it to work with her. He often looked at the little girl; she was one of the reasons he had decided to marry. To have such wonderful beings around him was mesmerising and the little girl, Violet, had no fear of him and having no father, tended to follow him around the house.

Hallam had an office there too, but was rarely in it. Jay was grateful that Hallam spent so much time with the men. He knew that they thought Hallam one of them. He and Jay had to not look like a partnership, but almost against one another, so that the men and their families could feel secure. Seeing the men talking to Hallam and not to him, he had grown used to the idea. He was building the town but Hallam and the men were doing the work.

Late in the evenings they would sit down and talk, and he liked how Hallam always had different views, another side to offer, another idea to examine. New ideas were the best things of all.

The two men refused tea. Having been on the wrong side of the law for so many years, Jay was suspicious, and when they had refused to sit down, he was certain something was very wrong.

'We are grieved to discover that there has been a murder,' Billings said, all self-important.

Hell, Jay thought, you didn't get many of those in the dale. Domestic disputes, mostly; if somebody had killed somebody, it was an argument over money or drink or too many children, and that could hardly be the same thing. Somebody had found a kitchen knife and gone berserk, as you would in the dale where attitudes didn't change and few people prospered. The two policemen were making the best of it; Billings was now shaking his head.

'One of the farmers, Mr William Dixon, has been slain in his own home and his daughter, Ruth, is missing. We understand that this woman was very wrong and bad. She was – she was—' Billings turned to his compatriot for help but without joy. 'She had brought shame on her family.'

'Shame?' Jay said. He wished Hallam could hear this. He would choke with laughter.

'Aye, she was – well – she was,' he stopped, coughed and didn't go on. 'We think she quarrelled with her father when he tried to put her out because some lad and she had done the dirty.'

What a charming way to refer to something which was in his experience usually very pleasurable, Jay thought.

'She murdered him. You should have seen the blood.' Billings shuddered in a theatrical manner that would have got him on the stage in Darlington or Newcastle, Jay thought. 'He had been stabbed many times. We found a kitchen knife, a horrible weapon. She ran so she must have done it. And having shamed her family, and her father kept her there all that time, she became too much for him, a wicked woman through and through.'

A tiny girl murdered a man? Jay wouldn't believe it. Ruth was but six stones, he guessed.

'We have looked everywhere in the dale and can find nothing. She should be easy to spot, she's – well, she's outsized.' Outsized, Jay thought, that was a new word for a woman bearing a child. And then he realised what had happened and what Ruth had had to endure.

'She must have been huge to kill a man, unless of course he's very short,' Jay said. Farmers were not usually particularly slight, Jay thought; their work made them hardy and strong.

'Nay, he's a big man, a six-footer – he was a quarryman. She might have had help from somebody, likely the man who made her— who did what he did. And then they were afraid to take the blame and ran away. So we just wondered if you had had anybody coming in here like that.'

'This is a school for orphans and a place for married people to work. We have not had a huge woman come here who could have murdered a big man.'

Billings sighed.

'We thought not; we just couldn't trace her and you have a lot of folk coming in here.'

'Only families who need work and a place to live. That's the whole point of it,' Jay said.

'A wicked woman,' Billings said again.

And Jay thought, yes, every woman who was not an obedient wife or daughter or sister was wicked, according to the law. Having had a vast amount of experience in all different ways with women, he concluded that evil was caused by lack of food and shelter, too many children and too little work. The need for sex bettered people. Whoever had designed the world – and he had never believed in something eternally good – had not given a thought to poverty and childbirth while creating beauty in landscape. People starved in their millions. Could that ever have been the plan?

Jay was aware that Maddy had seen the two men, and he thought it right to tell her what was going on. He made sure that they were alone; they were outside and it was a cold bright day, so he walked her away from people and buildings. He told her about the policemen. She didn't interrupt.

'Do you think I should tell Ruth about them? I'm not sure whether she overheard or not.'

'If she doesn't ask, then perhaps best not for now. I'm so sorry for the girl,' Maddy said. 'Do you think they will come back?'

'I hope and trust not. I don't want to frighten her now by telling her that she killed him, but neither do I want her worried about whether they might come back, or he might. Isn't it difficult?'

'Almost impossible. Would you like me to tell Sisters Abigail and Hilary?'

'Yes, but not Sister Bee. I think she might think even more badly of Ruth if she discovers the truth.'

'Possibly. I will swear them to secrecy. But I would rather they knew, just in case there is a problem with that of any kind. I will watch her carefully.'

He thanked her and left, glad that he had confided the problem; it eased his worried mind.

Ruth ate a little more each day. They gave her warm goat's milk with bread softened in it and then she slept. When she began to get better, Maddy and Hilary agreed that she was the most beautiful girl they had ever seen. She was like something out of a fairy story. Her long red hair looked like something you could have warmed your hands on and it reached down past her waist.

They washed it and gave her a comb so that she could sit over the fire and sort out the knots. Her skin was pale and her eyes were bright blue. Slender and long-limbed, she was tall when she stood up straight, nothing that they had thought she would be. She didn't seem to know any of this and they were pleased. Perhaps her looks had got her into the terrible trouble which had been her ruin. All they could do was look after and pray for her.

Jay went to see her every day but it took a while for her to speak to him. It happened one day when they were alone, the nuns having gone out to attend to lessons and meals for the children. He was amazed at her. Her eyes were shining on him.

'You're the person who found me,' she said.

'Yes, I'm Jay Gilbraith.'

'I thought you were Jesus.'

'What?'

She smiled and shook her head and then her face crumpled with dismay.

'I thought I'd died, and hopefully gone to heaven, and then I got here and knew I was in hell.' The tears dripped and because she had stopped looking at him, they dropped off her chin end.

'Why?'

'Because. Because I – will go to hell for what I did.' She was so scared. He hadn't seen anybody that scared since he had left Newcastle. 'I had a bairn and no husband and then – I hurt my father and I'm terrified he's going to come after me. I have to leave and run away as far as I can get, because if he's still alive, he will come here and kill me, I know he will. I can't sleep for thinking about it.'

'There's no need for you to worry. This is my town and nobody gets in or out without my say-so. You must stay here and let us take care of you.'

'I don't think the nuns want to.'

'What makes you say that?'

'I'm a fallen woman. I don't think nuns have much time for fallen women.'

'You're nothing of the sort. There is no such thing.'

'They want rid of me; I heard the head one, Sister Bee, talking about it. I'm too sinful to stay here and I don't want to be where I'm despised.'

'I will talk to Sister Bee and we will sort something out. Don't worry about it. All you have to do is get well.'

*

Sister Bee was looking thin and white-faced, he thought, but she was finally functioning as she should have and was in her office. It was a small place on the ground floor, bare but for a cross on the wall, a curtain across what was presumably her sleeping quarters, and a table and two chairs. She greeted him politely. They didn't know one another well since she had been ill most of the time and he had dealt with Maddy. She asked him to sit down on a rickety chair across the table from her, which would hardly hold his weight.

'I want us to talk about Ruth Dixon,' he said.

'A very sad case. I am rather hoping that when she feels better, she might go as a maid to one of the local farmers, if any of them would have her in their home, which I doubt. Other than that, I don't really see what we can do with her. She is too old for the school, and not old enough for anything more, and nobody will ever marry her after what has happened to her. A girl like that is, well, she has nothing to offer a decent man.'

'Do you know what happened to her?'

Sister Bee's face coloured.

'No,' she said, 'and I know that it is wrong to judge, but it seems to me that she has behaved badly with some farm boy and this is the result. Presumably he ran away.'

Jay considered whether to tell her that the girl had been raped and impregnated by her father and then – as far as he could tell without asking – she had killed him when he tried to touch her again. Then he decided it would not help Ruth if the truth got out. Also he was worried that he had made the wrong decision by not telling Ruth that she had killed her father, and that he knew what had happened. But he thought she had sufficient to deal with, and he could always change his mind later.

There was no way he would give her up to the law, so the

fewer people who knew her history, the better it would be. And this was a more plausible story and an easier tale. Women were supposed to resist rape. How they were meant to do this, he had no idea, he had not been able to when he was a boy, and he had been much stronger and bigger at nine than Ruth was now.

Sister Bee muttered, 'Shameful,' but he didn't respond.

'I don't know the circumstances,' he lied, 'but I don't think we ought to send her away.'

'Then perhaps you can think of something else to be done; we cannot really keep her here.'

Jay thought he could go off Sister Bee if he spent much time with her, but then, she was old-school. She had probably been badly brought up in some poverty-stricken area in Ireland, by her accent, where new ideas were unheard of, rather like the dale. Perhaps because of that poverty, she had been forced to become a nun, regardless of her own desires for life.

Maybe she had fled overseas when it was frowned on here, or there might have been a lad she wished to marry and he was unsuitable. He didn't know, but people were all the result of their childhood experience, and so was Ruth and hers had been horrific.

He said to Sister Bee that he would be grateful if there was no talk about Ruth, and that he would sort something out for her over the next few days. Nobody must know that she had had a dead child, there must be no gossip. Sister Bee flushed and told him that nobody beyond the four nuns here knew, and they did not gossip. People would soon lose interest, if the general people there were interested in Ruth at all.

He didn't think so; she had barely been outside, and although she stood out hugely because of her fiery hair and fragile looks, he didn't think any man in the place would look twice at her. They all had sufficient problems without getting mixed up with some unknown young girl. Experience had taught them caution.

Thirteen

Eve thought of Jay as her best friend. It was silly, really, to think of a man that way, and it was not as women were supposed to think of men, but she began to rely on him for all sorts of things. She had never had a best friend, either man or woman, since she had always had governesses and not gone to school. She was always the outsider; her position in the village as the doctor's daughter had prevented such things from taking place. She was below the landed people and above the working people and she had nowhere to be.

She had no men around her but her father and Kyle Miller, who looked after the horses, and the two men who did the garden. But there was nobody young on her level, so the first time Jay came to see her in the middle of the day when her father could not possibly be at home, she was at first surprised and then rather gleeful.

Nobody had behaved towards her as he did. Giving his horse into Kyle's care, he joked with the young man and said to her afterwards that two of Kyle's family worked up in the new town and that they were good people. She liked how he spoke to Kyle as though they were friends, and Kyle grinned and said how lovely the mare was. Phyllis was Jay's horse. He said that it was just as well Phyllis was more intelligent than he was, since he had never learned to ride and had had to rely on her to get him around. He felt she must have known how stupid he was, how inept and inexperienced.

No one she knew would have dared to treat her as lightly as Jay did, and almost immediately she became proud to know him and to have him visit her, though she was not sure what his intentions were. He saved her from boredom and she was truly grateful. He admired and liked her, she could tell, so perhaps he needed a friend, a woman he could talk to, rather than the other men up there who helped him. She already knew that he liked her father but she was flattered to think that he liked her.

She knew no one who was anything like him. He was not educated; she thought he had probably never read a novel or heard decent music. Or perhaps he was just too clever, making her think that he had nothing before he reached her.

At first it was casual; he would talk to her about her father. He did not drone on and on about himself. He was interested in the books she read and the flowers she planted, and he would walk around the garden and let her tell him all about the shrubs and the birds and the seasons. As a city boy, he said, he knew nothing of such things.

Since her father spent so much time up in the new village, Jay could not go on pretending that he came here to talk to her father. She liked that he enjoyed finding her at home. In truth she had few places to be, and did nothing other than take walks by the river, trying to avoid all the old biddies of the town who bored her stupid with their conversation about who had got married and who had had children and who had baked cakes for the church sale.

She liked silly things about him: how confident he was, how

tall he was, how in charge. He had started up something which she had never thought anybody might. A whole new town. How ambitious, how scary. He was her equal in so many ways, though quite different. She liked that they were separate sorts of people.

His visits were brief, and she was always glad to see him arrive and sorry to see him go. She looked for him more and more, and took even more pride in her appearance, just in case he should come to see her that day. He had lifted her whole life on to a different level.

She became so much happier, so much more content somehow, and contentment was something she had not known before now. She hardly dared to think that he was going to ask her to marry him, though she saw that she would be disappointed if he did not. That was new. He came to matter a great deal to her.

She thought of them wandering about the gardens while she explained the flowers. She loved her herbs best.

'Rosemary and thyme. Surely these are for sale in Newcastle.'

'I didn't do a lot of cooking,' he pointed out and they both laughed. She was happy, almost dizzy, and yet something was lacking. She had no idea what it was. Perhaps it would come in time. For now she had him smiling at her and his shadow was big in the garden and across the lawns.

She liked the attention and she had never been able to bask in such a feeling before. Other women would envy her that she had captured his attention; he could afford to look after her, to take her to special places, to buy her beautiful gowns, to give her a secure future. She would get out of there because of him; she would no longer have to exist in this ghastly little town in the middle of nowhere.

*

Jay had been in love before. It had been ten years ago and he had thought it would never happen again. He hadn't wanted it to happen; for a while he was content to pay women to sleep with him. They were high class and beautiful and he could have them for as long as he wanted, but Hallam was right; it became tedious. It was bed and nothing else, and for some men that would be wonderful, but he had the feeling that those bastards were married men who enjoyed deceiving their wives. That was not him and it was not Hallam.

They were just two lads from the street and greedy for those things they had never had. Perhaps men always were. In Eve, he saw a home and a woman he could come back to, and decent food on the table, and maybe even a child, so despite Hallam cautioning him, he decided to ask her to be his wife.

He did what he had not done the first time he courted a woman: he spoke to her father before he approached her. He only knew Mr Gray professionally at first, and then they had dinner together two or three times. He knew that if he didn't speak to him, there was no point in going forward.

Women who had no mother made much of their father, as you would if you had only one parent, and Eve was like that, he had discovered. So when Mr Gray ended his clinic one dull afternoon, Jay asked the man into his office.

Hallam was busy but would be in soon. It was Jay's favourite time of day. They tried never to work in the evening unless there were problems, so they ate and drank and sat and smoked outside. And they still made plans: things they would do in the future, cities they would build, countries they would visit.

It was therefore a good time for him to ask the doctor. But the doctor had no idea what was happening and assumed either that Jay was ill or that somebody he loved was ill. He looked enquiringly at him as Jay closed the door.

'Would you like a drink, Mr Gray?'

The doctor looked surprised and rather pleased. He obviously didn't often get asked.

'Have you got a drop of whisky?' he said.

Jay poured single malt generously for the doctor and himself into little squat glasses. The windows were open and the early evening sun was making shadows on the floors and the walls, and yet Jay hesitated.

Mr Gray sipped appreciatively. He obviously knew decent whisky when he tasted it. Jay reminded himself to send the doctor a case of whisky if this worked out.

'There's nothing wrong, is there?' Mr Gray said, face all concern.

'No, no. I just wondered—' He couldn't get the words out.

'Oh dear,' Mr Gray said, 'would you like to sit down?'

'I should have asked you whether you would.'

'I'm fine. Tell me whatever it is and I will help you if I can.'

Jay didn't want the doctor to turn on him as Henry Charlton had, and he had a feeling that the man would when he knew that the upstart from Newcastle wanted his daughter to marry.

Mr Gray laughed but gently.

'It can't be that bad, surely, laddie.' It was the way he called Jay 'laddie', like it was some part of a poem. The doctor's voice was rhythmic, concerned, kind. Nobody did that; he was nobody's laddie and never had been and possibly never would be. You didn't get used to not having parents; you groped your way through life in a kind of darkness which other people did not understand, unable to reach out because of the idea of rejection.

The more rejected you were, the less you could reach out, life had taught him that. Nobody had ever wanted him. His only friend was Hallam. He hesitated.

'You're scaring me, laddie,' the doctor said, and his tone was almost a caress as he tried to smile, to make whatever was bothering Jay the easier to bear. He did it well.

Jay looked at him.

'I wondered whether you might let me court Eve,' he said.

The doctor looked taken aback but not in a bad way. Indeed, the doctor looked sympathetically at him.

'Why would I not do that?' he said.

'Well, because – because I have no family. I don't know about my background. I have no education. I know nothing. I don't even know how to address her. But I thought that perhaps if I asked you, then if it was no good, I wouldn't try and therefore upset things. Do you see?'

The doctor let go of his breath.

'Oh, I do see now,' he said. 'And you like her?'

This was surprising. As if nobody had ever liked the most beautiful girl Jay had seen in years.

'I like her very much.'

'And does she like you?'

'I don't know. I didn't dare ask because if you didn't like the idea of the match, she might get hurt.'

The doctor looked thoughtful.

'You know I came here with nothing and my family thought very little of me. And Mary's family' – here he looked very sad – 'they didn't really like me, either. So I always said to myself that when Eve found a man who wanted to marry her, if she loved him, I would say yes, no matter what I thought, because nobody should have to go through that. But the thing is, I think you are a fine, upstanding young man, and I would be glad to have you for my son-in-law.'

The doctor's tired eyes were shining. Jay couldn't believe it. It was the first step.

'Are you sure, sir?'

'Don't "sir" me. I am quite sure. I admire what you are doing here; it is something which has not been done before in this area as far as I know. If you want to talk to Eve, then do so, and you will have my blessing when you marry. You will treat her well?'

'I swear it,' he said.

The doctor went off home and Jay could not stop smiling. Then he began to worry that Eve did not like him, would not accept his idea of courtship, and all that night he couldn't sleep. He had gone from one problem to the next. He had no idea how many more rungs of this ladder he must climb, but at least he had made a start.

He swore that if she turned him down he would never do this again. It would be too much to be turned down twice. He had tried to forget the first time; it had been almost ten years earlier, and he was only now recovering from the slights and cuts of being unwanted. Perhaps he might be wanted now.

He couldn't wait. The next day was Saturday and the men were given the afternoon off and the whole of the next day. He was determined they should have time to rest and be with their families. He took himself at his word and got on to his horse and rode down into Wolsingham.

It was the prettiest afternoon they had had in weeks. The sun set a little sooner than it had before. Autumn was upon them and yet it was unseasonably warm and when Jay rode into the yard of the doctor's house, the groom, Kyle Miller, was there and greeted him amiably.

'Mr Gray had to go to an emergency,' Kyle said, 'but Miss Gray is in the garden.'

Perfect, Jay thought. He gave his horse into Kyle's capable hands and walked through into the garden. It was one of the prettiest gardens he had ever seen, with big lawns and rosebeds, and he could see Eve. She was talking to one of the gardeners; she had gloves on her hands and the gardener was smiling at her and nodding. Then she saw Jay and waved and took off the gloves and came over.

'We're just talking about new plans for the place,' she said. 'We don't agree. Mr Sams wants vegetables everywhere and I think the back garden is the place for that. I want more roses. It's lovely to see you. Have you business in Wolsingham?'

'No, I just thought I might come and share a pot of tea with you.'

'Really?' She looked disbelievingly at him, suddenly excited. 'Then I will tell Mrs Florence. We could have tea out here in the shade of the big tree, if you like.'

He said he did and then she ventured into the house and came back with the joyous information that Mrs Florence had just made coffee cake and she would bring it out to them.

Jay could not have eaten anything, he would have choked, but he made what he thought were the right noises. So they waited for the tea. At least he didn't have to make conversation. Eve managed that all by herself, though he was half convinced she was nervous.

Neither of them ate. He barely managed half a cup of what had to be good tea and then he said to her, 'I like you very much, Eve, and I wondered whether you might permit me to – to ask you to marry me.'

He hardly dared look up.

'Marry?' she said.

'Yes, but only if you like me.'

'Jay, I already like you.'

'Do you?' He ventured a look into her face.

'Very much,' she said. 'I will have to speak to my father.'

'I did ask him if I might approach you. It seemed the right thing to do.'

'He goes on about you all the time.' She raised her gaze to the lovely blue sky.

'Does he?' Jay saw then how desperate he was to be liked. For a man as clever as the doctor to like him, that was precious to him, almost as much as the doctor's daughter. 'So will you, will you marry me?'

She nodded; she was smiling and the smile reached her eyes.

'Yes,' she said.

Fourteen

Maddy was not sure when she first knew that Sister Bee was really ill. Sister Bee had been tired ever since she got there, and was coughing and sneezing, but she did get better. Then it was only a short time before she seemed exhausted again. Maddy could not remember Sister Bee ever complaining about being ill before they got here. You couldn't really call it complaining. Sister Bee was not the kind of person who was ever out of temper. She was not exactly formidable, but you took notice of her when she asked you to do things, and she always asked. Sister Bee was too tactful and too polite to tell anybody what to do, but you did it because she was always right.

All Maddy knew of her was that she came from some part of Ireland, and had an accent so sweet that it felt like a warm blanket; it filled the air with good things. She and Mother had been in France together for years when Catholicism was looked down upon here in England. Or perhaps 'there' was the word for it. Here in the north, people were more worried about finding food and shelter for their families than to enquire how men regarded God. They didn't talk of such things – perhaps for fear that they did not worship as they should do – but among the poor, it was hardly an important question. All the men wanted was work, so that they could hold up their heads, and provide a home and good food for their families.

Sister Bee kept to her office a good deal after she began to feel so tired.

The first thing that Maddy noticed was Sister Bee trying to hide how tired she was. She kept falling asleep in her chair; Maddy would knock and hear her clearing her throat and coughing and then saying 'come in' when she thought she was sufficiently awake to understand what was happening.

She had a cold and a cough and during the night she wasn't good, and Maddy would go down and look after her. There was nothing so bad that it should concern her. Yes, they had a lot to deal with, but they were used to that. Although it was hard, the four of them had managed, but now it was three of them since Sister Bee was so unwell.

They had sorted out the dormitory for the children and since there was only one little boy, the children did well together. The nuns had a room to themselves. They had chosen another room for dining, and the kitchen itself was large. They chose a special room to be their chapel and put in it a table for their altar. There they observed the offices as well as they could, considering that three of them were doing the work of four and it was never finished.

Mr Gray, the new doctor who had come to the village to help, said at first that Sister Bee had a chest infection; she was wheezing and lethargic. But he also said privately to Maddy that he thought the change of lifestyle, the responsibility and coming here like this, probably did not help.

Maddy began to worry. Mother had thought Sister Bee the right person to do what Hilary called 'leading the expedition'. Eventually the chest infection went, but then the fatigue replaced it. Mr Gray kept saying that she would get better but she didn't, not properly.

That was when Mr Gray would call to see the children and he would ask how Sister Bee was. Officially there was nothing wrong with her, but the trouble was that she was so often asleep or tired that Maddy had to start doing things in the school and all around without asking her. She was short-tempered when she was awake and dismissive of what anybody else thought. Maddy couldn't quite work out what was happening, but since she began to hesitate outside the door of the office, instead of going in with requests which would always be turned down, she stopped doing it. She knew that until they made compromises, they would get no further.

Mr Gray enquired whether Sister Bee had been ill back at the convent in Newcastle, but the answer to that was that she had never been ill in the past four years, that Maddy could remember.

The other two were also worried.

'Do you think Sister Bee will die?' Abigail asked and looked straight at Maddy, tears in her eyes.

'I don't think so.'

'But she isn't eating very much and she has no energy.'

Maddy didn't like to say that Mr Gray was perplexed. He hadn't said it, either, but it was obvious to her that he didn't know what was wrong with Sister Bee. Maddy wondered about telling Mother but it was too early. Perhaps things would come right if she waited.

Nothing more was said between the sisters about Ruth after Hilary and Abigail were told the truth. Sister Bee told them that Mr Gilbraith had said he would come up with a solution about her. She didn't say she would be glad when the girl was gone, but they all gained that impression.

Hilary and Maddy had been good friends right from the beginning, so when they were hanging out the clothes one cold, blowy morning, Maddy should not have been surprised when Hilary asked her about Jay.

Maddy was so startled that she almost dropped a clean white sheet and had to take a better hold on it, thinking of how much extra washing it would need from the dirt on the ground.

'He was a colleague of my father's.'

Hilary knew all about Maddy's father and looked curiously at her.

'Wasn't he a bit young for that?'

'My father thought highly of him.'

'And did you?'

Maddy could not help blushing. Hilary was watching her in such a close way. She had few secrets from Hilary or Abigail. They were the dearest friends she had ever had.

'He asked me to marry him and I refused.'

They went on pegging out the clothes – Hilary saying she hoped they wouldn't blow away in the wind – but after the two nuns stood there for a few more minutes, she said, 'Didn't you care for him?'

'Very much, but my father wasn't well, and he had spent such a lot of time looking after me when my mother died. He was horrified that Mr Gilbraith had even asked me. I couldn't disobey him.'

'And then he died and you were left and now you've met him again.'

'It's quite different. I'm a different person and he is going to be married.'

'He isn't married yet,' Hilary said.

It was not as unusual as it sounded. In their order, they took their vows every year. It would have been odd but not unfeasible for Maddy to leave.

'We're different people. We're ten years older and have gone in such different ways.'

'But you still like him?'

'I like him very much.'

'Not love then?'

'I don't know much about love, but I think what I have here with you and the other sisters and my life is – is very good. I don't think I would be a better person for marrying anyone and I certainly don't think I could be happier. Also I think there are sufficient children in the world; look at those here with no parents. I think things are better as they are.'

Maddy was resolute at the time but afterwards she did wonder at herself. She wasn't sure that it was true she could hope for nothing more. She had been contented with the nuns, but this had all changed since she had seen him again, and the more she saw him, the more she admired him.

He had been so kind about the orphans; he had been better than that about Ruth. What he would do now about Ruth, she didn't know, and she wondered whether his betrothed would want her in her house. It would be interesting as to what happened.

She tried not to dislike people, and she had never met Miss Gray, so it was unfair to judge her because she was going to marry Jay. Maddy had had a chance to marry him and felt that she couldn't; she should not automatically feel negative about a woman she had never met, nor even glimpsed in the distance.

He sent her a note asking if she might come to the farmhouse and help him with some buildings. He apologised beforehand for intruding and said that he knew she had a great deal to do, but he needed help. He thought that if she could just spare him a couple of hours, it would make a great difference.

Maddy did not mention to Sister Bee that Mr Gilbraith had asked for help with his houses. The village was built on several levels, the butterfly house being at the top. New houses were being built not just up there, but all the way down the hill. He had made good progress, she thought, while they had been here. At the bottom of the hill was the farmhouse where the two men had offices for their work.

It was beautiful, she acknowledged, quite different from the butterfly house but still great, with stone mullioned windows and oak doors and clinging ivy all across the front which had been planted for beauty. There was no garden around it. The land sloped gently towards the stream.

There were no walls to shut it off from the land, which made her think that however long it had been there, it had been a safe and good living. It was sheltered so it needed no walls, and nobody had thought to plant anything that looked like a garden.

Around it were many fields; she could tell this by how comparatively new the buildings around it looked. When it was the only house – which it had been for many years – the very openness of it was enough. Jay could have had his headquarters anywhere but she thought he had chosen well. Short of the butterfly house, which she had come to love, and she thought not quite as old, she liked it very well. There were buildings in this area which had been there for hundreds of years.

She banged on the door and after a short while, he answered

it himself. He urged her inside in a friendly manner which she found difficult to resist.

'I wanted to talk to you about the house I'm having built for when I marry. I hope you don't think I'm stupid to ask.'

Maddy faced him.

'Not at all,' she said, and he rewarded her sincerity with a smile.

'Thanks. I think you will be able to help me – not just with this house, but with other ideas I have.'

She was emboldened to say, 'I'm not my father, you know.'

'I would have given so much to have had him here helping me. I am sure he would have liked it. I know he didn't want you to marry me, and I understand it better now that I'm so much older, but I think he would have enjoyed the project. He could have been such a help; I just need a bit of reassurance. Will you come with me and take a look at the house I'm building for Eve?'

She said that she would be pleased to, and was glad that they were now on such a footing where they could be open with one another. The house was not far from the pit – too near, if anything, Maddy thought privately. It was close to everything, as it had to be. It was but a few hundred yards from the butterfly house, and yet was by itself on the fell top.

Maddy was almost carried away by his enthusiasm, and yet as soon as she saw it – and she had seen the men completing the outside recently – she knew that it was not the kind of place any gently bred girl like a doctor's daughter would want to live.

Eve Gray had not seen the house, he told her, and that in itself was worrying. Why not? Maddy thought she should have done, but perhaps he had not asked her because he was not sure whether she would want to leave what was reputedly one of the prettiest houses in the dale. Perhaps she was reluctant to come up here, to the middle of nowhere? The community was not yet established, and among it she would find no peers. Maddy was fascinated to see the place.

As soon as she saw it, she loved it, but then she was not a prosperous young woman who already had a house so much better than this, in a village by a river, where the air was softer and the winds did not blow as they did here up on the tops. According to what Maddy had heard, the house was to be hers and had been in her mother's family, somehow in the female line, for centuries.

No wonder Jay was worried. Here Eve would be stuck where howling gales assaulted the buildings and the people. But then all Maddy had ever known was the damp house by the river where she had lived with her father, so she was not the person to judge.

It was bitterly cold the day that they chose to go up. The puddles were thickly iced and the wind was screaming across the fell, so that the odd sheep was seemingly almost windborn by its fleece, though they did not move, looking for something to eat while they were still upright. There were low grey stone walls, and the most sensible of the sheep were in against them. But you got the odd one that they called in Newcastle 'the dizzy bugger', who was out there come what the hell, munching, regardless of the wind that cut your face in half if you turned the wrong way.

The house was beautiful. It wasn't as exquisitely shaped as the butterfly house, but it was lovely, all proud and by itself with big, square stone walls and a sound roof. Now that it had doors and windows and was glassed, the minute you got inside, you were aware of its hold. The wind was singing low across the grass that day and she loved the sound of it, like a hive of humming bees.

He had built it to let the light in and if ever the sun ventured there, it would be glorious. It was the wrong way round, in a sense, because the kitchen faced the fell and she would have put the living room there. The far side near the road would not have the cutting wind, but this side had the view, such as it was.

The fireplaces were built of local Frosterley marble, grey and white with fossils like white smudges in it, which she loved. Her father had used it very often in his buildings, and there was a huge range in the kitchen. She didn't say much as they wandered around, until she knew she should make some remark, because he was waiting to hear what she had to say.

'If you want a garden on the fell side, you will have to put up high walls against the wind and rain and snow.'

'It would limit the view.'

She wanted to laugh. Nobody who was not from this area would consider the great flat expanse of fell with the odd tree and the stone walls to be a view.

'Why is that funny?' he asked.

She hadn't even known that she was smiling. She shook her head.

'You have sufficient room to make gardens around the back.'

'I was going to build stables and a carriage house there,' he said. 'If I do that on the fell side, the view will be ruined.'

'You should turn that idea around. Nothing will grow on the fell side, so you could put buildings there, to either side, since you have so much room. Though in bad weather, that might be problematic. You need a defence to keep out the wind, rain and snow. Also you need a couple of extra fields for the horses, land which could be reclaimed from the fell.'

'I've got this all wrong,' he concluded.

'You need to think it through a bit more and see what compromises you can make.'

There was one long room which had no apparent use that she could see, and when she enquired, he said, 'It's a billiard room.'

That was when she did laugh.

'Does Miss Gray play billiards?'

'Well, no, but—'

'You will come home in the evenings and play billiards?'

He gestured in a futile kind of way, waving his arms about as she had never seen before, so disconcerted was he.

'I just thought it might be nice.'

'So where is the south-facing room which should be warm for Mrs Gilbraith to write letters and read over the fire? Also a small dining room, about half the size of the one you are proposing, because you'll never go in there. It'll be too cold three quarters of the year, despite the fireplaces. I know you have plenty of coal, but you don't want people on permanent coal duty, surely. You need to eat near the kitchen and that room is much too far away. The food would be cold before it got to you.

'The rooms for you – a study, if you like, and perhaps a library, or both together – could be on the open side so that you can see the fell. The drawing room, or whatever you want to call it, should be left at the back, where it's warmer and also looks towards the road leading to Scotland. That's a decent view, though if you build houses on that part of the road, you will lose it. It should be made into a sheltered garden. You have a lot of fires so you will need servants – a cook and a gardener and a stable lad and people to clean.'

He stared at her.

'Miss Gray is a lady,' Maddy said. 'She isn't going to want to go into the kitchen or build fires. If the help is to live in, you will have to make sure there are sufficient rooms so that everybody can have space and you and your wife can have privacy. Also you have light to consider. You've made the best of your windows, but during the winter there is little light here. You have the best light on the fell side, though it isn't much. You could do with windows in the roof.'

'Wouldn't that weaken the roof?'

'It can be done.'

He stood, looking out at the fell and didn't speak for quite a long time. Then he turned and said, 'I haven't thought this out properly. Eve will never want to come and live here.'

'Why don't you show her around?'

He hesitated.

'I did ask her to, but she didn't seem very interested.'

'You have to make it her house, and let her have it how she wants it,' Maddy said. 'Some of these rooms could be divided, so that you could have more cosiness.' She took him through the whole of the downstairs to illustrate what she was talking about.

She couldn't stop thinking about the idea that Eve didn't want to see the house. Perhaps the wrench from her father was proving too much at present, but presumably she would get used to the idea. It would be like being torn in half at present, Maddy thought, with her strange mother no parent to her, and her father left alone with the servants and his work. How very difficult.

Fifteen

Ruth was astonished that anybody wanted her. She was so afraid of her father coming for her, she was so worried that she had killed him and would never be allowed to do anything again, that she began to enjoy being at the convent.

She liked the little girls and especially the little boy; there were only the six of them to begin with. Since she was so much older, they began to rely on her. She found that she liked them all and wanted to help look after them.

Having had no siblings, she was astonished and pleased at the power she had and how the smaller girls relied on her. Ruth was so much older and they looked to her for guidance. She had never done such a thing in her life, but it was rare now that one child or another did not creep into her bed for comfort in the dark hours of the night. Even Hannah, amid her songs, would find a few tears and lie against Ruth sobbing and saying nothing. Ruth did not ask. In time, if they chose, the children would tell her what their problems were. In the meanwhile, she was there for them and they were a comfort to her.

She had initially longed for a room of her own, but when Sister Bee called her into the office, and informed her coldly that since Mr Gilbraith had found nowhere for her to go, she could at least have her own room and be out of the way of the younger children, Ruth found herself saying, 'But Sister, the children like having me there and I like being there, for when they have nightmares. Is it that you need my bed and I should go away?'

Sister Bee's look softened.

'No, no, child, nothing like that. We thought that being older, you might like a room of your own with a bed and books and . . .'

'I can't read,' Ruth said. 'I wish I could read stories to the children when they are frightened.'

'What do you do then?' Sister Bee asked.

'I make them up.'

Sister Bee smiled and it was the first time that Ruth had felt welcome.

'You shall have a room of your own in case you need it. It's very small and beside the dormitory. It's for your things and for you to go when you choose. You may also stay with the children, so there will be a bed in there for you as well.'

Choice was a new idea for Ruth.

'And you can go to Sister Madeline's classes if you like, and learn to read and write.'

'Then I could write my stories down,' Ruth said.

'Yes, indeed,' Sister Bee said.

In a way, Ruth felt so damaged by the birth and loss of her baby that she needed to be near children. Although at the time she had been glad that the pain stopped, the pain in her heart still hurt her. She grieved over the loss of her baby, even though it had been conceived in the most awful circumstances imaginable. Stupidly, she even felt awful for her father. He had not had an easy life and he seemed to understand nothing. Mixed in with all this, was the idea that she would now never have a child of her own or a husband, or anybody with whom she might form a family. She didn't quite know why she wanted a family. Anybody with any sense, she thought savagely, would want to stay away from such stupid ideas. Yet every time she thought about couples and their children, she longed for somebody of her own.

After the other children began sleeping with her, and she told them stories, she began to feel better and accepted – and even acceptable, somehow. She had found her place in the storytelling, and also in that the children took her as they saw her and they so obviously liked her. She found that she laughed more and that she felt better; looking after children made you put your fears and horrors to the back of your mind, and at night when the devils would come down on you, they could not if a small person was sleeping beside you. She thought that all of these children had suffered in different ways and since she was older she might help. Her awful experience made her feel the more for them. She had not thought that having a bad time made other people so much dearer to you. Every night she thanked God that he had given her the rest of her life when she might have died, and that he had moved her on to be useful and helpful and still able to enjoy what she was doing.

They were not country children, so she made up stories about animals she had never had, about sheep and pigs and hens. She gave the animal names, so that the children clamoured for more stories, and it seemed to help them get better. They slept and they ate and the nuns praised her good work, as they called it. She was doing such good work with these children; they were so glad to have her there, she was like one of them.

Sixteen

Jay had insisted on Ruth not being sent away. Sister Bee had called him into her office and demanded of him where Ruth should go. He said that she should stay here, and must be properly looked after. She must have good clothing and anything else that she needed and not be required to do menial tasks.

'Ruth is in my charge,' he said, 'but you know very well that I cannot have her live with me as things are. She must stay here. I will pay for everything you think she might need.'

Sister Bee didn't say anything to begin with and then she met his eyes and she said, 'Ruth has more worth than I gave her credit for. She is very good to the children we have here so far. We are expecting more children; things are so bad in Ireland, and I hear tales of what it is like on the Liverpool docks. Those that have made their way here, we will take in and we thank you for it. Ruth may prove to be an asset yet. Did you know that she tells them stories in the evenings?'

Jay wasn't convinced that this was the best thing for Ruth but he didn't know what to suggest. He was pleased that Sister Bee thought she was now an asset, but he had the feeling that the nuns were wanting everybody to help them with everything, and Ruth had been through a great deal. She was still so very young.

He decided to talk to her by himself, so he went to the school just as they finished breakfast. He asked Sister Hilary, who was supervising the meal, whether he could see Ruth.

He was always surprised when he saw her. At first she had been in awful pain, and he had not seen her except at her worst. After that she had barely spoken to him. But now she was again different. The horrors of her life seemed to be receding a little, and though she was very thin, she was putting on weight. She even seemed taller to him. He wanted to say that to her, but thought how very old it would make him sound. But to her he was old, he could have been her father. But then again not, considering what her father had done.

She was shy. She went outside with him. It was a crisp, clear morning and when she raised her eyes, she looked worried.

'Have I done something?'

'Hell, no.' He was so surprised that he swore. After she hesitated, she managed the ghost of a smile.

'Do you want me to leave?'

That made him feel impatient. This was a lot more difficult than he had envisaged and he didn't know how to lighten it. Yet somehow he must break through the barrier of him finding her in such distress, and she thinking he was Jesus. He smiled.

'What?' she said.

'You, thinking I was Jesus.'

And she giggled just like the young girl she had never been.

'I've seen pictures of him and he was nothing like you. He had blond hair and blue eyes.'

Jay didn't point out to her that since he came from the East this was most unlikely.

'You did save me, though,' she said, somewhat wistfully.

'It wasn't me, it was Phyllis.' He told her about the mare and how she stopped and wouldn't go on, and that made her smile too.

'I just want to say to you that you don't have to stay at the school, where the sisters are undoubtedly making use of you. Is there something you want to do?'

'Do?'

She had so obviously not been asked the question before. She looked astounded.

'I don't know. I quite like being here with the little children and helping them. I'm telling them all kinds of things they don't know. Some of them have never seen a rabbit. Except in a stew.'

Jay waited because he thought she had something to say, and that if he stopped humouring her and let her think, she might say it.

'What did you do with my baby?'

'I buried it under big stones in the churchyard in Wolsingham. The vicar said I might.'

'That was nice of him.'

'If you want to, I can take you there and show you some time. Any time you want.'

'I miss my baby. You do know that I – that I didn't want to do that.'

'Of course you didn't.'

'And you know that my father – that I couldn't hold him off.'

'I know.'

'How did you know?'

Ah, here was the problem. He had fallen into the trap that she had unwittingly set for him.

'I just knew that you could never have wanted such a thing.

And you were badly hurt, too. There were a lot of bruises and you were very distressed.'

'But how did you know what I had gone through?'

'Because when I was a small child, I went through something similar. I know what it feels like, how helpless you are, how unwanted. And worse still, you had a child because of it. I was lucky in that way; at least I couldn't have a child.'

Ruth's eyes were glinting at him and her mouth trembled.

'But it makes you feel stupid, and as though you aren't worth anything.'

'That isn't true. You aren't stupid and you are worth a great deal. You will go on and do other things in your life. You will always be aware of what happened to you, but people who have had a hard time are more sympathetic to others having a hard time.'

Here she nodded.

'I think that's why I like being with the children. I tell them stories which make them feel better, where the children are safe and they have animals and they grow carrots.'

'Growing carrots is a serious business,' he said, and then to his surprise she thumped him lightly on the chest. She said, 'You are being silly now.'

'Aren't you glad?'

'Yes.'

'All right. So just remember that I am here for you always. You can't come and live with me, because Hallam and I are there together and there is no room for you. But I am your new family, and if you get stuck for anything, or you want to alter anything, you can come to the farmhouse and talk to me. I won't have you upset or hurt anymore. If anybody gets in your way, you tell them that I will sort them out or come to me.'

Ruth had never known what it was like to love anybody before now, but that morning, she fell in love with Jay. Yes, he was old but he was not old like her father. He was big and clever, and he had clear eyes, and he smelled good and looked good and made her laugh. She thanked him and went back inside. She helped wash up since Sister Hilary was always complaining nobody went to carry the dishes into the kitchen after breakfast.

The houses had gone on being built steadily all that autumn until the tents disappeared and it was just as well. There were flurries of snow in October, and the frosts, though few, appeared in November. Before Christmas, the howling winds came down across the fells and the people there were glad to be inside. The winds brought great snow flurries and everything froze for days on end.

Maddy was pleased that the mines produced so much coal that it was free for everyone. By then every child had thick clothing, the beds had blankets and the rooms had fires.

Advent was important and Christmas was the most important feast in the calendar, except for Easter.

They tried to keep what offices they could, but they had so many things to do, what with the children and the practicalities of feeding so many people. And then the population, having realised that Mr Gray was there three times a week, would sit outside until the sisters took them in. This had become a regular practice.

Maddy was very much aware that Jay paid the doctor to come here for the families, because from what she could discern, nobody paid for medical treatment. She thought that was unheard of, except in those places where the workmen paid weekly. She liked Jay the better for the fact that he looked after the people.

It was useful for him too, she accepted, because sick people did not work and he needed them to work. But it was also several steps forward from the thinking of a lot of other businessmen. He was creating a dream here, as far as she could see, and it was a huge enterprise, a risk, since dreams so often verged into nightmare. But she admired it in him, that he would attempt such a thing.

The doctor was there almost every day and she was aware that his practice in Weardale must be feeling the lack. He needed to be. People who came in had almost starved and were weak. Maddy thought she had realised the bottom of life, when small children and babies died as she and the doctor watched over them. They were too weak when they arrived, but she felt that each death was a heartbreak.

Maddy had not known what a defeat it was to watch a child die, when you had done everything you could to stop it from happening. Families coming in had the same problems: no work, no money. Now they were being given just a little bit of hope. They had sound houses to live in, and everything was done to help them, which was exactly what Jay had wanted, Maddy thought.

Mr Gray told her that a child dying was not something you became used to; it was dreadful each time it happened. She thought this was right. You should never grow used to anything that robbed people of the years they should have had. Maddy admired his skill and energy and was grateful that he came to aid them so often.

Also he helped with the clinics they set up for people who had moved in. Here were all manner of mostly minor problems.

Mostly what these people needed was decent, dry lodging, work for the men so that they could afford to live and somewhere they could buy decent food for their families. These things the school now provided with help from the doctor and Jay.

Seventeen

The children they had taken in now included two small boys, Gordon and Philip. Their mother had died and someone, hearing about the nuns' work, had dropped them off. An aunt, they said, though around here aunts were not necessarily family. Perhaps somebody could not afford or did not want to keep them. They had not waited around in case of questions, she thought. Now that the children were all clean and fed, and were a bit more confident, they could be taught. Hopefully they would be able to take in some hard work, like reading and writing.

Children were still coming into the town, though most of them had parents. Maddy was pleased to see that Jay tried to house those who hadn't with couples who already had children, and he would provide for them. This worked very well.

So far the new school had been a careful and slow venture. She had the feeling that a lot of these children had had no schooling at all, and she wasn't sure where to go from here. But in the end, with Mr Nattrass helping, she got them all into the big room which she had set aside for this purpose. She had found a piece of wood, and to this she pinned a large piece of paper. She told the children of the things around them, and on the paper she wrote down the names of things and showed them. First of all was the goat, Rachel. That made them smile.

They loved this. She told them about how Rachel had happened in and how that perhaps the Lord had sent her (though daily she waited for an irate farmer to claim Rachel as his). From there, she could talk about the milk the goat gave them, and why she had the milk, and how goats gave birth and fed their offspring. She kept it simple and clear, no graphic details. She told them a lot of facts which turned their eyes round, nothing that could be disputed or worried over. It was a useful lesson for her as well as for them. You had to suit your material to your audience.

Also she told them about food: how mills worked, how flour was made, how porridge came about from oats and oats from the fields. From there she told them about seasons. She would have liked to go on to flowers and such, but since it was winter, that didn't seem like a good idea.

These children needed stories so that they could relate to what was happening around them. She told them Bible stories, which they loved. The Bible stories were even better than she remembered, and they learned and were entranced all at the same time.

Daniel and the lion, Moses and the bulrushes, Joseph and his coat of many colours, David and Goliath. She thought you could not better the drama of the Bible and the children loved the old stories best. Her favourite was Ruth and Naomi but she thought the ideas in it were too advanced for young minds. Simplicity was the key thing at the moment.

She and the other nuns also read to them, but not the Bible. The language would discourage them at this stage, and she wanted them all to find reading a solace in time.

Sister Bee was well enough at that time to read them poetry, but it was nursery rhymes which they might understand. Though Sister Bee might not want them to recite at that point – their learning for the most part being slight – sometimes in the late afternoons, when it was growing dark, Maddy would hear the class reciting 'Jack and Jill went up the hill', and pause to listen and be glad. Sister Bee would read the line and they would read it after her. She had a good idea of how to treat children well, and she wanted them to learn; it was a rare thing, Maddy knew.

Advent was in a sense the beginning of Christmas, and more welcome this year than ever. Maddy was starting to feel quite proud of what they were achieving. Though having the same amount of space, they had managed to find somewhere to sleep for the children who came to them. Often they were there temporarily because they had taken ill, rather than been left alone. She was glad of that.

They managed a clinic that Mr Gray attended three times a week. Sister Abigail was the experienced one with bandages and she kept their spirits up.

During Advent, preparation for the birth of Christ, they lit a candle on each of the four Sundays prior to Christmas. It was the time of year they liked best, except for Easter Sunday. Maddy didn't like to say that she preferred this because the north was cold and dark. She loved the cold and the darkness, and she loved how the light brightened it, especially the candles.

The altar was draped in purple cloth and they went out and gathered greenery for the wreath. It was not necessarily a Catholic tradition, but being a country girl, Hilary liked it and was the main instigator. Evergreens denoted the hope of eternal life, she said, and there was nothing wrong with the celebration of it since Christ himself was the light.

They had brought with them painted figures for the nativity scene, and they took the children into their makeshift chapel for a special service and let the youngest of them put the figures into the barn and the baby Jesus into the manger.

Maddy thought that the children loved the candles and the scene and the wreath. Sister Hilary found a big turnip – it had to be a round fruit or vegetable, to represent the world – and she put a candle in the middle of it, which was the light of Jesus, and then red ribbon around it, for the blood of his sacrifice.

The candles were surrounded by raisins to represent the produce of the earth. They had prayers and services, readings and singing, and taught the children carols. They all seemed to enjoy it very much. Maddy just wished they could have afforded a small gift for each child, because to her that was what the heart of Christmas represented.

They had no musical instruments of any kind, but with Hilary to lead the chanting and singing, they needed nothing more. Her voice was so pure that Maddy thought Mother must be thinking of her, and missing her more now than at any other time of the year.

On Christmas Eve, the world was white and yet the snow did not set as ice. Maddy was glad of it and pleased. She was glad to see that Jay had made sure all of his workmen and their families had good fires, sturdy homes and plenty to eat.

Things were more organised by then. The shops in the village held foodstuffs in plenty and people could choose where to shop. They were fairly paid and the sisters helped as much as they could. So far that winter, there had been nothing but colds and coughs, but Maddy knew that in this area it was after

Christmas that the really bad weather set in. It could be savage until April. Had she not been a nun, she would have crossed her fingers.

A storm set in even as they called the children and their families for the carol service. The snow began falling in great white square flakes, sideways and up and down, and they all knew that it was what you called a hap up. That was the local name for it. When it fell very thick and fast, nobody could go anywhere, but luckily they were all together.

They were hoping for a quiet evening, when they could sing and spend time with the children. Sister Hilary said she wished the doctor could be with them. He was safely at home by then. He had been there that morning, and to one of the clinics they had established. He was most attentive, but he could not come now; he had no way up the hills in weather like this. Something always happened when there was no doctor and a snowstorm, Sister Hilary said.

They were just about to go to bed, having made sure that all was secure, when Sister Abigail thought she heard the sound of voices in the chapel. She listened for a few moments, and then went into the kitchen where Maddy and Hilary were just finishing up, and said, 'I think there's somebody in the chapel. You don't think it can be those policemen back? After all, they could get in here on a night like this, and have nobody see them. What if they grab Ruth and try to run off with her? It's late and dark and Mr Gilbraith isn't here. Whatever will we do? We can't all go into the chapel. I tell you what: I'll go in very quietly, and you two wait outside of the door, and I will yell if it's anything important.'

She went very softly and rather worried. They were all scared that the policemen hunting William Dixon's killer might still be around, and they had suspected Ruth. In the end, they didn't quite close the door because it was too nerve-wracking, Hilary said, and possibly too dangerous. Abigail went in there very slowly and carefully. There was no light, but the moon obligingly came out from behind a cloud at that moment. She could see the people who were in the chapel and they were small. They were children. Abigail heaved a sigh and gestured to the others. All three went in. The children were meant to be in bed, but she could see a boy and a girl. Their backs were turned to her and she hadn't made a sound. They were standing by the crib and not actually doing anything, but as she waited, the little boy, Patrick, reached over and took the baby Jesus from the crib and handed it to Shannon.

Then they turned and saw Abigail.

'What are you doing in here?' she said in a friendly voice. 'You're supposed to be asleep. Christmas Day cannot come if you stay up half the night.'

'She wanted the baby,' the boy said.

'He has to stay here with his mam and dad,' Abigail said, approaching but slowly. The other two hung back, as they did not want to frighten the children, who were, after all, causing no real harm.

(As she said later to Maddy in confidence, 'I thought some bugger was going to nick the candlesticks, like I tried to when I first got into the convent.')

'Why?' Shannon said, holding the baby closer.

'Well, because he needs looking after.'

'We could look after him. We've got no mother and father. We thought he would like being with us.'

'All right then, but you have to promise to bring him back in the morning, otherwise I'll get wrong off Sister Bee. We can't be singing all them carols with an empty cradle, now, can we?'

Shannon held the baby very close to her and they promised to bring him back. Abigail made a mental note to make sure they did, because if the crib was empty in the morning, Sister Bee would have a fit.

Abigail took the children, plus the Christ child, back to bed, and Hilary and Maddy had a little bit of a giggle. But most of it was relief.

'I sometimes wish that Mr Gilbraith didn't live at the bottom of the bank,' Hilary said. 'It's a long way for him and Mr Hallam to belt up here if something goes wrong.'

Maddy had thought about this ever since the two policemen had called on the village. She just hoped that Jay was not over-confident about his powers. If something did go wrong, there were men in nearby houses they could call on, but she was not sure they would hear if problems went on inside the chapel or the school. She couldn't sleep when they finally got to bed, and when she dreamed, it was of men breaking in and picking up the children and running off with them.

Eighteen

It was not long after Christmas and Maddy had gone down to the farmhouse to help Jay with the building of a new street. He had said he couldn't work it out.

A row was going on. She stood just inside the door and closed it carefully so that it made no noise. She hoped they heard her, in one way, because she didn't want to intrude, but in another way, she thought they were so intent on what they were talking about that even if she had slammed the door, they would not have heard her. She recognised the man's voice; it was Jay. There was a young woman's voice and she was angry.

'You promised we would be married by now,' she said. It was a sweet, middle-class voice, but accusing and sharp.

'We will be. In the spring.'

'You said by Christmas.'

'Eve, you know we need somewhere to live and I promise you—'

'Oh, don't make me any more promises, Jay, when you know very well you can't keep them.'

There was a slight scuffle of somebody's steps and then the girl came out of the room. Though Maddy had heard plenty about Eve, she had not yet seen her. She was very young and stunningly beautiful, wearing a dark blue riding habit, gloves and boots. She had white-blonde hair, not really visible under a jaunty hat with a feather. She slammed out of the house without noticing Maddy. So he did see beauty, after all, she thought.

Maddy watched her mount her horse from a big block and ride away. Maddy was surprised that he was going to marry a girl so much younger than he was. She couldn't have been more than eighteen or nineteen and he was, well, he was almost forty, she surmised. Which she had to allow was not that old, but it felt old. That hurt. Maddy was about to let herself out when his voice came to her. She wished she had gone straight away. His hearing was acute and he knew who she was even though he couldn't see her.

'Sister, come in.' And also he said with a smile, 'We're getting married shortly and the house isn't finished. I've had so many other things to do.'

They went into a big room with huge tables, and on the tables were various drawings. It reminded her so much of her father and how he went on that she gasped.

'I wanted him here to help me,' Jay said, smiling that they understood one another instantly, 'and then I found out that he had died. When I first looked at this place, I was so entranced. I thought if I got him out here, he would see the same vision and we would build the town together. It seems foolish now, but I thought it would work. So I was sorry not just for you, but for me, when he died. I know he didn't like me, but I thought he would have been inspired by the whole concept of this place.'

Maddy couldn't help being pleased at what he said about her father, especially since the two men had parted in enmity. She looked at the drawings. His gaze followed hers.

They sat down and he asked her what she thought. She

stuttered for a couple of minutes and then she forgot that she was a nun. She forgot that her father was not there to talk to him. She told him what was right and what wasn't, and he kept telling her, with such enthusiasm that he infected her, that she was right. She was glad to help.

'Yes, of course. I should have worked that out,' he said, over and over again. She kept on doing this until all the sketches were looked at, and then she started to rework them. Then she remembered who she was.

He didn't notice this. His face was shining, and he said, 'You are your father's daughter. I couldn't sort these things.'

Maddy stood up, astonished firstly that he had needed her help, secondly that she had found this easy – whereas he so obviously did not – and thirdly that she was more pleased with herself than had anything to do with the humility which nuns were supposed to aim at. Failure and success in one go.

'I shouldn't have stayed so long. Sister Bee will wonder what I am doing,' she said.

'Thanks for coming here. I am getting on much better with the fell-side house after you advised me.'

Jay had taken Eve to see the house now that he had altered it in accordance with what Maddy had told him, but he was worried about it. She showed a distinct reluctance to fall in with his plans, and he didn't know why he hadn't worked this out. He had wanted to build a house for her; it seemed such an essential thing to do for his new bride and their new life. They could begin again, start something new. But he could see now that he had got this wrong, and worse still, he had not listened to her.

To be fair, it was a horrible day. It had started off fine and then the rain began. With the wind sideways across the fell, he had to hurry her into the house. He showed her around, waiting eagerly for her to say something positive about it, but she did not. She turned this way and that with a swishing of skirts that did not make him feel any more confident. She went in and out of the various rooms as though she had a train to catch. She didn't smile or speak. In the end, when there was nothing more to look at, she stood by the window and looked out at the fell. When she obviously thought that she could not put it off any longer, she turned to him with a determined look on her face which did not bode well, and she said, 'We talked about this and I thought you understood that I cannot leave my father. Yet you went on with this project.'

Project, that was all it was to her? A project that somebody else had designed, somebody else wanted. Why had he not understood that she would not come up here? He had gone on regardless, somehow thinking that once the house was there, she would fall in love with it. Had she really said such a thing?

'I think your father would prefer we have a house of our own,' he said.

She went back to staring out of the window. You couldn't see the fell; you couldn't see anything beyond the rain that was throwing itself sideways at the windows.

'He may have said that to you, but why would he want that? I have always lived with him and he has not had an easy time of it. Why would I wish him to be by himself now? His wife is mad. Why should he not feel lonely?' she shot back at him.

Jay almost recoiled at how savage her tone was.

'He has a difficult profession which takes up most of his working hours,' she continued. 'If I'm not there, he comes home to the servants. He has no friends – he doesn't have time – and anyway, people shy away from madness. I have no friends, either. Don't you understand what it would be like for him if I came and lived up here in the middle of nowhere because you are insisting on it?'

'I am not insisting on it.'

'Yet you went ahead and built this—'

She was going to say 'monstrosity', he felt sure, but she stopped herself.

He took her home. There was little more conversation, and in a way, he felt relief when he was on his own again.

That evening when their work was finished, he and Hallam sat over the fire. They talked about the problems and possible solutions, but when Jay offered talk about Eve and the house, he wished he hadn't.

Hallam didn't say much about her, but Jay had the feeling that Hallam disliked the little he knew of her. Jay knew by the way that Eve did not talk about his partner and friend that she thought Hallam uncouth. Hallam, when he did not like people, acted differently.

'You thought she would like the house because you like it?' Hallam said.

'I suppose so.'

'It's much prettier where the doctor lives.'

'I know.'

'You could use it for something else.'

'I don't want to use it for something else.'

'You've got a problem then, haven't you?' Hallam said.

Nineteen

Eve made her way into the house. Her father had just come inside from doing his rounds before starting evening surgery. He was sitting in the kitchen as he so often did, just himself and the housekeeper, Mrs Florence.

Mrs Florence had tried to remonstrate with him a number of times over the years and had long since given up. In vain did she tell him that he ought not to eat in the kitchen, that he should take his meals in the dining room as good Christian men did. He said that he had no time for such flummery. Mrs Florence had been housekeeper to him for at least fifteen years, having started off there as the kitchen maid in the years when the mistress was still well – at least Eve presumed – so had licence in such matters.

She was also aware that her mother could not have managed without Mrs Florence. She didn't remember her mother ever stepping outside of the house. Her father had tried to explain why that was, but Eve didn't understand, only that her mother might just as well have not been there, for all the use she had been to her husband or daughter.

She rarely came out of her room anymore. She took her meals up there. Eve had only seen glimpses of her, since the few times her mother ventured downstairs when Eve was a small child. She had never allowed Eve into the room, had never spoken to her or held her that Eve could remember. It had upset Eve so much at one time, but she had long since lost patience and tried not to care.

'Eve?' he called, as he heard her come inside. And then she was in the kitchen, refusing cake and drinking tea, and he thought that she looked as if she had been crying.

That was the first time he wished he had taken his meals in the dining room. Mrs Florence tactfully left, so he didn't have to make a decision, as ever. He said to Eve, 'Are you all right, lassie?'

'He won't set a date for the wedding.' She sat down with a thump.

'He has a lot on his plate.' Her father was always so reasonable; she wished he would come down more on her side. She knew he was right, but she wished he had told her that he understood. All she wanted was to have Jay to herself and it didn't look as though that would happen.

They were never alone, and even though had he not come here she would never have met him, she was frustrated. She didn't care about the damned house or his wretched village or anything else, she just wanted to have him to herself. Even a short time would do. He never concentrated on her. It was one thing a man saying he cared for you, and quite another when he never demonstrated it.

'You always say that, but at the moment I feel like an intruder. He is so intent on living up there, but we could move in here with you.'

'Nay,' the doctor said and she cried. 'If you insist on him coming to live here, it will be a mistake. He will always be at work.'

'If I go and live up there, he will still always be at work.'

'But he will come home to you. Eve, there is nothing in the world better for a man, than to have a wife to come back to. You need to make it so comfortable that he wants to come back to you.'

Eve felt like saying how did her father know such things, but she didn't want to hurt him so she held the words back. He obviously didn't understand what he had said but was only thinking of her.

'And what is he to do?' she asked.

'Work for you and your children, be faithful to you and God-fearing—'

'I don't think he fears anything.'

'Although he has a great deal of experience in some ways, I don't think he has known much love. Men are not minded of God when they resent him. You can teach him how to be gentle and all those other things he lacks. He has the makings of a fine man but he needs the right wife.'

'I don't know if I am that wife.' She hadn't meant to say it and wasn't sure that she meant it. At least, she hadn't before now. She was doubting herself and him and it wasn't easy. She knew nothing about wives, if her mother was anything to go by, but she wasn't her mother.

Over the years she had repeated to herself a thousand times that she was not like her mother, she was nothing like her; she would make a huge success of her life. Somehow she would get away from here, where her mother's presence cast a horrible mood on the house and her father was at work all the time. It was as if having not been able to live with the way that his wife was, he had run away. The trouble was that Eve wanted to be away and she had not managed it. She had been hoping that Jay Gilbraith would do that for her. Now she was in doubt.

Her father did not answer for what seemed like a long time, and she felt her throat and neck and cheeks burning.

'You are the only person who does, but for goodness' sake, if you aren't sure, don't marry him, because it will only make you both miserable.'

'I have thought hard about him. I never imagined myself marrying a – a workman.'

Her father just smiled at that and shook his head.

'Oh Eve, he's a good man, with the finest intelligence I have ever met. He works hard and he doesn't ask a lot. He cares for people; he gives them opportunities they might never have had and he makes money at the same time. And he gives that money back. That's how things are meant to be. He wants to build a hospital of some kind so that we can look after people.'

'I just wish he could find room for me.'

'He has found room for you, but you must compromise,' her father said. 'And so must he, but you may have to show him how. He is a good match for you.'

'I don't understand that. Surely socially he's well beneath me.'

'A doctor is not as important as you seem to think he is, but that isn't the point I was making. He is different than you. You each have special things to offer the other. Your experience and background are so diverse that it would be a marriage of progress.'

'You're talking about children now,' she chided him, 'which you have no right to, especially when speaking to your daughter.'

'Aye,' he said, smiling, 'I know. But I'm right about such things and you wouldn't be bored with a man like him. You would test his mettle in every possible way. It would be very lively, I'll warrant. And probably very successful.'

Eve wished she could have fallen in love with any man other than the one she was now betrothed to. She didn't much like him anymore was the truth. She had fallen under his spell to begin with because he was clever and rich, and because he had fallen in love with her and she had been flattered. There was nobody like him around here.

Since then she had discovered that he was obsessed with work, and short-tempered when he was busy, which was always. He was not at all like the man she had imagined herself marrying. When they had first met, he had been very polite.

He dressed like a gentleman, wore an expensive suit which had so obviously been made for him by a master tailor. He was tall and slender, and he had clean hands and well-kept nails, very neat, shiny hair and cool blue eyes. He had altered since he had become so involved with the work up here. There was a hardness about his very self which she could not leave alone; she wished she had almost every day.

From the beginning of this venture up here on the tops with his new town, he had shown what he was really like. He would work night and day; his vision was the most important thing in his life. She thought at first that she could help him fulfil his dream. She was no longer sure. There did not seem to be space for her. It was all so basic, nothing to do with the things she cared about, music and literature and painting. As far as she knew, he didn't read, and he certainly knew nothing else but the life he had made for himself.

He knew little of culture. She dared say he had never been to a concert or read a book for pleasure. He knew little of church; she could tell when they finally went there together, to talk to the vicar about getting married. He knew nothing of how a Sunday morning service went. She was inclined to be amused, until she knew him better and saw that he was doing such a thing only for her.

This was flattering in its way. He was rich, not as other men were rich, who had land and education. He had fought his way from some back street in Newcastle. Although at first she thought that in its own way it was charming, his grit was so far away from anything she understood that half the time she was inclined not to marry him. She was offended by his lack of cultural knowledge.

He had a determination about him which half frightened her. He was not a man to cross and she knew herself to be quick-tempered. She had never been crossed in her life, but he would take the view he chose. She liked that in one way, but in another she felt he would thwart her if he considered that he knew better.

Most infuriating of all was that her father liked him. She had had so little to kick against in her life, and she could not kick against her mother. She rather wished she could have rebelled, and had her father be horrified that she had chosen to marry such a man.

Her father had first met him when the town was nothing more than a few tents, and a rough road up from the valley to the tops, and a man had been injured down one of the small pits this man owned. There was now a foundry and more than one quarry and men were pouring in to work for him. He had decided to build a town, and he was widely reputed to pay well, though he expected good work.

She wanted to laugh at first at the very ambition, at the gall, and then her father had brought him home to dinner. She was so prepared to dislike him that she almost managed it. She could tell that he had not been invited to dinner at many houses. He watched how her father picked up his cutlery, how he dealt with his napkin and sipped his wine. That was the thing about Jay. He only had to see something done once and he perfected it.

He had yet to take her into his arms. She wasn't sure whether this was deliberate. She would have preferred that he could not help but want to, and yet she knew from the moment he did, that she would be lost, and she didn't want that. She needed control. Perhaps he had been careful with her so that she should be sure of her mind.

There had been nothing but a slow, sweet kiss when she agreed to marry him, and even then it had been measured. She had the feeling that he measured everything in his life, and she was not sure what would happen if she did not measure up. What if she could not have a child or that child was not a son? Men always wanted sons. Yet when she had as politely as possible approached the subject, he looked hard at her and said, 'Would I care if we didn't have a son? Why should I care about that?'

He looked at her as though he was examining every feature of her face with love, but also with respect and a question.

'Men do.'

'I never had a father or a mother and I know nothing of children. I don't know much about people at all. It's always just been me and Hallam. All I know now is that I want you for my wife. I would be so very proud, because I never thought that a woman as good as you would agree to marry me. I will do everything I can to make you happy. I haven't been married before, so I just hope I can do it.'

The more she knew of him, the more she was surprised, and it was not a comfortable feeling. The trouble was, that having secured her for his wife, he no longer pretended to be anything he was not. He never had time to dress up and go out; he spent long hours poring over papers and he was everywhere in the village, helping and showing people what to do and organising the workmen. She was astonished that he had all that energy, but not for her.

Maddy thought March was very cold for a wedding, but she also understood that Miss Gray had run out of patience. Maddy surprised herself. She didn't want him but neither did she want him to marry this beautiful girl. She was not usually so mean.

She had tried hard to be content with the life she had chosen for herself, but she dwelt unduly on his marriage. It was not good of her, she knew. He was not hers. He never had been hers. And she felt now that if she had ever really cared, she would have defied her father and gone to him. She knew that she had felt responsible for her father, and she saw him more coldly now that he had been dead for so long.

So many people, she felt, remade their parents to suit what they chose with their best memories. They possibly thought more kindly of them than they might have done, because it was easier without them, or because it seemed uncharitable to think badly of the dead.

She didn't feel like that. For some reason, she had clung to the idea that she had to be loyal to her father, even though she had been able to acknowledge to herself that he had not been a good parent.

She didn't know now whether there was any such thing. She had no evidence because she had had no other parent; maybe they were all like that. She didn't want to think of him as doing any wrong. He was a large figure, an important and very talented man. Men had called him a genius and she had been so very proud to be his daughter and there it ended.

She knew that a caring parent would not have made her live in what she now knew was a small, damp house by the river. She had tried to deny this to herself. But if her father had really cared for her, he could not have let her endure such a thing. Then she had told herself that he just didn't see it and that excused him. But in the end, now that he had been dead for so long, she saw him not just as her father but as a man. And while men were doing their best, she could not help but wish he had been able to see her as an independent being, and not just as his daughter.

She knew that a lot of men felt the same, but they were doing their daughters a great injustice. It was not right that he should regard her so, and then leave her with no one to care, with no money to help, with no friends or assistance of any kind.

His wonderful buildings counted for nothing and she had taken her pride and gone to the sisters for aid. And yes, poor people lived there, but her father came home only to sleep sometimes, so although he was giving the impression of doing good, he was doing nothing of the kind, as far as she knew. He had an office in the town. He always said he needed a respectable place to carry out his profession.

She had been there only once and could not believe that it was so luxurious. It was a stone building and inside, there was gleaming mahogany, leather chairs, ornate oak desks and brass stair rails. There were big fires, and her father's clerks and architects and designers spent their days in this luxurious place. She could not believe it. How could he do that and allow her to live in such squalid circumstances? Yes, it was his work; that was when she knew that his work meant more to him that she did.

The day over, he went straight to his club. So although they lived together, in that they sometimes slept under the same roof, they rarely met.

She heard whispers that her father had a woman and stayed overnight with her two or three times a week. She tried not to think about it, to discard it. She tried not to think whether he kept that woman lavishly. Perhaps that was part of why he did not consider her comfort; he was not there to experience it.

Sometimes father and daughter had breakfast together. But he kept the house short of money and then complained there was nothing much to eat for breakfast. He said that if she could not afford to give him bacon and eggs, he would go to his club for it. When he was not there, she had toast and jam. It was all she could afford on what he allowed her, and yet she felt she could say nothing. She didn't understand why she felt like that. Maybe she somehow felt guilty that her mother had died, though as far as she knew, it was nothing to do with her.

Very often the coalhouse was empty. He would pay for only one servant and Maddy did a lot of the work herself. There was very little left over from the meagre household allowance, so she bought few clothes, and those second-hand. If she mentioned such things, he would go into a rage and that she could not bear.

She thought how hard his lot was since her mother had died and left him with one daughter and no son. She was sure that he cared, even though he did not say so. She could feel his patience being tried when he thought that she was being stupid. A son might have followed him into the brilliance of his light. He never considered that any son of his might have wanted something else. Sons were not allowed to choose different things; they had to follow on, it was their duty to do so. Daughters were part of oneself.

Her father was lauded in Newcastle for what he did for the

poor, but he kept his own household so short of money that often she had despaired.

Looking back now, she knew that Jay could have lifted her out of that poverty, not just financially, but in other ways. She felt lonely, she had no friends. She could keep no servant, because they left as there was too much to do and they were so badly paid. She was always alone.

After her father died, she had gone to the convent for lack of any place else. He had not left her a penny, nor a home to live in. Then she had been relatively happy; the sanctuary of it was such a relief and it was an easier life than she had lived thus far. She was happy here too and grateful for it. She liked the work and her sisters, and the whole idea of women living together, using their minds and bodies to help others go forward. She did not grieve over her father for long. She felt guilty for that, but in some ways she saw how selfish he had been once she led a different life.

But there was a small, ridiculous part of her that thought about what it would be like to have a man to come home to her, as her father must have done when her mother was alive. She was not sure whether she remembered their lives together. Had they been happy or she had built up in her mind a past which had never existed?

But it was all settled and Jay was marrying Eve on the Saturday morning. No one had been invited but Mr Hallam and Eve's father. It was to be very small, with a quiet wedding breakfast before they left for Paris.

Twenty

Ruth surprised herself because she had thought that she was content with her life. She was now accepted in the school and had her own room should she choose to use it. Most of the time she stayed with the children in the dormitory, and she was learning to read and write with what Maddy assured her was great speed. Also she had learned that she was good at making sketches. The nuns provided thick cream paper and coloured pencils so that she could draw the collies and the kittens, and scenes about the town and in the fields, which everybody seemed to like. So it took some time to work out that she didn't want Jay to marry Eve Gray.

She was astonished and not very pleased with herself. He was quite old and she had decided that she would never like men for what her father had done to her. But her memories of Jay – she didn't call him that, it would have been disrespectful, it was only in her mind that he was Jay – were good. She tried telling herself that it was just that he had been kind to her, the first man ever to do so, but there was just something about him which she could not get past. She would push to be where he was and tried to stand nearby whenever she could. Worst of all, having discovered he was getting married, she soon learned to hate Eve Grey – for being so beautiful, so well-spoken, for being the doctor's daughter and living in the biggest house in the area. It seemed to Ruth that Eve had everything and she had very little. She called herself names and tried hard not to hate Eve, but it was difficult.

Miss Gray only occasionally came to the farmhouse and so Ruth did not see her, but the talk was that very often Jay was in Wolsingham in the evenings and at weekends, especially Sundays. Ruth came to dislike Sundays because he was absent, even though she rarely saw him. But as time moved on and the wedding day drew nearer, she wished she could have wiped Eve Gray from the face of the earth.

She wanted to pray and ask God for something to stop the wedding day. Perhaps that Eve might change her mind – though she never would, the horrible grasping person she was – or that Jay might realise that she was not the right woman for him and cry off, but nothing happened. She knew with a clean, pure thought that Jay must marry nobody but her. It didn't matter that he was so much older; she loved him so very passionately that the feeling was part of the same violent dislike that she felt for the young woman he was meant to be marrying. Ruth knew that she could not just stand by and let it happen.

And that was when she took matters into her own hands, and prayed for something to happen that the wedding would not go ahead. She felt slightly guilty about this, but she could not bear the idea of him married, and having to watch him go home to that awful woman.

She knew also from general talk that Miss Gray did not like the house that Jay had built for her; consequently, they would live with her father. There was talk of the house being made into another place for the nuns to use for the children, but so far nothing had happened.

Ruth tried not to go near the house, but since it was just along from the butterfly house on the very edge of the town, she found it impossible. So one snowy afternoon, when she would not be missed, she went there. She had thought there might be workmen about, but since it was Sunday, nobody was there.

She was therefore in front of the building within very few minutes and almost straight away wanted to run back to the school.

It was those few moments before the sun sets. It had been a cold, white day, and the sun was twinkling in the low sky as if it had nothing better to do. It was therefore shining on the house, and Ruth thought it could never have looked more beautiful than it did now.

The view along the fell was spectacular, the sheep almost lost against the snow which had fallen that morning. Now, as if to compete with the sunshine, the snow began to blot out its rays, falling softly to blanket the scene.

Ruth was so taken aback at the idea that Eve Gray disliked this house that she learned to hate her right from that moment. Eve Gray had everything, whereas she had nothing. Jay had built her this exquisite house. How could she not long to be there with him? She would have him all to herself; she would belong to him and he would come home to her every night. She would be able to see him during the day, as he went about the village helping and directing, and on cold nights, like at this time of the year, they would sit in front of a big fire and talk.

Ruth could not imagine anything better. So why did Miss Gray cause problems like this? Did men build houses for women every day? Ruth had never heard of such a thing. She was so envious that the hatred in her heart settled hard like iron. Eve Gray did not deserve Jay. Ruth wished hard that Eve Gray would leave him alone. She determined to pray that this happened, that Eve Gray would never marry Jay. She was not the right woman for him, she would not make him happy, he would be much better off without her.

It was also known generally that Jay would take Miss Gray to London and to Paris for several weeks after the wedding. When they came back, Ruth would see him even less because he would be in Wolsingham. She found that hard to stomach. She was only just getting used to living near her idol. Once he was married, he would have little reason to come to the farmhouse. So she was unhappy as the weeks went on and the day of the wedding moved forward.

The darkness fell and Ruth walked slowly back to help with sitting the children down for tea. But when she went to bed, she held in her mind a picture of Eve Gray not marrying the man that Ruth loved so very much.

Eve's father was reluctant to take on an apprentice doctor, but they had decided it was a good idea since there was so much work to do, and so he had done it.

Eve had almost convinced herself that he would not arrive, and that when he did, he would be fat, gawky, awkward and short. So when she got back from visiting her Great Aunt Daisy in Stanhope and found a neatly dressed young man in the drawing room, she was agreeably surprised.

Noel Esher was most courteous, getting to his feet as she entered the room; he was wearing a very neat suit. He spoke in soft, cultured southern tones. He had warm brown eyes and shiny brown hair and he was smiling as he greeted her.

Mrs Florence had put on a very good dinner and when they

sat down, Eve could not help but ask about London, which she thought she liked best of all the places she might visit, except for Paris, where she hoped to go after her wedding. This was the epitome of sophistication to her.

He spoke warmly of his father's practice, though he did not boast; it was only an impression she gained. He talked about his sisters and his mother and of how much warmer it was in the south. How dull the dale seemed to Eve then, and how common the little town which Jay thought was his whole life. It made her feel impatient with her betrothed. She was almost ashamed of him.

She asked her father if she might show Mr Esher the area and her father said yes, he might have that first day off. She drove him about in the pony cart, and where she saw dullness, he saw beauty, and she liked him the better for that. He loved the waterfall at Eastgate and the ford at Stanhope, and he looked up to where the sheep and cattle grazed on the high hills and said how wonderful it must be to live in such a place.

'I feel the opposite,' she said. 'I long for town life.'

'I don't suppose it's what you imagine,' he said. 'My father has a busy practice and hasn't been in good health lately. And there are a lot of poor people who can never pay. You don't see the like here because you live in a close community, but London is full of beggars. My father has to charge, as I'm sure yours does, but it means that sometimes he cannot do all that he might want to. The streets are dark and cold and dirty, and people aren't open as they are here. And there are so many of them that it's difficult to make friends.'

She didn't want him to misunderstand, so she told him about her betrothal and what her husband-to-be was doing. He said how brave and ambitious it sounded.

'I would like to see it,' he said.

This was easily accomplished, because the following day her father asked Mr Esher to go to the new town with him. With the help of Gilbraith and the nuns, he had begun several clinics within the school itself. Although the air on the tops was very healthy, and people ate well, there were various problems and he needed the aid.

Mr Esher loved the place from the moment he saw it, Eve felt. He was enthusiastic; he wanted to help straight away. Jay showed him around the place and he talked of helping Mr Gray to set up more clinics. With two of them, they could do twice as much – well, almost twice as much, since he was not yet qualified – he said with a modest smile.

After that, Eve saw as little of Mr Esher as she did of her father, and mealtimes were transformed because they talked of nothing but work. Having always been a doctor's daughter, they were unaware of speaking out of turn before her, but Eve knew that her father trusted her not to betray his confidence. She was interested in what they were doing. Mr Esher especially liked seeing to the orphanage children, and making sure they ate well and had plenty of fresh air.

Mr Gray always maintained that the champagne air up there was as good as any tonic. People ailed less when they had good frosts in the winter to kill the germs, and plenty of outdoor time when the weather was better. The men were less inclined to come to the doctors for help, but Jay would not stand for this, and many a sheepish man stood there, cap in hand, in the queue for the doctor.

Even when they injured themselves, they were reluctant to go and have their injuries seen to. Eve knew that her father liked these best; he was interested in setting bones and how the healing proceeded. What he dreaded most was disease, but up here with clean water and good food, these things seemed not to happen. Eve was proud of her father and the new doctor, and how healthy they enabled these people to be.

The decision had been made. The wedding was to be on the last Saturday in March.

Twenty-One

On the Friday morning before the wedding, Mr Esher was doing the clinic. As many people as cared to wait went to that clinic and the two other clinics that were on hand that week, on Monday and Wednesday. Everybody would be seen. Eve knew well that it was not from the graciousness of his heart that her father spent so much time up at the new town. It was known throughout the area that Gilbraith paid him handsomely.

Sometimes Mr Gray came and took the clinics himself, but once a week he let the junior doctor try his hand. He would only come at the end so that any difficult cases might be seen by both of them. Mr Esher was well liked right from the beginning. He always had a word with each patient; he spoke to the children instead of over their heads and was endlessly reassuring to their mothers, who came with them. Men were a different matter. Few would come to be seen unless Gilbraith had insisted. They seemed to think of illness as a personal fault.

Being a Friday, it was the shortest clinic of the week. Monday was the heaviest, after the weekend. Wednesday could go either way. Mr Gray always did Monday and Wednesday and would visit those who could not come to see him. He was content to go into their homes when they were too ill to attend.

That Friday morning, the clinic was almost finished when there was the biggest bang that Maddy had ever heard. The butterfly house shuddered as though its roof was about to fly off and its walls to break.

She and Mr Esher ran outside and joined a lot of other people, mostly women, running towards the pit head. There were several small pits around the area, this was the one inside the town. The air reeked of fire and was thick with smoke.

It was only one bang, the men were saying, as though that was good, but Mr Hallam insisted on going down to have a look. If it was bad enough, Jay would follow him. Down he went to assess the situation. Maddy was horrified and scared and had never seen anything like this. She had not seen disaster before. She could feel and smell the fear and anxiety around her. Each second was so long, and each minute felt like an eternity, as the people of the village gathered and waited. They stood about as though they had seen such things before, and she didn't doubt that a great many of them had.

There was what felt like a long wait before the cage came up. Men were in it, walking out, and there were many glad cries – that they were not just alive, but uninjured. The talk was that there had been a fall, not a big one, and several men had been trapped. But Mr Hallam had taken charge, and as long as nothing else came down, they would all come out of it.

There was another long wait and it was cold. Sister Hilary brought a thick cloak for Maddy. She was glad of its warmth. Womenfolk and grandparents went to claim their men with joy and then the cage came up again. This time two men were injured, though not badly, according to Mr Esher, who cheered them on as though he was used to such things, though Maddy doubted he was. She liked him all the more for it.

Gilbraith went down to help so that it should be known they were both doing everything they could to ensure that all the men were out. There was a long time when the cage brought up no more men. Maddy heard them talking about the risk of explosion, but they had to get the other men out.

'What causes it?' she asked one man, whom she vaguely knew.

'Firedamp, pet,' he said, forgetting who she was in such circumstances. 'It sets off a spark and the air changes and then it blows up.'

'And how many men are down there?'

'Not many, sweetheart, the joys such as they are of a small pit. They'll get them out unless there's another explosion.'

She filled her time helping with the wounded; none of them was badly hurt, just cuts and bruises, and shock, of course. Mr Esher remained cheerful and the men talked as though it was nothing and were taken home in triumph.

The talk was that three men were hurt, and so another long wait. Then the cage came up and in it – her heart sank – two bodies. Maddy had never seen anything like it when the bodies were brought up. They were treated so gently that at first she thought perhaps she had been wrong and they were injured.

There was, however, a cry of grief from one woman; perhaps she had seen such things before. She ran over but she was the only one. Maddy recognised her, Mrs Hope. She and her husband had been here for a very short time; he had been some kind of engineer and was a lovely man. He had intended retiring, and boasted smiling that his wife could not bear having him at home, so he had decided to come here and give Mr Gilbraith a helping hand in any way that he could. Maddy had gained the impression he was bored at home and that he had enough money, but liked industry, having always been in it. He must have been fifty-five or even sixty, but he wanted to be there and had been a huge asset. Jay spoke of his tremendous ability and what an asset he was to himself and to Hallam.

Maddy tried to remember any children, and thought if they had any, they would have long since left the nest and made their own lives. She couldn't remember whether there were grandchildren or if they lived nearby, but it would be easier on Mrs Hope now if she had support. Ruth, standing close beside Maddy, stared and then she said, 'The second man is Mr Russell. He came here with his two little girls.'

Maddy remembered. She had talked to him just after he got his house. He had come here keen to start a new life, all the way from Cornwall. He was a bonny, auburn-haired man with what must have been a ready smile in good times. But his wife had died on the way of some fever, and the smile these days could have been painted on; it did not reach his eyes. His daughters, Pansy and Primrose, were old enough to understand and huddled together now.

'Oh no,' Ruth said. 'I can see them. I don't think they should be here. He was just settling in and I was hoping he would bring them to school this next week.'

'Why don't you take them back to the convent now?' Maddy suggested gently.

Ruth paused, as though reluctant to leave, and Maddy knew that she was concerned for Jay. The two women with so much of life between them had become quite close. But after a minute or two, she nodded and went across to the two little girls.

By then they were holding hands, as though they knew that

life had been cruel to them once again and in such a short space of time. Ruth tried to coax them with sweet words, but the girls just looked across to where the two dead men lay.

'That's our dad,' Primrose said.

They were twins but not identical. Strangely, Primrose was dark, as though to confuse everybody, and Pansy was fair. Coincidence, Ruth thought, was a strange thing.

'Can we go to him?' the girl enquired.

'Primrose—'

'He's dead, isn't he?'

No pretence here. Passed away was not the right expression for children. They wanted to hear the truth.

Ruth was beginning to wish that she had urged Maddy to do this; she was so much older and knew more. And then she realised that it was not so; her bad experience had prepared her just as much as anyone else for the hard things, in other people's lives as well as in her own.

'Our mam died and now him. Can we go and see him?'

'Wouldn't you like to come over to the schoolroom? Sister Hilary will give you some cake.' She felt dreadful but she didn't really want them to see what his injuries were. They could be horrific.

Primrose looked at her sister and then disparagingly at Ruth.

'We want to see him,' she said, so Ruth took them across.

Ruth was minded that they would not forget such negative images of him but Mr Esher, perhaps thinking that this might happen – she thanked him with a smile which was all she could offer, for being so sensitive and so thoughtful in such horrible circumstances – had wiped the blood from Mr Russell's face, and the rest of it was covered in dust and dirt. Mr Esher merely smiled – just a little, in a friendly way – at the twins as he showed them the face of the sole parent they had had.

'He doesn't look dead,' Pansy pronounced. 'He looks asleep.'

'They are very similar,' Mr Esher said, getting down to the twins' level.

'You are sure he's dead then?'

'I'm afraid so.'

Pansy turned to her twin.

'I want my mammy,' she said. Her face worked for a few seconds and then the storm broke and the tears cascaded down her small face. They worked their grief over her cheeks and down to her lips, then her mouth opened and great sobs poured out; her body began to shudder. Ruth didn't know what to do but her sister did. Primrose took her sister into her arms while Pansy broke what was left of her heart, Ruth thought.

Time went forward. The evening had turned into night and night into morning without Maddy noticing. Ruth took the two little girls back to their new home, and after trying and failing to get them to eat anything, she sat down with them and let them cry.

Early on the Saturday morning Mr Esher got a message saying that one man was badly hurt and the doctor was needed down there. Maddy had never seen anybody go so white in the face; she thought he was going to faint. It had not occurred to her that he might be afraid of small, dark places and danger. Why wouldn't he be? She had put from her mind that Gilbraith was down there. She understood now that another explosion could kill them. While he hesitated, she said to him, 'I will go with you.'

'Yer canna go down there, Sister,' said the man in charge, who had called her sweetheart and pet. 'The boss would kill us.'

'I could probably be of help and I don't think I need your permission,' she said tartly, as she thought she needed to be. 'Come along, Mr Esher, we can go down together.'

Twenty-Two

Jay played a game with himself as to which day was the worst of his life. At one time it had been the street, when he was starving in Newcastle and horrible men had forced themselves on him. That was always first. The second was the day that he had hoped Maddy's father would care about him and let him marry her. But this day, when two good pitmen had died, was the worst day of his life. He thought carefully about it, right from the beginning, because he was so afraid that things would get worse.

He had awoken not quite happy even though he knew that within twenty-four hours he would be a married man. He knew that he should have been happy, but he doubted Eve's love for him — and on another level, he doubted his regard for her. He wanted a wife. No, that was not quite true. He had wanted a wife when he met Maddy; now he wanted a trophy. He called himself stupid, but Eve was young and beautiful and clever, and he had doubted that she would accept him. He wondered whether she was already regretting it and whether she might leave him at the altar. That would be another first.

He wished that he had not let Hallam go down the pit without him on the Friday morning. He would never forget that. He had tried to argue, but he was aware — they both were — that Hallam was always second in this venture, and of late he seemed to have wanted to be more involved. Jay thought it probably would not be much of a fall and Hallam would come back up and show him and tell him. Then he would go down with Hallam and they would sort it out together. Tact, he thought, was important.

Hallam went down and they began to bring the men up, mostly unhurt. Then Jay got into the cage to go down and assist, and there was a rumbling and a huge noise. The cage shook until he feared he would die, and when he got safely to the bottom, the second fall had been mighty. It shouldn't have happened, he told his not-quite-believing self. He had done everything he could to make sure it was safe. He knew that mining was never safe; the earth was sometimes like a huge and mighty animal. It was unpredictable, varying each day, and as if it hated men taking its bounty, it exacted revenge.

He kept hoping that nobody was badly hurt. The men who had been involved had mostly got free, and were only slightly hurt, dazed from the noise and the shaking, but nothing important. He wanted to be able to breathe freely and then he came upon the main fall. One man was trapped and another two were dead. Even though they were free of the fall, the stones had killed them.

And that was when Friday turned into the worst day ever. If it became harder than this, he would die himself. The dead men had to be taken to the surface and Jay remembered that one had not been there long. His wife had died before they reached the new town and he had two little girls. The other would be taken to his wife, a lovely woman, and another brave soul who had come here to better herself and her husband. And now look. Saturday did itself out for awfulness – it was the worst that he could remember.

It was as though God laughed at him for trying so very hard to help people. He was paid out for his arrogance, for his huge attempts.

The man who was trapped was Hallam.

Eve could not believe what she was being told, that her wedding day was not to happen.

She stared, not taking in what her father told her after he had a message from the village, one of several. He had been anxious because Mr Esher was on his own, but there were a great many needy patients in Wolsingham, so he had had to contain himself and let the young man cope.

'He's still down the pit.'

'But it's his wedding day,' she said. 'We are getting married in – in just a little while. What has happened?'

'This note is from Mr Esher. Most of the men are out now, but Jay won't be able to make it to the church in time for the wedding. It will have to be cancelled.'

'Cancelled?' She stood, staring, and the tears leapt into her eyes. Her mouth quivered, she could feel it. 'But – but – there must be somebody else, what about Mr Hallam?'

'Mr Hallam was already down there and they are doing what they can. Now I will go round and see the vicar and then I must go up there.'

'But everything's booked, everything's—'

'Don't worry, my lassie, we will sort it out. Everything will be fine. A short delay will cost nothing and the food and drink in the house will keep for another day or two. You can be married soon. There is nothing to worry about. Now you go and tell Mrs Florence, and I will go to the vicar. Then I will go up to the

village to see if Mr Esher can cope. Poor laddie, he's not used to
our northern ways, he is probably very worried and trying not to
show it.' Her father smiled at her and then he left.

Mrs Florence came through and Eve told her about the wedding being postponed and Mrs Florence, being of a practical
mind, clicked her tongue and said they were lucky it wasn't a June
wedding or everything would have gone off in the next day or
two and spoiled. As it was, the pantry was doing grand work and
there was nothing to be concerned for.

Somewhat relieved, Eve followed her into the kitchen and
tried not to think about it. She remembered her father's words.
It was only temporary. It would sort out and they would be
married. Perhaps tomorrow or the day after, she thought. The
vicar wouldn't mind; he was a kind old gentleman and would be
happy to help them.

And then she thought about the note. Why had Jay not written
a note to her himself? Had he completely forgotten about her?

How bad could it be? There was plenty of help up there, it
wasn't as if Jay had to manage by himself. She was quite comforted by the idea of Mr Esher. Though not nearly as old as
Jay, he was to be relied upon. Her father liked him very much,
possibly more than he liked Jay. They certainly had more in
common.

Eve disliked Hallam. They had met briefly and he had looked
sideways at her and not spoken. She did not look forward to
marrying Jay and then having to be civil to his brutish friend.
The only good thing about Hallam was that he would surely
look after the place so that she and Jay could escape to Europe.
After that, she dreamed the dream that she always did now, of
beautiful dresses, diamonds on her wrists and fingers, carriages
taking her to the play and the opera and the theatre. They would

have a house in town – the town being London – and they would go further afield, and then Jay might decide that he would not go back, and they would have a wonderful life hundreds of miles away from this boring existence.

Twenty-Three

Mr Esher shook his head and would have gone alone but Maddy didn't let him. She got into the cage with him and when the cage went down, she left her stomach above. She didn't think she had ever felt quite so sick. The feeling passed and was succeeded by sheer terror. She had never seen blackness like it. It felt so thick you could touch it, but thankfully there were lamps and they had a guide. The roof at first was high but soon it was so low that it frightened her even more.

When they got further in, she could see the problem. The explosion had brought the roof down and a man was trapped. As they got there, Gilbraith, barely visible, just the whites of his eyes in a black face, glared at her and at Esher and then he said, 'What in hell's name—'

'We have come to help,' she said before he could go on. 'What's happening?'

He hesitated, but he had other things on his mind than her presence down his pit, and she had relied on that.

'It's Wes. He isn't moving. We got everybody out and then the roof fell in again as we were about to leave and . . .' His voice trailed away. 'Everybody else is accounted for. I thought I could get him out, but I don't know whether I can without doing further damage,' Gilbraith said, voice unsteady. 'If we move him, we may hurt him more. And if we try to get him out, it will weaken the roof. What do you think?' he asked the doctor.

Mr Esher went and knelt down in the muck, and he seemed to her to be down there for a very long time. When he got up, he didn't speak for a few moments and then he said,

'He's still alive but only just,' and he shook his head.

This was the worst news and Jay didn't look up. Then he asked in a hoarse, unsteady voice, 'Will it help if I shift the rock and then move him? Is it worth the risk?'

Mr Esher shook his head. Jay gazed at him for a few seconds and to Maddy in the lamplight, it felt like an eternity. The cold eyes glazed, trying to accept what he was being told.

Jay fell to his knees.

'Dinna gan and leave me here, for God's sake,' he said. 'Wes, don't. I can't do this without you. Please, don't die on me. Please.'

There was no response. Noel Esher got down in the pit muck with him and he felt for life in Hallam's neck.

'I don't think he can hear you.'

'Yes, he can,' Jay insisted. 'We can't let him die down here. I've got to get him out.'

Noel got down closer beside him and tried to look into his face, even though Jay turned away. And then Noel said softly, 'Jay, you cannot get him out. He's dying. For God's sake, let him go.'

Maddy was amazed at how sweetly the doctor spoke to him, how soft his voice was. The intimate use of Jay's first name was just right.

'He cannot die down here. He cannot. He cannot leave me like this. I've never been anywhere without him. He cannot die. He cannot.'

The doctor felt for Wes's pulse and slowly shook his head.

'He's gone.'

'No.' Jay's voice broke. Maddy didn't know where to look through the all-consuming black beyond the little light that they had.

The pitman behind them, who had brought them down, now jostled the doctor's arm. Noel understood and nodded, even though neither of them said anything.

Then all of a sudden, there was another unholy noise and the roof came down. Maddy had never been as scared in her whole life. She didn't want to die down here, suffocating in all this muck. As she felt the roof give, so she felt Jay grab her and pull her out of the way. When she collected herself, she saw that the pitman had pulled Noel out too. But the roof had come down and buried Hallam. She couldn't see him at all now; all she could see was a wall of stone. It was a huge fall. Even in front of him, the roof had come down. They had had to move much further back. She began to cough and couldn't stop, and the pitman gave her some water from the bottle he carried on him.

They waited for a few moments until Jay collected himself and then the pitman said, 'We have to go.'

'No,' Jay managed.

'Mr Gilbraith, it will take all the rest of the day to move the stone from his body, and even then you know the risks.'

Noel looked vacantly at him and the man said, 'We have to get out in case there is another fall.'

'I can't leave him here,' Jay said.

'With respect, sir, you should come to the surface. It's the only thing to do.'

'No.'

And then Noel waded in and Maddy admired him for his perception.

'You cannot endanger the village by staying here now. Come on.'

'If you could just—'

'He's dead,' Noel said, and looked as straight at him as he could manage.

'I want to get his body out.'

'And what are the chances, what about the roof?'

'You go up now. There's nothing more you can do. I have to get him out.'

'You are going to spend a lot of time, which you don't have, according to what the men on the surface said. These people are your responsibility. You have to let go of this man.'

Jay shook his head; he had not taken his eyes off his friend.

'Go up and take her with you.' He nodded to the only other man who was there, the one who had brought them down. 'Take them up.'

'You must come too,' Maddy said. And that was when she saw the man she was dealing with for the first time. He could not betray his friend, but in doing so, might betray the whole village and everything he had striven to bring about here.

'I'm going to bring him out.'

'You can't. You heard the doctor, you'd be endangering your life.'

'It's mine to endanger.'

'What about Eve?'

Nobody said anything for what felt to Maddy like a very long time.

'Take them up, Bradley,' Gilbraith instructed abruptly and he didn't even look at her. She saw that she had no influence with him, and why would she? If she had married him when he asked – but she couldn't go there. She blamed her father, she blamed herself, she couldn't think. She told herself she was too upset and that he must do what he thought was right, but the idea of him dying down there with his friend wouldn't rest with her.

'Why don't you ever listen to anybody?' she said, resisting even as the pitman touched her arm.

'Get the hell out of here,' Jay said.

'You cannot stay down here and risk the whole village.'

He didn't answer her.

'Come on, Sister, we have to make sure of you and the doctor before the rest of the roof comes down,' the pitman said shortly. His grip on her arm was firm as he guided her away.

'We can't leave him down here,' she kept saying, but the two men made her go along the way they had come. This time she didn't even notice the narrow roof, the horrible air, the way that the whole place smelled so hot. They got her up and out of there as quickly as they could, and all the time she wanted to go back and help him. She thought she would remember the roof fall in her dreams. The idea of suffocation would go on and on.

Mr Esher left the scene very quickly to see to other people, but she lingered, trying not to cry.

'Why won't he let people help, if he insists on bringing that man's body out?'

'Because he won't have it,' the pitman said. 'Howay, Sister, I'll take you back to the convent.'

'No.' She pulled away. 'I'm not going anywhere until he comes out.'

'That could take some time because the stone has to be moved off Mr Hallam. He won't have anybody else down there in case the roof comes in.'

'I don't care.'

Ruth was not there; Maddy guessed she would have stayed with the Russell daughters. But Hilary and Abigail were, and Maddy had to tell them that Hallam had died.

'Mr Gilbraith insisted on staying down there and moving the stone by himself so that he can bring Mr Hallam's body to the surface.'

'Should he have done that?' Hilary asked.

Maddy felt herself swaying and the scene in front of her eyes wobbling. She closed her eyes for a few moments and said nothing and steadied herself.

'He insisted.'

'What if the roof gives again?' Hilary said.

Maddy said nothing. She choked. It was nothing but coal dust, filth, she told herself. She didn't understand him. She knew that Wesley Hallam was his friend and they had known one another for a long time, but they were not related. He was not Jay's father or his brother. Surely it was a stupid thing to do.

She didn't understand why he couldn't just face the facts and let him go; it would have been kinder for all of them.

Jay set to and began to clear the stone. It would have been a lot quicker and easier if he had been half a dozen men, but in view of the way the roof was coming down without warning, he was not prepared to risk anybody's life but his own. All that mattered now was that he should bring Hallam's body to the surface.

The falls had been huge. In a way, he was lucky that only three men had died. Lucky, was that the word for it? He began to cry. That was of no help, he told himself, licking at the salt as the tears ran into his mouth.

His hands caught on the stone and began to bleed. He thought of what it would be like without Hallam. They hadn't been apart for more than thirty years. Whatever would he do? It could not be happening to him.

They were still businessmen in Newcastle and this was just a horrible dream. He had never started up something that would take Hallam's life. It was all his fault; it had been his idea and he had urged Hallam towards it. Now look.

The trouble with tragedy was that you got no warning. Nobody said, 'Why don't you go down instead of your best friend?' No, no, you ended up down here, your friend lifeless. And as you moved the stone, you saw more and more of the person you had loved and did love and always would love, and they would never move, never speak to you or anybody else. It was over.

He went on tugging at the stone and moving it, and in a stupid way it made him feel better, that the fault was not all his. The place, the pit and everything concerned, was finished to him. The blood began to run down his hands and he wiped it off on his trousers and then on his shirt. He could smell the blood so warm, and Hallam's still-warm body now beneath his fingers. He thought he would never sleep again, he would never be easy again, he would never eat or take pleasure in anything, now that he had caused his best friend, his only ever friend, to die like this. How could he have been so careless when Wes had done so much for him, had done everything for him? Watched his back, laughed at him, laughed with him, got drunk with him, sorted out men down alleys when they came at Wes and at him for their money and fine clothes.

He had somehow thought they had a charmed life. How stupid that was now and how carelessly he had let it go. Time ceased, above ground and below, and in the end he wished that the roof would fall in and kill him, because he could not stand the idea of his life going forward. He knew that it was against all the ideas he could ever remember, but there was nothing left.

The hours crept by. Maddy knew that the stone would take one man a great deal of time to shift, but as the day went on and on interminably, her fears grew. Surely they should have been up long before now. What if the roof had fallen in again and nobody knew? But there would have been a lot of noise, wouldn't there? If not, then why was it taking so long?

The night grew even darker and colder and it was almost dawn, the first faint pink and black streaks in the sky, when the cage finally came up with the two men in it, one alive and one dead. Jay held his friend's body in his arms. Maddy was scared.

Mr Gray had sent his assistant home. He tried to urge the sisters to go to the butterfly house. The dawn was beginning to break when Gilbraith brought his friend's body up from the depths of the pit. Maddy always thought afterwards that she would henceforth hate winter dawns, so bright, orange and pink and black, and doing all those magical things which dawns did, despite what was happening. The dawn played itself out in all its majesty and she hated it for its disregard.

Gilbraith put Hallam down so gently upon the blankets, as

though Hallam could still feel pain. Jay spent a long time gazing down at him and then he came to Maddy. His hands and arms and face were covered in blood from his treatment of them getting the stone off his friend. He seemed to her to have aged a hundred years, and that was when she knew that she did still love him. She hated that she was proud of what he had done, and despised him too, for the risks. She was not even swayed when he spoke roughly to her.

'You shouldn't have been down there,' he said, and he glared at her.

She glared back at him. The temper she had thought long since conquered raised its head like a hurt dragon.

'Don't you tell me what I should and shouldn't do,' she managed through her teeth. 'I'm glad I'm not marrying you, and if you cared about that girl at all, you wouldn't have stayed down there like that for the sake of a friend. Some friend you were to him. It wasn't as if you could save his life.'

She was horrified once it was out, but it was too late. To her horror, sobs choked her. She hadn't cried so much in years; even when her father had died, she hadn't given in like this. It was a torrent of feelings that she couldn't stop. He stood there and let her cry, while in the background the men took Wes's body away.

'I'm sorry, Maddy,' he said. 'He was the only real friend I ever had. I couldn't leave him. There was a part of me that didn't want to come out with him dead. I felt I owed him a lot more than that. I felt like it was my fault, and I didn't deserve to be here when he wasn't. This was all my idea and he came along for the ride.'

'I thought you were going to die,' she said.

'Well, I'm still here.'

Hilary came across and put an arm around Maddy's shoulders and led her away. Maddy thought that Jay did not remember it had been his wedding day yesterday, and that a young woman was waiting for him, knowing little of what had happened. Hallam had been his only thought, his only vision.

Twenty-Four

Ruth tried not to think about what had happened. She had Primrose and Pansy to think about. She did not have time to consider what she had done, but she had to face it. She had called on God to make the wedding stop and he had answered her. Thinking of it made her feel sick and she tried to shrug it off, at least for now. She had done terrible things. First of all, she had badly injured or killed her father, and now three men were dead because of her. Why on earth had God been listening to her now when he had never done so before? And what was he trying to prove, why had he made her so wicked? She was, she had done awful, awful things and she felt that she didn't deserve to live.

At first the two little girls seemed to accept what had happened, and she was able to sit them down and give them a meal. It was when she put them to bed that the problems began. Primrose cried and her sister joined in. Ruth lay there with them and let them cry themselves to sleep. After that she was wide awake, trying to think of what had happened. She could not dismiss from her mind the idea that it was all her fault. She had asked God to stop the wedding and he had done just that. Her mind crawled with guilt and threatened to overwhelm her. She began to moan, but stopped herself when the girls both half awakened. She had no sleep that night.

She suggested to the little girls that they might go to school the following morning, but they hid under the bedclothes. She had no idea what to do next so she scrubbed the house. She was just beginning to panic and lose herself to her mind again when she heard a noise and found that Sister Maddy had arrived. She instantly wanted to blurt out her cares and her worries, but she thought that Maddy would be horrified at what she had done. Was she never to do the right thing?

Sister Maddy was big with praise as she always was but Ruth managed to detach herself sufficiently to see that the sister was tired and her eyes were full of concern. Ever since Sister Bee had recovered from her summer cold and then grown worse in other areas, Sister Maddy had had to take on more and more responsibility.

Sister Bee was almost like another person. When she was able to lead them, she was apt to tell Sister Hilary that she must not see Mr Nattrass, as though there was something wrong in it. She forbade Mr Nattrass the schoolroom. She told Maddy that she must not ask Mr Gilbraith to come to the convent and she must not go to see him in his house; it was not the thing for nuns to come into such contact with men.

She complained when Hilary made her special dishes. Abigail fared best; she kept out of the way. But after a week or two of this, Sister Bee became very tired. That was when they found a room for Maddy that was well away from Sister Bee's office, towards the back of the building, with a big window that looked out at the fell. She began to run everything from there, grateful for what peace and quiet she could get.

Best of all, Ruth thought, she would spend an increasing

amount of time with Sister Maddy and she liked that. Now this barrier was rising between them and she had to hide her feelings. Her hopes were gone and all she could aspire to was making these two children reasonably happy over time.

The little girls heard the voices and came downstairs. They were hungry, which was a good start, Ruth thought. Maddy stayed with them while they ate. It was only bread, warm milk and sugar, but it was what they had asked for so they got it.

'Mr Nattrass is bringing his new puppy to the school this afternoon,' she told Ruth, ignoring the little faces which lifted from the bowls of bread and milk.

Nobody said anything to that, but eventually Primrose said, 'Is he like Dobber and Bonny?' The dogs were famous in the new town; all the children knew them.

'No, he's what you call a Jack Russell, a kind of terrier. He's so small that he can be picked up and cuddled. He's brown and white with a little black button for a nose.'

After that, Sister Maddy went out back to prepare for Mr Nattrass's visit. Ruth sat the little girls down and she read to them. Her reading was coming on a treat, she thought, and so was her writing. She was hoping that they would find this a dull book; she made it sound as dull as she could manage, and after two pages the talk turned to the new puppy.

'Has the new puppy got a name?' Pansy wanted to know.

Ruth said she knew nothing about it; it was the first time since the puppy had left its mother. This led her into hard depths about birth, weaning, and why puppies left their mothers and how old they had to be. She skimmed over the details and after that Primrose decided that she thought she would like to see the puppy and then it became easier.

The little girls were washed and dressed and they left the

house without tears. Since Mr Nattrass was just arriving at the schoolroom with the puppy, they were the first to see it and the first to hold it. Mr Nattrass said in front of the whole class that he was hoping somebody might think of a name for the puppy. It was a boy puppy. While the children were occupied, Ruth was able once again to think of herself and of what she had done. She attempted to brush away her worst thoughts.

She liked the schoolroom. Of all the places here that she had come to love, this was her favourite. Maddy had told her she was a very quick learner. Whether she just said that because it was like a carrot, Ruth didn't know, but if it was a carrot, it worked because she tried all the harder.

Writing gave her a freedom she had known nothing of. She loved the feel of the pen in her hand. Even the act of dipping it into the ink and the scratching of letters brought her a kind of dumb satisfaction. After a life of nothing but housekeeping, she plumped for helping outside as much as possible, but she was so excited that she went between the garden and the schoolroom with energy and delight. Reading was such a treat.

Most of all, though, was being around Sister Maddy. The other two had their allotted tasks and these were many. Mr Gilbraith had arranged other women to come in and clean, wash and help Sister Hilary in the kitchen, so to Ruth the whole thing was getting bigger and bigger and more and more interesting.

Everybody called Jay Mr Gilbraith, and of course that was how she addressed him, but in bed at night she would say his name over and over. She liked to hear him say her first name. She thought it was the prettiest word she had ever had in her hearing.

She liked being in his presence. To her chagrin, he took little notice of her – she was almost superfluous to him – but she was able to stay in Maddy's new office with the two of them as they talked about new ideas that would be put into place.

Sometimes Mr Gray was also at these meetings and he seemed to like her being there too. He included her in everything he said, and kept looking at her as though he needed her approbation for what he planned to do. There was much talk of the new hospital. Up to now they hadn't found any place for it but it was not forgotten.

Ruth was aware that she cared a great deal for Jay, and she had to stop herself from doing childish things, such as wanting to sit next to him, follow him outside or try to be where he was talking in the village. She wanted to hold long conversations about him with Sister Maddy or anyone else, but she could do none of these things and it became troublesome to her.

She wondered how old he was. He couldn't be anywhere near as old as the doctor, who had a grown-up child. She tried not to bring the grown-up child to mind; she could not stop hating Eve Gray. She wondered how young he thought she was. But if she had been thought very young, then presumably she would not have been allowed to act like an adult, both at the meetings and beyond. She was now close to all the children and helped them with their schoolwork, their dressing or anything else they might need. She was growing to love them too.

Marriage? She dared not think about the wedding. Jay could marry nobody but herself. She thought about the only marriage she knew, that of her parents, and how horrific that had been and how her mother had run away. Sometimes she wondered whether her mother had come back and found the place empty, she gone and her father dead, and then she felt guilty all over again.

Sometimes she wanted to ask Jay if he knew anything about

it, but she had the feeling that if he heard that her mother had come back, he would tell her. And why would she come back when she had been so desperate to get away?

What if they married and he turned into her father? What if he hurt her in the same way and she had another child? She did not think he would do such a thing, but there were a lot of women in the village with children, so presumably they had gone through something similar to what had happened to her. It was disgusting. Also they had obviously done it more than once, some of them had four or five children.

All these thoughts did nothing to dent her regard for Jay, now she had betrayed him and herself in the worst possible way. She had made a bargain with God for his life and everything had gone wrong.

Eve waited for her father and Mr Esher to come home. She hated waiting for things, always she seemed to be waiting. The longer she waited, the more she worried. Would her father have to go down the pit to help with things?

Her father, she knew, was concerned that Mr Esher was an apprentice and not an experienced doctor. He could not be left with the problems alone. But she knew also that her father could not wait to get there. It was what he did.

So it was daybreak when Mr Esher rode his horse into the yard. Eve was already outside and to him just as he dismounted. Kyle, of course, would not have slept either and was there to take the horse. Kyle had lit lamps so Eve could see how tired Mr Esher was.

Mr Esher looked like she had never seen him before. He did not meet her gaze. He was dishevelled, his clothes were covered in coal dust and his face was lined where the coal had etched itself. When he did finally meet her gaze, his eyes gave him away. They were glazed as though he had not been able to take in what he had experienced, and so much older than when he had set out.

'Is Jay all right?' was the first thing she thought of and he merely nodded his head. 'Will he be coming back soon?'

'No.' Mr Esher didn't even nod in recognition as Kyle took his horse. He trod into the house as though his feet would barely carry him.

When he got inside she gave him brandy; that was what her father would have done. They sat at the dining room table. The rest of the house was quiet, though Eve knew that Mrs Florence had not gone to bed, but was giving them time. She had made sandwiches and covered them in a damp cloth for when the men should come back. Eve took a plate and put sandwiches on to it but Mr Esher said nothing until he had swallowed several gulps of brandy.

'I thought I was going to die,' he said finally. 'I've never been afraid like that before. I've seen a lot of things since I wanted to be a doctor, but nothing on that level. There is no light in the pit at all. If you put up your hand you wouldn't be able to see it. The roof came in and the dust and chaos of it all was horrible. I didn't think we'd make it back out.'

'Mr Hallam?' It was selfish, she knew, but Hallam was Jay's right-hand man. If Hallam had died, would they be able to get away? She knew she was an awful person for thinking it. She tried to banish the mean thought, but all she could think was that Jay was all right and Mr Esher had come back. She was about to ask how her father had faced it when Mr Esher said, 'Mr Hallam died and two other men. He was trapped and couldn't move.

The other two men had been killed by rocks falling on them. Mr Hallam was still alive but only just when I got there. I had to try and persuade Mr Gilbraith to leave him there but he wouldn't.'

'Jay is still down there?'

'He wouldn't come out without bringing Mr Hallam's body, though we told him how dangerous it was. The roof had already come in once while we were there.'

'Jay could be dead?'

'No. The other men wanted him out but I think he must have thought it would be all right, otherwise surely he wouldn't have stayed. He must have thought of you.'

Eve was about to say that he never did think of her, but she couldn't get beyond the idea of Jay dead.

'Your father is so good, such a comfort to people. At least he didn't have to go down there. He sent me back. I have to go to bed, I really do.' And he staggered out of the dining room and took the stairs like a man of eighty.

Eve's father came back filthy with coal dust much later and all she could think to say was, 'Papa, is Jay all right? Is he? What about my wedding? What is happening? Is Jay coming here today?'

She had run out to the yard when she heard his horse. She had waited and longed for him to come home.

'I know, my dear heart, but he has been down there all night and has just brought Hallam's body up so he is worn out. Why don't you go and sleep and I shall do the same?'

'But everything was arranged and even though now it's a day late, surely we can be married.'

'People understand. There will be another day. Jay needs time to grieve for his friend and the two other men who died as well.

I know you don't want to hear these things, but one of them had just lost his wife, and his two little girls will now have to be cared for by the nuns.'

'You think I'm selfish.'

'No, I just think you need to get things into perspective and not blame Jay for something that was not his fault, though people will say so.'

'Why?'

'Because the roof fell in.'

'It shouldn't have?'

'Of course it shouldn't have, but it happens. He is doing his best and his best didn't save three good men from dying down there. He will have to learn to forgive himself and Wesley Hallam was dear to him.'

A few days later, Eve was still torn. She had been hoping that Jay would come to see her so why had he not?

'Papa, what am I going to do?' It was Sunday and Eve was all dressed up to go to church.

'Do? About what?' Her father and Noel were dressed the same, and had just sat down to breakfast. She had had breakfast hours ago and was on a different time scale, unable to rest until she had seen her betrothed.

'About my wedding. Ought I to talk to the vicar?'

'He does know what happened.'

'Yes, but . . . I am supposed to be getting married. I have a white satin dress upstairs, a long veil, I have tickets and reservations and I have no idea what's happening. Do you think you could go and talk to Jay?'

'Not just at the moment,' the doctor said.

'But somebody must. What am I supposed to do?'

'Why don't you just go to church?' the doctor suggested. When she had left and the door was nearly closed behind her, she heard him say to Noel, 'You want to go home?'

The young man looked gratefully at him. 'Would you mind very much, sir? I'm afraid I didn't acquit myself very well.'

'That's not true. The men were full of praise for you.'

'I couldn't have braved it without Sister Madeline. She was remarkable.'

'She probably thought God was there with her and perhaps he was. But you went. You did your duty and you are very young to face such things. You did very well, the men said so, and they don't say such things lightly. You can go home any time you like, but if I were you I would give myself a few days. You need to recover from the shock of this. We all do. Just rest and then you shall go back to your family.'

Eve was immediately jealous as she hurried across the street to the church. Why had that nun been there with Jay while she, the woman he was about to marry, was ignored, and in such a way? Nobody had given her a thought. The food was spoiled, the arrangements were now of no use and worst of all she had to go into the church where she was meant to have been married only a few days before.

Everybody would stare at her. All the life she had planned seemed to have been dropped, vanished as though it was nothing but a dream. This nightmare had succeeded it.

Twenty-Five

Going back to the farmhouse knowing that Hallam was dead was the worst thing Jay had ever had to do. He avoided it to begin with, but there came a time when there was nothing else. He would have to arrange the three funerals and take into consideration what the widow wanted, but at the moment it was as if his head had turned into a fog.

Mr Gray had tried to persuade him to go home, as he called it, but it could not be a home without Hallam. Eventually somebody took him back to the farmhouse at the bottom of the hill, led him almost like a prisoner. Jay found the door being opened and closed for him and the two cleaning ladies who looked after the house didn't know what to say. They fussed around him about food and tea and how awful everything was. In the end he just took himself away from them, though when he got to bed he didn't want to be there. He didn't want to be anywhere.

He felt a little better when he heard their voices as they left the house. There was the smell of stew, which they had wanted to give him, and recent banking down of the fire, as though they had done everything they could, as though they could halt tragedy that way. He thought that women had done it for generations, perhaps always, keeping places neat and providing the basics like clean beds and food. He sighed in relief when they left and turned his grimy face in among the white of the pillows.

Peace descended but somehow it didn't last. He must have slept because the two women were back, and one of them, Mrs Tempest, came up the stairs and she said, 'Tea, Mr Gilbraith,' as though things were normal – which was, he thought admiringly, probably the best thing she could have done. She poured it out and she brought him buttered toast and Jay sat up as she pushed back the curtains further to let in the light. He ate the toast and drank his tea and then she said, briskly, 'We are going to have a hot bath sorted out for you so that you can get into something clean, and then you can go to sleep again,' and she left him.

Jay had not been told to do anything for so long that he just did it, and was glad when he had. In the meanwhile, they had changed the bed, but he didn't want to go to bed. He sat down in the living room and tried to think about what had happened.

He kept waiting for Hallam to come in. Every time he heard a sound, he knew that Hallam could not have died, but nobody came, nothing happened.

He was therefore rather surprised when Eve appeared in the sitting room. She was wearing a ridiculous riding outfit, as though such things mattered. He looked blankly at her.

'I thought I ought to come,' she said awkwardly.

'It was good of you.'

'How are you feeling?'

Jay had no idea how he felt; nothing was coming through, nothing to aid him.

'I feel silly coming here like this but I had to see you.'

As she spoke the vicar was ushered into the room. Jay got up to welcome the vicar and the old man took his hand and said, 'I'm so terribly sorry.'

The vicar merely nodded and smiled just a little at Eve, having seen her at the Sunday service, Jay knew. He had tried to go but somehow couldn't. If he went forward, he could not stand still, and at the moment it was the only thing he could manage.

'Thank you,' Jay said and then strangely he felt comforted. He didn't know the vicar at all well – couldn't even remember his name – but somehow the sight of the man helped a lot. This man had buried a lot of people. The idea made Jay want to laugh in one way, but he was glad.

The vicar asked about Hallam and then about the other two men, and it was such a relief to sit there and talk about them, to think that the vicar understood. It was so soothing. The vicar said all the right things and although Jay knew that it was his job to do so, he had not understood before then how much it mattered. The vicar did not say stupid things like, 'God's will be done.' He said how sorry he was, what a loss they would be and how he would help to make sure that the children of the one man and the widow of the other were helped in every possible way.

He asked Jay so many things about Hallam; Jay was able to talk about how long they had been friends and how much he would miss him. He talked about their childhood in Newcastle. The vicar made notes about what Jay wanted for the funerals and said he was going to see what the widow wanted; he would try to incorporate everybody's wishes. Jay said that he would provide food and drink for the gathering after the funerals and would do everything he could.

The vicar also said to him that if he needed anything, he

should come to the vicarage; the vicar's door was always open to him. Jay felt bereft when the vicar left. He saw him to the door and outside and then he went back in. He had almost forgotten that Eve was there.

'Don't you have anything to say to me?' she said.

He stared at her.

'What?' he said.

'Our wedding.'

'Oh. Yes.'

'When is it to be?'

He stared again.

'I haven't thought about it yet.'

'I have my wedding dress hanging on the wardrobe door and my trunks packed. Everything is supposed to go forward.' There were tears in her eyes. 'What am I meant to do?'

'Wait.'

'For how long?'

'I don't know yet. Until – until I've buried Hallam.'

'I've been waiting for so long to get married. Is there always going to be a good reason for you not to marry me?'

He said nothing, just stared.

'We could still be married. My father said the vicar would marry us tomorrow – or the next day. It might even help you, take your mind off such things. I'm sure it isn't disrespectful in the circumstances.'

'I can't do that right now,' he said.

'But what am I supposed to do? Surely you could find someone to help and we could go away as we planned?'

Her mouth was quivering and the plea in her eyes was huge, but all Jay wanted now was to get away from her. He couldn't talk about this or think about anything else. Did she not understand?

'I have lost my only friend and I will need time to think, time to put things into some kind of order, including myself.'

'I have waited so long to get out of this place.'

'Then you must learn patience like the rest of us.'

'Jay, I can't go on and on waiting and waiting. I'm going to die in this place if I can't get away from my mother and the – the sheer awfulness of it. Please, take me away from here, I'm begging you. If you love me, don't make me stay here any longer; I can't bear it, can't stand any more. Please, Jay.'

She had by now taken hold of the lapels of his jacket. Tears were running down her face and she was shaking. Jay was horrified at her behaviour and her language. She had not even told him she was glad he was alive, or that she was sorry about Hallam and the other men. She was the very opposite of the way that the vicar had behaved.

'I can't do anything right now,' and when she clutched at him, he got hold of her wrists and put her from him. Then he turned around and walked away.

She ran after him and she was sobbing now openly in the hall.

'Why have you put this off so often? I don't think you really care about me at all. I think you cared more about your friend than you ever did about me. First of all, you were too busy, then the house had to be finished, and now you don't even come to me when it's all over. I have nobody but my father to ask. We are supposed to be getting married and yet you leave me alone.'

Jay stared at her. He didn't go any further but as she wept, he turned and looked at her.

'You want me to get married and go away and leave other people to bury Hallam's body?'

'He's dead!'

He wanted to hit her. He had never hit a woman in his life, not even been tempted, but he was so hurt and so aghast that he had to get away from her. She stepped back. The tears had run all the way down her face but Jay didn't care.

'I think you should leave,' he managed.

'What?'

'Go away.' When she didn't move, he left the house and began walking very quickly up the hill towards the works.

Hallam was the only person who remained from his childhood. Jay remembered so very little now, perhaps he had wiped it out, but Hallam had taken with him that enormous chunk of his life where there had been so few people, so many problems and heartaches.

He and Hallam had sat under bridges to keep out of the weather, the cold, the raging sun, the few times it offered itself as such. There were those who said that in Newcastle there were only two seasons, winter and summer, and he thought they were right. It went from icy cold to red hot; most of the time you sat under the fucking bridge, wishing things otherwise. Hallam was always there.

He could not bear to be in the farmhouse where he and Hallam had been together. He went to the house which Eve had so despised and lay there in the moonlight, or the thick cloud, or the rain and wind, and he thought about Hallam and all he had lost. The future was gone.

He was dreading the funeral but, like a lot of things, it wasn't as bad as he had feared because he took charge. When all else failed, that was what you did. It gave you some illusion of power, when really you had none because the Lord had denied you a stake.

He gathered the workmen – and there were a great many of

them together – the day before. He told them that Mr Hallam was to have a funeral and be buried the next day in Wolsingham and that they would have a day off. They could go to the funeral if they wished, but they would be paid however they spent the day. Even if they played games, or went for a walk with their wives and children, he wanted them to remember that day with some pleasure.

He did not want it all to be grieving. He told them that he was going to put on a supper for them and that they could take their wives and children and relatives. It was to be a kind of celebration of Hallam's life. There would be music, Newcastle folk songs, the only kind of music that Hallam had acknowledged.

There would be various places for them to go – the butterfly house, his new house, the farmhouse – and everybody would be accommodated. For the Methodists there would be tea and cake and savouries. For the Catholics there would be whiskey, and again lots of tea and cake. For everybody there would be sherry and beer. Hallam had liked his music; why would they not do it now? And if they needed to sit quietly, the chapel in the butterfly house was always open and the nuns were there to aid anyone who needed it.

He thought that many people would accuse him of levity, but he was determined that he would have this day as he chose and as he thought Hallam would have wanted.

He sent a note to Mr Gray's house and explained his intentions and said they were all welcome to come to the funeral if they so wished, but he would understand if they did not want to be there. He also invited them to the supper in the new village.

*

Eve didn't know what to do. She had stood there thinking that he would come back to her – he had to – but she'd waited and waited and still nothing happened. All she could think of now was how it ought to have been, how they should have been on the way to Paris, how everything that had been booked would be wasted.

Her wedding dress was like a reproof with a big cover over it against dust and possible smudges. Her bags were packed, everything was ready. Now she had to stay here and pretend that she did not mind, that she did not care, and had nothing else to do but to wait until Jay got used to his under-manager dying and was prepared to go ahead and marry her. She did not think she could be patient for much longer.

When she'd seen that he was not going to come back, she controlled her sobs and she turned around and walked away. She wished that he was dead and that she was dead or had never been born. She wished she didn't care, that she had never seen his damned horrible house on the fell.

'I'm not going to the funeral or to his stupid meal,' Eve announced when her father gave her the note.

Mr Gray stared at her.

'Out of respect for Jay, you ought to, however disappointed you are about what has happened. This man meant a great deal to him.'

'I thought I meant a great deal to him. I have waited and waited for him to marry me while he built that monstrosity of a house. He knew I didn't want to be there, I told him over and over, but he just didn't take any notice. He is so conceited that he thinks the world begins and ends with him.'

'Eve—'

'He risked his life to bring a body from a pit. He could have died. Then what? How would people have managed? He hasn't even apologised to me. I meant so little that he said nothing. I'm tired of waiting for him to get his life together so that we can be married, and I'm not going up there to live a lonely life among his wretched villagers. I'm not doing it.' And she left the room.

She ran past Mr Esher as he came into the hallway and she took the stairs so rapidly that he did not have time to speak.

Later that day when Mr Gray was out and Mr Esher was packing, Eve passed his door. He stopped her there and beckoned her just inside, leaving the door open for respectability's sake, and he said, 'I couldn't help but overhear what you said to your father, and while I understand Mr Gilbraith's view, I think I see yours better. The thing is—'

Eve stared at him and let him continue. He didn't look at her.

'I just wondered whether there was any chance that you might be persuaded to come to London with me.'

When she stared at him he looked earnestly at her. 'I have learned to love you so very much. While you were about to be married, I could say nothing – and perhaps I'm wrong now – but if you would like to go with me, we could be married in London. My parents and my sisters would welcome you, I feel sure.'

Eve took only moments to make up her mind, but it was not the first time she had thought about it. She had seen for some time now that Jay's deficiencies were more than made up for by Noel's presence. This was the kind of man she would have chosen to marry, had she been given options. He was well educated, well spoken, and the people respected him because of his profession. Now it seemed as though everything was falling into place; perhaps this was how it was supposed to work all along.

Finally, she was going to have some good luck and marry a man who would put her first, something Jay would never have done, she knew that now. She came last with him, behind his village and his people and his pits and his iron works and everything else. They had nothing in common and were not in tune. Had they been, he would have built her the house that she wanted and not the house that he wanted, up there and alone on that awful expanse of nothing they called a fell.

'Yes,' she said, 'I will go with you. I want to get away from this place and never come back. And while I don't know you very well, I think I would like to be your wife. You can offer me so much more. Let us leave while the funeral is on. Nobody will notice if we slip away, and by the time my father gets my note, we will be gone.'

'I don't like to deceive him. He's been very kind to me.'

'He'll probably be relieved to get me off his hands. He's been very good while Jay didn't marry me, why shouldn't he be glad that I am to be married to someone like you?'

She was now excited all over again and couldn't rest for the novelty of running away and letting everybody know how she felt about the way that she had been treated. They deserved nothing more, neither Jay nor her father. She packed as furtively as she could. Nobody suspected anything, they were all concentrating on the funeral. And so the following day, when the men and their families trooped down the hills, she left. No doubt Jay had wanted them to come to the funeral; she heard rumours saying that he had paid them.

She and Noel slipped away as the funeral began and the village descended into quietness. They did not have to go anywhere near the church. They were driven to the closest station and got on a train. She had but one large bag with her; it contained nothing other than her clothes. She felt so much better when she was on her way to London. She imagined her father and Jay finding out that she was not there and being sorry for the way that she had been treated.

Twenty-Six

After the funeral and the burial, the men all trooped back up the hills towards the new town and Jay went with them. The nuns went by pony carriage. It had unprecedently been all faiths together. It was most unusual for Catholics, Protestants and Methodists to come together, but they did on that day and a great many went back up the hill to eat and drink and be relieved that it was over.

Hallam would have been pleased, Jay thought, that the men had had the day off, that they and their families had come to the church.

When the doctor appeared, Jay went and thanked him. He sat him down and attended to his needs. He asked if Eve and Mr Esher had decided the funeral was too much for them, and Mr Gray said that he thought so. It was the day after the funeral and Jay was glad to get back to anything that looked like normality, even if he had to pretend that Hallam was somewhere else in the village. The work would help and it did. He was glad to see Mr Gray there, ready for surgery that morning, but he thought that the doctor looked as grey-faced as his name. Jay went to him when he stepped down from his horse and said to him, 'You've done too much. Come and sit down.'

Mr Gray shook his head.

'I must speak to you.'

'Well, come into the house.' Jay led him the short distance to the new house. The doctor followed him without a word, but when they got inside Mr Gray flapped a paper at him and said, 'I want you to read this.'

Mr Gray had gone back to the house after the funeral and then he found the house empty – Mrs Florence and the staff had all gone up to the new town – and there was a note for him from his daughter.

Dear Papa,

I know that you will not blame me for having gone to London with Noel. He has asked me to marry him and I have said that I will, the moment we get there, all very respectable. He says his family will be happy to have me among them and I have grown so tired waiting for any kind of excitement. You will understand.

I hope you will not think badly of us; we did our best, but he will be much better for me than Jay. You had probably worked that out. I can no longer bear the Durham dale and the loneliness and the boredom and the lack of opportunity and new things. I think I will be happy here, so don't worry about me. Perhaps when you have forgiven me for leaving, you will come here and we will have good times.

Your loving daughter,

Eve

Jay read and was astonished. He had not expected such a thing. He had not thought that she despised him so much over what he had done that she had no feeling for him anymore. He read the letter twice before he handed it back, but the doctor waved it away. He was looking down as though it was his fault, as though ashamed. Jay felt sorry for him; this was not his fault.

'I am so sorry,' Jay said finally, remembering how she had entreated him. He thought that had he said the right things at the time, it might have made a whole lot of difference. Her only experience of death was her father's profession; how should she understand? She was too young and too involved in her own selfish needs, as the very young were. He wished so hard now that he had said the right things, but he could not find anything beyond the images of Hallam dead down the pit and could lend his mind to nothing else.

'In a way, I don't blame her. What place is there, here in this dull existence, which men like us thrive on?' he said.

The doctor shook his head and said in mitigation, 'She had no friends; she had nobody until you arrived. I don't think Noel is the right man for her. She is having the same chance as her mother had and that isn't progress. People need to move forward and marry people who are different and more interesting. But she couldn't see past what is, after all, the small intelligence that doctors are.'

Jay sighed and now he looked coldly at it. He was able to look coldly at so many things that it was awful, as though ice was all he had to offer. He felt sympathy for her, but rather as though she had been a distant relative. A girl like that, so much younger than he was, so naïve and hopeful – he had given her nothing she wanted. He had tried to mould her into what he wanted. He felt sure that men very often did this with women. Somehow, with having lost Hallam, he understood so much. How awful that he should feel more now. The ice was beginning to break, until he wanted to howl for the whole goddamned bloody world.

'Don't upset yourself,' he told Mr Gray. 'You have clinics to do and people to look after. Maybe this is for the best. If Eve can be happy there, that might be enough. I don't think I would have made her happy.'

Jay wanted nobody at the new house. That was how he thought of it, nothing but the place he had been so proud to build for his promised bride. He had thought they might call it Snow House because of the howling white gale which besieged the area in winter, but now it was the fell house, the only place of comfort he could find. It had few good memories, other than those of Maddy telling him he had made a mess of it. He found that made him smile and that was a rare thing at present.

He had already asked the carpenter who had made the doors and windows to build him some more furniture, he didn't know quite why. Perhaps there had been some part of him that sensed disaster, or maybe he wanted to turn this house into somewhere he might like to be and make use of, even though he and Eve had agreed to live in Wolsingham with her father.

He had the big tables on which he worked brought up from the house at the bottom of the hill, and then he had a bed made and tables and chairs. The house had never felt so big, and night after night he remembered Eve hating the place. Since he hardly ever built a fire, the wind howled around the building, and he saw now why she had so much disliked it. Very often the wind swept cold across the fell top. He found it comforting.

Problems were springing up like weeds in a field. He wished he could bat them away, but he couldn't. They were multiplying so fast that all he wanted to do was leave himself, or get drunk and sleep, because he didn't think he would ever sleep again.

His mind would not let go of Hallam dying down the pit, the guilt that he felt since it had been Hallam and not him. When he cried, it was not for Hallam's death, it was for himself and for the great empty space that Hallam had left behind him which would never fill.

You had to let go, he knew that, but you had to let go slowly, and that was a very hard thing to do when somebody died so quickly. His sensible self told him that he must be practical and find another under-manager, but every time he thought about it, he felt sick. So he went on, day after day, discovering more and more work that was not done because Hallam was not there to see to it. Hallam had also had a way with the men which he didn't have.

When they fought, he couldn't break it up as easily as Hallam had with a word and without blows. They respected him but they had cared for Hallam. He was not quite one of them, but Jay was nowhere close and they would not accept him. Jay was the master, so although they minded him he knew that one or two spat with disdain when he tried to manage them.

Day by day they came to him with their problems and he saw Hallam, ghostly by his side, watching him getting it wrong. At night Hallam stood outside his bedroom door and longed for life. When the day came, it was another day to get by, to get through, there was nothing in it but work and continuing on. He began to wish he had not started this, because his stupid mind told him that had he stayed in Newcastle, this would not have happened and Hallam would still be alive.

He would not be bludgeoned on a street corner, garrotted by thieves such as had happened to him when Hallam had saved him. That was such a bitter memory. They had been safe in Newcastle; they knew the territory so well. Hallam was not a pitman by trade; he had been the survivor whose life had been lost because of his friend's stupidity and ambition, and Jay could not forgive himself.

Twenty-Seven

Maddy went to see Jay at the new house and was unhappy about it. He was there completely alone and the place was already a mess. Papers were strewn everywhere. There was no smell of cooking, and worst of all, there was a half empty whisky bottle on the table. He looked awful. She understood that he felt awful, but she was inclined to ask about the state of it. She said, 'Where are the housekeepers?'

He shrugged.

'Did you turn them off?'

He looked disparagingly at her.

'They didn't want to come.'

'If you're going to drink like a fish, you can hardly blame them,' she said sharply. Sharpness was wanted here, she knew.

'I'm not drinking like a fish.'

'I am not going to argue with you. I don't know what you're going through, but you have a whole village to look after, so you have to get on with it.' She got hold of the bottle and went into the kitchen and tipped its contents down the sink. He didn't attempt to stop her.

'Now I'm going to go down to the farmhouse and see about Mrs Tempest and Mrs Neville. And you are going to have a cup of tea and pull yourself together.' Part of her felt rotten at this, but she could see a slight amusement come into his eyes, and it was the first time since Hallam's death that she had seen anything of the kind.

The kettle boiling, she made the tea and set it out for him on the table. Then she went off and left him, throwing up a quick prayer to God that he wouldn't open another bottle, that he hadn't had more bottles stashed away, and that he would drink his tea and let his senses better his sense of loss, at least for a little while.

'I'll be back to check on you later,' she threatened, as though he was a child, and made sure she slammed the outside door when she left.

When she reached the bottom of the hill, Mrs Tempest and Mrs Neville were cleaning and putting everything to rights. They both looked guilty when she came in without ceremony and asked why they weren't up at the new house.

'We haven't finished here yet,' Mrs Tempest said.

'Well, it could hardly be any cleaner,' Maddy said, glancing around her and sensing a new problem. 'I think Mr Gilbraith needs you up there. Being alone is the worst thing that could happen to him at present.'

Mrs Tempest – who, true to her name, was large and dark – didn't look at her, but said that her son and his wife and five children had just moved to Sunniside, and that they had asked her to go and live with them because there was so much to do. Mrs Neville, by contrast, was a tiny woman with a very small voice. She barely spoke above a whisper, but now she managed to convey that she had been offered a better job cooking for a very respectable family in Wolsingham.

'I thought you liked it here. And doesn't Mr Gilbraith pay the best wages?'

They looked woefully at one another and then Mrs Tempest confided,

'We did like it when Mr Hallam was here too.'

This was unlikely, Maddy thought. Hallam had been a surly, difficult man, as far as she knew. He spoke little and looked less at anyone but the men and the work.

'Mr Gilbraith still needs looking after, perhaps more so after what he has been through. Don't you feel any loyalty to him?'

'I don't see why we should,' Mrs Neville said stiffly but not looking at her. Then she seemed to repent her words and she looked directly at Maddy for the first time and she said, 'We don't think we would like the new house. We don't want to be there.'

Maddy was clueless. She thought of the big beautiful house and its views. She thought of how Eve Gray hadn't liked it. She thought Eve took some understanding, and that a lot of it had to do with her mother being locked away.

'What is it about the house that you don't like?' she asked.

The two women looked at one another and finally Mrs Neville said, 'We think that Mr Hallam's spirit is there. No disrespect, Sister.'

Maddy couldn't think of a single thing to say, she was so astonished. She knew that, especially in the country, many people were superstitious, but she didn't think it as bad as this anywhere. It shocked her and made her want to speak impatiently but she couldn't.

'Mr Hallam didn't live there,' she managed when the silence threatened to take over the day.

Mrs Neville put up her chin.

'I went up there yesterday to see Mr Gilbraith and he was talking to Mr Hallam.'

'I think that's just to do with how he misses him.'

'And that house feels funny.'

'Funny?'

'The wind was howling around there, like it does in graveyards.'

Maddy had not credited Mrs Tempest with such an imagination. Her eyes were fairly bulging and she was a large woman, so it made her look strange. Mrs Tempest shuddered. 'I could never go back there.'

'He cried,' Mrs Neville said. She was quite small, but given to calling a spade a spade. They were holding nothing back.

'What?'

'Mr Gilbraith, he cried, down the pit, over Mr Hallam's body, so I was told. Men don't do things like that. It isn't natural. He would have been better to leave Mr Hallam where he was, for all our sakes.'

Maddy wished she could have refuted this; she hated how people talked. But of course they did, you couldn't hide things like that, and it was true. Everybody knew that Jay had cried, and to a lot of people it made him less of a man because he was grieving openly and hard for his friend.

'Mr Hallam was all the family that Mr Gilbraith had,' she said.

'He wasn't family,' Mrs Neville said. 'It isn't the same thing.'

And then Mrs Tempest put the boot in.

'He's soft,' she said; 'that's why he's so nice to everybody.'

Maddy didn't waste her breath; she went back to the school. She didn't tell Abigail or Hilary about it, but that night in bed she let a few tears fall for Jay, alone and bereft in his beautiful house, where the wind was no doubt howling around the building, producing all kinds of sounds amid the gorse where the sheep would be sheltering against the big stone walls. If Hallam's spirit was anywhere, then perhaps it was true that he was up on the fell. She hoped that perhaps Jay might somehow find him there.

Ruth heard the conversation stop as she moved into the kitchen. Two of the women who helped Sister Hilary were pretending that nothing had been said. Gossip was not encouraged here at the foundling school. She tried telling herself that it had been nothing important, but Hilary came in behind her and she had sharp ears and she looked hard at both women. Then she asked Ruth rather sharply what she wanted; they were in the middle of making dinner.

It was unlike Hilary to be out of temper, but since the pit accident everybody had been different, not least Ruth because she couldn't sleep or eat. She was getting through the hours in a kind of daze, until Maddy stopped her that afternoon and asked her what was wrong. She told her that it was nothing.

'I understand that the accident affected you very much,' she said.

'It hurt all of us,' Ruth said.

'Yes, but you had already been through too much for somebody your age, so if you should feel it more than other people, it would hardly be surprising.'

After this Ruth thought she was comforted, but an hour or two later she had gone back into the awful guilt which she thought now would never leave her.

After dinner was served and everything cleared up, the two women took a break and had some tea. Ruth could not help now hearing what they were saying before she went around the corner into the hall.

'That poor man, having all that to contend with after what he's been through,' said the first.

'I never liked her.'

'Nobody ever liked her. When he comes back to his senses, if he ever does, he won't regret not marrying her, the little whore. Who would have thought that a well-brought-up young lady like that would do such a thing?'

Ruth half feared that somebody would come up behind her before she had heard any more, and so she dodged around the corner, causing the two women to start and said quickly, 'What has happened?'

'You know what Sister Hilary said,' said the first.

'But I don't know anything about it.'

'You must be the only person who doesn't then. It's all the talk. Miss jumped-up Eve Gray has run off with the doctor's apprentice.'

Ruth couldn't believe it. She did and then she didn't. She just stared at them.

'The talk is that she confronted Mr Gilbraith and told him that if he didn't marry her right away she wouldn't have him no more, and this before Mr Hallam and the other two men were buried. Disgraceful, I call it.'

'Fancy,' said the second woman, 'running off like that with one man while betrothed to another, and he the best man in the world. Who wouldn't have had him? Every woman I know wishes they could marry him and she was lucky enough to be chosen, and this is what she does?'

'She won't never come back. He's better off without, I say. He'll find somebody a lot better than her. She was bonny, mind you, but never had a nice word to say. She really thought she was somebody, and now look. The doctor must be so ashamed, his only bairn, behaving like that and after years of him being saddled with a mad wife an' all.'

They went back to the kitchen. Ruth didn't know what to do. She hadn't thought that things could get worse and now they had. She felt sick. She ran from the house and threw up out the back where the sisters generally hung up the washing. Nobody was there. Nobody saw her break down into tears. She could have flung herself on the ground and sobbed until she couldn't breathe. Wasn't it bad enough that she had prayed for things to go wrong and God had answered her prayers in the roughest imaginable way, and left her to deal with it even though she had no idea how to?

God was not done with her. If Jay could have been happy, if he could have married the woman he loved, then perhaps Ruth might not have felt so bad, but she was done for now. God had completed the task he had set himself and he had decided to destroy her. Jay was alone now, his best friend was dead, his men had left a widow and two small children and his happiness was gone. Eve Gray had struck the last blow but she, Ruth, had set it in motion. All she wanted was to run away and die; she could not stay here like this. She couldn't bear it. God had expected too much. He had not cared what had been done to her young life, all he wanted now was her complete destruction.

Twenty-Eight

Eve was looking forward to the sights she had never seen — the galleries, the plays, the Georgian houses and the lovely terraces – but she seemed to be interminably on the road. She had known that London was a long way; she had not known how difficult it would be to get there. The railways seemed to have no cohesion, so she and Noel were spending a lot of time waiting. The coaches no longer ran as they had done years ago, though she didn't know this; the railways had proven too great a foe. Now it was only a determined traveller who ventured this far.

The roads and railroads were dusty and everything seemed to take a long time. She could not sleep, the food she was given she considered inedible and all she had to drink was water. They were obliged to put up at hotels on the way. Why she had not thought of this, she could not imagine. She was travelling with a man and they were not married, so she must be viewed as wanton by all and kept a veil over her face.

For the first few hours she was excited, but as they went on, she began to regret what she had done and panic as to what might happen. She wished that she had stayed at home where her father and Mrs Florence made all well. She could by now have forgiven Jay his shortcomings. She thought of the lovely diamond ring she had left on her dressing table, which her father would have given back to him.

She had thought to punish him and was punished herself.

At the end of the first day, they had to find somewhere to stay and it was even worse then. Once she had spent a night at an inn with a man, she could never go back. That was when her nerve steeled her. She was being ridiculous. What on earth would she go back for? Jay didn't really want her; he wanted a wife and children in that stupid big house up on the fell. He wanted somebody to be there for him. She was not that comfortable, forgiving person who would play second fiddle to Wesley Hallam, and all those stupid masculine ideas where men didn't come home, but went to drink and gamble and have other women.

She understood now that she had always been jealous of the friendship between Hallam and Jay. They were so close. When she was with them both, she didn't understand what they talked about; it was like a secret language and she was not included. Hallam ignored her. She hated that. She wanted him to address her just once; if he had done, she could not remember it. Their laughter was not inclusive, it left her out. Their conversation she did not understand and even now, when Wesley Hallam was dead, she felt he came between them. Jay's treatment of her after Hallam had died illustrated that he did not care for her as a wife ought to be cared for, so she was right to do this. She was right to try for something else, something which she felt was better.

She wanted to go places and see things and meet interesting and exciting people, not be left in a ghastly little backwater like Wolsingham where nothing ever happened. Nobody read, nobody was fashionable, nobody knew anything about culture; there was not even a bookshop or a decent library. No musicians played Mozart, nobody knew Shelley's poetry. It was awful, boring day-to-day stuff – who was having a baby, who had died, who was ill. She reminded herself how much she hated it. She was trying for something new; she would let herself attempt it.

There was only one room at the hotel, Noel had to take it. He couldn't have asked for more than one and neither could he afford it. She soon saw that he was not happy either.

The room was at the back and was dark. The noisy city street in York was something she was not used to. She jumped at every sound. When she saw Noel looking at her she smiled and said, 'I've never been in a city before.'

'Never?'

'I had no one to take me. My mother has always been ill and my father could never take time off because he had so little help.'

'It didn't occur to me that we would have to spend time like this,' Noel said, looking at her with dismay.

'Does it matter?'

'I love you. I loved you from the moment I saw you, so no. But I will sleep in a chair, because there has to be respect.'

It wasn't easy. She had never slept in a room with anyone other than Mrs Florence, the odd time she had been ill as a child. But a man? What about when she needed to use the pot under the bed? What about when he did? How would she wash and undress?

In the end, he suggested to her that she should do what she needed to do and he would go downstairs and ask for some food. He would give her plenty of time and she must not worry about anything. Cheered by this, she did what she had to do, but she could not do the same for him.

In the end he didn't undress, and he said he had done what he had to do downstairs. She saw now that he was not that much older than she was, and yet he had brought her away with him. She could not help worrying about what his parents would think and say and how they would treat her.

The food came. She had not thought that she was hungry until they were seated at a little table by the window on two rickety chairs with a single candle between them. There were beef sandwiches, cheese and beer, and she thought she had never tasted better.

She felt so much more positive when she had eaten, to the point where she became very tired and told him he must sleep on the bed, but he wouldn't. He was such a gentleman, she thought, such a decent man and right for her. No matter what anyone said, they would be married and she would live in London with him, the kind of life she was sure they both deserved.

The beer did it, she thought afterwards, or perhaps she needed an excuse, because Noel found the floor too hard and lay on the bed with her. Then they were turned towards one another and he kissed her. It occurred to her then that if Jay had kissed her like that, things would be different, but perhaps it was nothing to do with the kiss.

After it, there was another and another and they were deeper and deeper. Her body moved towards him in a way that she would have cringed over had she been in her right mind, but her right mind had long since left. She had never felt like this before, and when his hands stole under her nightdress on to her breasts, she heard herself crooning. Her body was moving forward, and then the kissing grew more intense and her body was giving and she couldn't stop.

When he took off the nightdress she wore, she was lost against him, so warm was his body and so intense his kisses. Had the roof fallen, she did not think she would notice. It felt right like nothing ever had done. Jay had never made her feel like this. She clamoured for Noel.

She had thought herself a modest woman, but she was not now. She needed him, she wanted him. She felt so powerful, and laughed and encouraged him. When they were skin to skin, she was eager, and when he took her she was so pleased. She had never thought to be immodest, but then women did not think so. Why not? Perhaps men had thought women should not be, but why was that? Women had children; women were built to marry and give birth. Why did men therefore think they were not strong? She felt as though she could build a house, or, even better, a child.

Her body gave and gave and she was vocal and screaming out his name and encouraging him. She was so pleased, so grateful, so happy.

In the quietness that followed when they lay apart, he said to her, 'Are you all right?'

She replied, 'I have never been so right. I love you so very much.'

'And I love you.'

Later, after they had slept, they did it again and this time it was even better.

In the morning they breakfasted on eggs and bacon and lots of tea and set off. She could not help blushing, thinking of what they had done. She was pleased that they would have another night on the road so that they could indulge themselves with nobody about. When they finally got to the inn, they could hardly wait until they were alone before they pulled off one another's clothes. The night could not be long enough.

She wished it would take them a month to get to London.

She was ecstatic. She was really in love as she had thought never to be.

Jay had not known loneliness in so long that he barely recognised it when it finally got to him. He tried to stare it down, but it seeped into his body, into his bones like an old and unwelcome friend. It was the first time he had remembered what life was like before Hallam. He was just a skinny child, half starved, and alone on the streets which he then despised because they had provided him with so little. He stole what he could, begged and was given nothing. Some days he barely spoke or was spoken to.

His life now was so unlike that early time in Newcastle that he thought he would get past the feelings which settled on him. They filled him up and cast out any thoughts of running the town. The men settled back into work and it was as if nothing had happened, as though Hallam had never been. Jay didn't go back to the farmhouse; he stayed up on the fell, telling himself that he had built this place solely for himself since Eve would never have lived there. She had never wanted it or saw herself belonging.

He got Rob Slater to deal with what had to be dealt with. Rob was obviously surprised and worried, but Jay no longer cared about the town or the people or the work. He told Rob to help the widow and the children. He paid Rob well so that he could make sure they had everything they needed.

Maddy had organised women to clean the house – at least, he supposed she had, because he hadn't. He tried to concentrate, but he sat hour after hour trying to make sense of the paperwork which held the village together. He told himself that he was needed, but there was so little he could do and he was very tired. Meals were put in front of him and grew cold. He didn't even go up to his bed; he stayed in the office, falling asleep from time to time over the desk. He berated himself that he was so ineffectual, that he could not pull himself together and get on with things which were not just important, but essential for the well-being of the whole enterprise. He wished over and over again that he had stayed in Newcastle and been less ambitious. His dreams had led him to this and the cost had been too high.

He also felt bad about Eve. He went again to the way that she had cried and pleaded with him. Yes, the timing was awful, but she was hurt and desperate too, and he had ignored her. When it had come to the crunch, he was stupid and self-obsessed and inadequate. He wanted to make Mr Gray feel better but there was nothing he could say. The doctor too seemed to have had the light punched out of him, and although he trailed up and down to his clinics, the joy of it was all gone.

That was another thing that Jay worried about. He had the feeling that he had been the first to think an apprentice doctor was a good idea. He felt still that it was a good idea, had the man been different than Noel Esher. But he couldn't feel bad about the man, because he had done everything he could to help. He couldn't even blame Esher for running off with his betrothed. The man was too shocked and too hurt not to run for home, and he needed the woman he had fallen in love with.

Jay thought he would never forget how selfless the young man had been. He feared it had been too much for somebody so young, and that Esher too would never be the same. Jay had been incapable of making the right decisions and so had made all the wrong ones. What a mess, Jay thought; what a terrible, awful mess.

And finally there was Ruth. She had taken up such a lot of his time and now he didn't know what to say to her. He didn't understand why she was more unduly upset than everybody else. She kept appearing, until he was convinced she was following him around like a sheepdog. She kept fussing and asking if she could do anything for him when all he wanted was to be left alone. He tried to speak kindly to her, but it was so much of an effort. When she had come to the fell house for the hundredth time and asked if he needed anything, he said, 'Look, Ruth, all I want is to be on my own. Is that too much to ask?'

Maddy went to the fell house with a mission. She had been trying to find a replacement for Mrs Neville and Mrs Tempest and she thought that she had solved the problem. She thought that Jay seemed all right, and there were no whisky bottles in evidence. Although the women who were employed were doing what they could, the place had a look about it, as though it was just an office, and somewhere to sleep when the work was done. She wasn't happy about that.

'I've found you a housekeeper.'

'I don't want anybody else here. I don't need anybody.' He hadn't even looked up from the papers he was studying, as though her presence made him impatient.

'Jay, I know you don't, but living with – with servants, and no housekeeper, isn't good for you.'

'How did you work that out?'

'Now you aren't thinking properly. What if one of the women here accused you of doing something improper to her?'

That was when he looked up.

'What?'

'To them you are a man with means and money, and although they may not be believed, I don't think it's a situation that would help, do you? You need an older woman here so that you don't have that problem. Somebody totally reliable and very good at what she does. There is a lovely woman living in Wolsingham. I've met her more than once going to the church there.'

'It'll be like Paddy's market; I'll never get anything done.'

'This place is enormous. I've seen smaller churches. You need somebody to run it properly for you. Miss Proud is one of the nicest people I ever met. She helps as many people as she can and she has nothing. Her father died and she will lose the farm. She would be just right.'

'How do you know that?'

'Why don't you go and talk to her before they put her on to the street? She'll end up here when they do, because I'm not going to see her starve. She is wasted if you don't take her on.'

Jay was still reluctant to go and see Miss Proud. He wasn't encouraged by her name. She would be stuffy and tell him what to do, probably as Maddy had taken to bullying him, but worse. He understood why she was doing it, and he knew that he needed help, but he was so very tired these days. Everything was an effort.

He put the pony into the trap and trotted down the hills to Wolsingham. Miss Proud's father had been a tenant farmer, the last house in the village. Her father having just died, she would be put out of her house and new people would move in. He knew that so he could not afford to be indecisive.

Jay halted the pony and trap at the end of the road. The little house had no curtains at the windows, the first sign of somebody moving out. He knocked on the door and waited. It occurred to him the moment he saw Miss Proud that she was nothing like he had imagined. He had thought she would be tall and very skinny, with cold grey eyes, and be wearing a grey dress and have iron grey hair.

The middle-aged woman who opened the door was not particularly tall. She was quite slim, but not skinny, and she was wearing the prettiest blue dress that Jay thought he had ever seen. It was not serviceable navy. It was a party dress and had embroidered flowers around the hem, red and white.

'Good morning,' Jay said. 'Miss Proud?'

'Yes.' He had thought he looked tired, but Miss Proud, older than he was, and about to lose her home, looked exhausted and scared. Yes, Miss Proud was worried about her future and why wouldn't she be?

'I'm Jay Gilbraith,' he said.

'Yes, of course. I have seen you around on that beautiful mare. Would you like to come in?'

Jay stepped inside. There was nothing to be seen beyond a very small stool, two big bags – which were all Miss Proud was presumably taking with her – and a rather large ginger cat pretending there was a fire on, Jay thought with slight amusement, though the grate stood black and empty.

'I'm sorry,' Miss Proud said. 'I'm afraid I can't offer you a cup of tea or even a seat. My father died and the tenancy moves on, you see. Mr and Mrs Peart and their five children will be moving in today. I am just waiting for them now. Everything has been sold.' Miss Proud's voice wavered at that point and she turned slightly from him so that he should not see her emotion.

'My mother died some time since,' she said, and Jay knew that she was keeping the chat going to hide her feelings, which could hardly be good ones at this stage. 'She came from good stock apparently, and always longed for a piano, but we could never afford one, you see.'

Jay did see.

'I understand that you are leaving your house, and wondered if you might like to come up to the new town and be my housekeeper.'

Miss Proud was looking at him now, unblinking and somewhat surprised, and why would she not be?

'Me?'

'I understand from Sister Madeline that you have a great many good qualities and that sounds just right. I'm sure you have heard that we have had tragedy at the pit and I lost my dearest friend, Wesley Hallam, and two good miners.'

'How very hard for you and for everybody concerned,' Miss Proud said. 'I have never done any housekeeping – I mean, from a professional viewpoint. I can cook and bake and clean, like every woman who runs a house, and people do say that my scones are very light, but light scones do not a housekeeper make, I would think.'

Miss Proud had what people called gentility, Jay thought. She was a delicately minded woman for all her circumstances, and he liked her.

He thought he would move further into the room and give her a little time to consider, so he moved towards the cat. Cats in general do not worry about people getting close, and this one merely looked to the side, as though waiting for Jay to lose interest.

'And who is this?' he said.

'That's Tiddles; he's all I have left. We had lots of cats and dogs and other animals, but Tiddles is the last.'

'So, will you come up to the new town and look after me?' Jay said. 'There will be other people in the house, but you will be in charge.'

Miss Proud looked at the cat.

'I can't go without Tiddles,' she said.

'Oh, you won't have to. There is lots of room and I live beside the fell, so Tiddles can do whatever he wants. But I suppose he will want to come and live in the house with you. You will, of course, have your own room, plenty of space and can order things just the way you like. Will you come?'

Miss Proud was blinking even harder at this stage, so he merely picked up her bags and took them outside. He stowed them safely in the back of the trap and then he went back and picked up Tiddles, who – knowing that the white knight had finally ridden over the hill, late as ever – sat in Jay's embrace.

Jay seated Miss Proud with two big rugs over her and Tiddles on her lap. Then he got in and they set off up the hills towards Miss Proud's new life.

'I haven't been up here before,' she said, when they got to the new town and up to the house on the fell. There was a little 'Oh' of surprise that passed Miss Proud's lips.

'You like it?' he said, rather pleased.

'Oh, Mr Gilbraith, it is a beautiful house,' she said, 'and it stands so grandly in the perfect place.'

'I've always thought so. I'm not sure anyone has agreed with me before now.'

'But the view,' Miss Proud said. 'I daresay you can see nearly all the way to Cornsay.'

Jay helped her down and walked her towards the house, Tiddles in her arms. They went in at the front, and there was the biggest sitting room that Miss Proud had ever seen. Sunlight was pouring into it and there in the middle of the room stood a piano. It was a huge grand piano and it shone in the sunlight.

'If only my mother could see me now,' Miss Proud said.

It was hardly surprising, Maddy thought, that Sister Bee should be ill now. She seemed to take everything badly. She could not attend the funeral or the events that surrounded it. Indeed, she kept more to her office than ever before. Maddy became more worried, but she did not like to burden the doctor with anything, as it soon became known that his daughter had run away with the apprentice.

Abigail was the first to hear about it. Somehow Abigail was always the first to hear of anything. While nuns were not meant to talk like that, when it affected them in any way, Abigail said they must talk about it. Maddy's reaction was to think about Jay, but she couldn't think of anything useful to say to him and in any case, it would make no difference what she said. He was beyond caring what anybody said. She couldn't believe that when he had just lost his best friend, the girl he was about to marry had run away and left him. She was horrified.

Sister Bee began to sleepwalk. Maddy heard the sounds before she understood the problem, but she had known that Sister Bee was more and more withdrawn. She was only waiting for what happened next. She did not cough or sneeze, she had no infection on her chest, and yet she could not eat and she went outside her office less and less.

It happened gradually. Maddy had already been doing quite a bit so she did not realise that things were getting worse until the night that she found Sister Bee sleepwalking. Maddy had particularly acute hearing, which was not always of help, and she wished now that she did not know Sister Bee was wandering about the butterfly house at night. She was becoming vague in what she did so that the others all worked harder. They didn't talk about her – it would have been unfair, when they all knew that she had been unwell almost since they had arrived. It was not that she was more difficult in what she asked them to do, or tried to put upon them in any way, Maddy thought; it was just that they were getting used to Maddy asking them to do what was necessary, because Sister Bee achieved so little. Sister Bee passed out twice in the week after Mr Hallam and the other two men died. This could not be a coincidence, Maddy thought. It happened once after prayers in the chapel, when she thought they had all gone, and then outside when they had eaten.

She had run outside, and Maddy had the feeling that Sister Bee had been sick and thrown up the little she had eaten. Since her body was by now very undernourished, she fainted from lack of sustenance.

Maddy had got to the point where she felt she ought to consult Mr Gray in spite of his personal problems. The very next time he came to a clinic, she took him aside afterwards and told him the situation, and he clicked his tongue over the fact that he had not been consulted earlier. He then berated himself, she could see, that he had not noticed – in his hurry to get everything right and his despair over his daughter – that one of the nuns was seriously ill.

Maddy knew that she must also find the time to speak to Ruth; the poor girl was looking worse and worse. Although Maddy had tried to find the right words to reassure her that things would get better, Ruth stayed out of her way somehow, or absented herself on purpose, Maddy thought. It was an effort for Maddy to find her or talk to her, and Maddy knew that she should. The poor girl was suffering even more badly than the rest, and it was hardly surprising after what her life had been.

Maddy tried to think what to say, and was always about to go and find her, when she was called on to see to something new. And although she knew that Jay was doing his best, she saw Rob Slater about the village more and more often, white-faced and unsure about the responsibilities he had had pushed on to him, so that Maddy thought Jay was unaware of Ruth's plight.

Twenty-Nine

When Eve and Noel finally reached London, she didn't mind the dark, dirty water that was the Thames, the horses' steaming brown leavings in the road or the smell of pavements filled with unwashed people. When she came into the station, however, she was aghast that people slept there.

She and Noel had to wait a long time for a carriage, and although she was desperate to pass water, there was no way in which she could. By the time she reached what would be her future home, her bladder was aching and her bowels just about to give up. She felt sick from the little she had eaten, her body was crying out for a soft bed and yet there was more to come.

He helped her down outside a fairly small terraced house. This was where they lived? She longed for a privy, for a wash, for something decent to eat. Instead of which, she was left in the dark, narrow hall with cold draughts coming through the front door, while apparently he told his parents that he had brought a bride home with him. She strained to hear their voices but the doors were stout.

She was kept waiting for such a long time that she wanted to cry. Could anything be amiss? He had told her that his parents and sisters would love her, welcome her, be glad he had found someone so wonderful to care for.

In the end she made her way into the kitchen, such a small room. There the girl who had opened the door was doing whatever she was doing, and Eve begged to be shown the privy.

They went outside and down the yard. Eve was appalled at how little and disgusting it all was, one candle left with her, but she was so needy that she didn't care very much. Back inside, the door of what she thought must be the living room had been opened and Noel was in the hall. He looked white and nervous. He motioned her inside. It was nothing like she had expected.

It was almost poor – a small room with a lot of ornaments, and chairs which she thought had seen better days. His parents, whom she had thought would be imposing, were nothing of the kind. They looked old, much older than her father; they looked more like someone's grandparents. His mother was very fat, and badly dressed in dark, sombre clothes, as people did who had no weekly washerwoman, in Eve's experience.

His father didn't get up, but that wasn't because he didn't want to; it was rather because he had difficulty in doing so, she could see. He was thin and ill, she could now see that too. His flesh had wasted and his clothes hung off him. His eyes were dull, as though he had experienced a lot of pain, and they were yellow and red in different ways which disgusted her, though she tried not to feel like that. These people were to become her family. She would grow used to them, she told herself, and to their way of life. Surely they would care for her since their son did.

'Miss Gray,' he said. He didn't sound hostile, so that was good, Eve thought. Then he added dryly, 'We weren't expecting you.'

Eve could feel her face burn. She had thought his father might be loud, and even violent, perhaps, to find what had happened, though she had told herself it would not be so. She had thought they were very well off; why had she assumed such a thing? Was it because Noel was what she thought of as well spoken, but not northern, something entirely different?

She had envisaged a large house in its own grounds, and many servants, and his parents being in society and doing wonderfully fashionable things. She didn't know now from where she had gained such an impression. He had never said any of that, just that his father was overworked and sometimes unwell, and it showed on him.

Eve had no idea what to say, whether to look at this poor, thin man with frayed cuffs and a shirt which must have been on him a week or more by the grey, sweaty line of it around his scrawny neck, or at this fat woman with the many chins in whose eyes she read dismay. It was Noel's mother who looked away first and Eve thought she saw a tear disappearing amid the fleshy cheek in a short series of highs and lows.

The atmosphere was broken by the appearance of the little maid from the kitchen, whereupon Eve realised that this was no maid, this was one of Noel's sisters. He had mentioned sisters; she didn't know how many. Was it six?

Mrs Esher brushed away the traitorous tear and said, 'Amy dear, would you bring us some tea? I dare say Miss Gray is parched.'

'Of course, Mother,' the girl said and she left the room, smiling politely at Eve as she did so.

Eve was also aware of other people in the house, movement upstairs. Perhaps there was another room – there must be a dining room at least, she thought.

'Do sit down,' Mrs Esher offered. 'You have had a very long journey.'

Eve sat. It was the most uncomfortable chair that she had ever sat on, lumpy and uneven. She longed to move to another, but had the feeling that none of them would be any better, so she made herself sit still.

Nobody said anything for what felt like hours. It was a relief when the tea came, but she could tell by the mismatched, garish cups and saucers in orange and brown that either Mrs Esher had no taste or she had no money. Or that she didn't care for such things; some women didn't, Eve thought.

The biscuits were stale and dry, the bread with a faint scrape of butter was several days old and tasted rancid to her, and the tea was dusty. She couldn't eat; she tried but the food stuck in her throat.

When the tea was finished, Mr Esher cleared his throat as though he had the same problem, but she instantly saw that it was not.

'Miss Gray, I understand from my son that you wish to be married, but I'm afraid that isn't possible.' He smiled as though embarrassed, as though he cared about her, as though he would have given anything to have not said this to her.

Eve stared. Not marry? Whatever did he mean? Of course they would marry, they must. They loved one another.

'Father—' Noel interrupted but his father merely looked at him and he stopped.

Eve was amazed at that too. Wasn't Noel supposed to tell his father that he loved her, that he couldn't live without her, that she was truly going to be his wife? She waited for him to speak up for them, to look at her, but he did neither. That was when she felt bad in so many different ways. She wanted to shout at him; she wanted to tell him to say to them that they must always be together.

'I know it must sound very hard to you, and that you are in love, as they call it, but I am in poor health, we have seven children and our only hope was that Noel, with your father's help, would become a doctor. We need rescuing, you see.'

He smiled slightly over this pleasantry. 'None of our daughters is married and we have no money to enable them to go into even a small kind of society where they could avail themselves of suitable partners. Also there is a young woman we wish him to marry—'

'I don't love her,' the young man protested with a quiver in his voice. Eve didn't dare look at him in case he was crying. She had never seen a man cry and wasn't sure she could bear the experience.

'She is not Noel's choice,' his mother said and she took hold of her husband's hand.

'I would never have chosen her,' Noel said. He sounded brittle like a sulky child but also resigned to his fate, as though it would happen no matter how he felt about Eve or she about him. And that was when it occurred to Eve that this was not a recent idea. He had known what was expected of him and still gone ahead and made her his. His what? His whore? What had he done to her? Why had he thought he could lie to her? Or was it just that he had not thought at all because he had wanted her? Had he known that she would give in, had he been waiting in a way that she could not like? Perhaps all he had wanted was her body and the rest was lies.

'You always liked her,' his mother said, trying to smile at him.

'Liking isn't the same. I've known that since I met Eve.'

'Is she a friend?' Eve said, somehow feeling she must contribute to this discussion.

'She's my cousin. She is an heiress,' he said bitterly, looking anywhere but at her, she thought.

'She's a lovely girl, fine and educated, unselfish and good, you know that. You always had a partiality for her company, ever since you were a small child.'

'Only like a sister.'

'I don't think you ever treated your sisters as you treat Cynthia,' his mother said in a kindly way. Then she said, smiling in sympathy at Eve, 'She is my brother's daughter and only child. He has done very well for himself in railways and he has helped us a great deal in our troubles. My husband has been ill for some time and can no longer work. He was a fine physician.' And even though she was speaking of him in the third person, they smiled at one another, like those who had been together for years and understood.

'I will write to your father, Miss Gray, and ask him to come for you,' Mr Esher said. 'In the meanwhile, perhaps you will forgive us that we were unprepared. My wife will go and sort out the domestic arrangements.'

'Father, you can't do that,' Noel protested but his father did not even look his way.

'But I cannot go back,' Eve protested, her voice fainter than she would wish. 'You cannot ask my father to come for me.'

'There is nothing else to be done,' Mr Esher said.

She tried to imagine her father receiving a letter which told him that not only had she run away and disgraced herself, but that he must spend precious time collecting her, like she was an unwanted parcel. She could almost see his disappointed face. This couldn't be happening to her, it just couldn't.

Mrs Esher thus went out and Eve wished she could go too; the atmosphere was so heavy. She was beginning to wish herself at home – not about to marry the man she thought she didn't love, but just not to be here. Surely this was a dream and she would wake in her bed in Wolsingham and it wouldn't seem half as bad as it had done before. She was safe there. She tried and tried to wake up but nothing happened.

Hallam had not died, it was the day before their wedding, and when she awoke, she would see the lovely dress hanging on the wardrobe door and her clothes packed and ready for her to go forward into a rich marriage. She would see Europe and everything would be wonderful.

She could hear several low voices outside the door, women whispering, obviously about her. She had sharp ears, but as they left for rooms upstairs, she couldn't hear much at all.

'Put some coal on the fire, there's a dear boy,' Mr Esher said with affection in his voice – which somehow made everything worse, though Eve didn't understand how or why – and Noel obeyed. That was the only thing that happened before the girl, Amy, came back and offered to show Eve where she would sleep. Eve tried to get Noel to meet her gaze, but he was avoiding her eyes. She felt he had dropped ten years since he had come home and was reduced to a small boy. His shoulders had gone down and his hair was hanging over his face, as though he knew that he had done something wrong and was penitent.

Amy led the way upstairs and then again. The second set of stairs was narrow and steep, and then they were in the attic bedroom, a room without a fire, so cold that it made Eve shiver. One small lamp let in what light there was. Three single beds stood in a line against the wall. There was a chest of drawers and a couple of little side tables, all with books on them.

'I sleep up here with Pen and Nancy. The others have a bedroom below. Nancy has given up her bed for you and will go downstairs with Fred and Belle and Lena.'

All this was said so casually that it made Eve feel worse.

'I'm so sorry,' she said. She wanted to be alone to think. She wished she could be by herself to try and take in what was happening – and worse still, what she had done. Noel could not forsake her now, he couldn't do it. Not after what they had been to one another.

'Oh, don't be. He's always falling in love.'

This was even harder to bear.

'Mind you,' Amy said with rare judgement, 'he has never been quite this foolish before.'

If Eve had not felt agony of mind before this, she did now. What had he been thinking of? Did she mean nothing to him? Why had he persuaded her to come here with him? Why had he kissed her and taken her to him, when he was promised to another woman, which he had to marry because he was poor and his family were relying on him? Had he not thought of that?

'But we love one another. We want to be married.' She knew that sounded desperate, but that was exactly how she felt – along with sick and horrified and lost, and so out of place like never before. Even Weardale had never felt like this. Boring was wonderful compared to how she felt now.

Amy's look was all pity.

'It can never be,' she said. 'Surely you can see how poor we are. Father hasn't worked in some time and although our family are kind, we cannot expect them to see to all our needs. Noel is my father's only hope. He cannot marry you; he hasn't a penny of his own. I presume he has just spent what he was hoping to save, coming back here like this. He will marry Cynthia.'

'Why should you rely on him so much?'

'He is the youngest and the only boy. None of us has married, and although we all have different jobs of various kinds – Pen is a companion to an old woman in the next street, and Belle goes out as a governess to half a dozen romping children – we make very little money. We cannot manage on it and nobody will ever make any of us an offer of marriage. If they had been going to, it would have happened long before now. But we could never afford to be seen or to go anywhere, and to be fair, none of us is beautiful. Cynthia got all the money and all the beauty and we can't even hate her, because she is so nice. I'm so sorry, Miss Gray.'

Eve said nothing.

'I'm thirty-two,' Amy said, and Eve thought, yes, she could see the lines on the woman's face now that she was closer. She was no girl and she was as plain as could be. She was wearing a dress which must have been hers since the day she had stopped growing; it was hideous, shabby and washed out. 'All I can offer you by way of entertainment, I'm afraid, is a book. Do you read?'

Eve was about to say that she had little else to do, and then stopped herself, ashamed. She had thought she was having a bad time. Compared to this woman, her life had been a wonderful gift.

'We will be having supper in a little while, I must go and get on with it. Please, if you care, stay up here and you can borrow my book.' Amy didn't wait for Eve to speak; she was out of the door and down the stairs in a very short time.

Eve couldn't read, she couldn't do anything; she didn't even panic. She sat there in shock and berated herself for her sheer stupidity.

Thirty

Maddy understood quite well that troubles came in threes, but she had yet to understand that, however big they were, they also equalled one another in size. Hallam was dead, Sister Bee was ill so that Maddy worried about whether to write and tell Mother and in the meanwhile, she was trying to run everything with the help of the two nuns, Ruth, and the women who came in to help. It ought to have worked, she kept telling herself, but it didn't.

So it was strange how the next problem loomed almost immediately. It was one which could not have been foreseen. Ruth had by now become almost one of them, and could be relied on to help with anything that came to hand. Indeed, often Maddy turned around confident that Ruth was right beside her. Ruth took care of the children so well; perhaps it was because she was so much nearer than any of the others to their age. She was particularly good with Primrose and Pansy, who by now had moved into the dormitory, although they were not happy. But how could they be? Ruth and Maddy and the others tried to keep their minds off what had happened to them.

It was Sister Abigail who first located the problem. It was typical of her; she was almost like the town crier, Maddy thought with impatient affection.

'I can't find Ruth. Did you send her out to do something? She was meant to be helping me in the schoolroom and I'm there on me own like a clod.'

A clod being a piece of turf, Maddy suspected not, but she knew what Abigail meant.

'I daresay she won't be long. She's never gone long for anything.'

'Well, she's nowhere to be found, and Primrose and Pansy are kicking up a fuss and I don't understand it, that's all,' and Abigail went back to the schoolroom, grumbling.

Even then it did not occur to Maddy that she had another problem. She went on with her paperwork. How did it mount up like this? But there it was: she had accounts to pay the various shopkeepers, she had to ask Mr Slater if he could do some building work and two of the women who did the washing had come down with something. She had to talk to Mr Gray and possibly send him to them if they were not well enough to come to the clinic. She was worried that if it was contagious, other folk might have caught it. And two of the children were bed-wetting, Primrose and Pansy, which was hardly surprising. They were usually happy up to a point because Ruth was devoted to them, but this was two nights running. This also she must talk to Mr Gray about.

So that morning she was too busy to think much about Abigail having to cope in the schoolroom on her own. But by dinner time at noon, Ruth had still not been seen. Frosty fingers closed around Maddy's heart, even though she told herself there would be an easy explanation.

By tea time when Ruth had put in no appearance, she was worried. Because she couldn't confide in Sister Bee and expect any real help, and she didn't like to burden the other two nuns, she told them she was just going out for a few minutes. Then she made her way over to the fell house.

This at least was something she had got right, she told herself, and took a little comfort from it. The fell house was so different now that Miss Proud was in charge. The place was spotless and somehow Miss Proud had stopped Jay from turning every room into an office. She had managed to confine him to one large room, which overlooked the fell, and Maddy thought she had probably worked out that it was the view he liked best of all. Miss Proud was clever and Maddy took credit for having got her there.

Jay even looked better: clean shaven, wearing what looked to her like new clothes, though she was certain that somehow Miss Proud had managed this, too, without him noticing. The smells in the house were of good food, coffee, fresh bread and some kind of stew bubbling on the stove. It was warm and welcoming and that day the fell was full of light somehow and he looked as though he was making a recovery. Miss Proud beamed at Maddy and showed her in to where he was sitting at a big desk with a lot of paperwork in front of him.

Instead of saying 'she will turn up' when she explained the situation to him, as most people, especially men, would have – worrying less about obvious things than women did – he frowned. He looked down at the work he had been doing and said nothing for such a long time that she thought he had forgotten she was there. Then he said, 'There's obviously something the matter. I'll get the men to search the village. And if they don't find her, I'll take a ride up to Stanhope in the morning.'

Maddy was astonished.

'She's only been gone since this morning and – did you think there was something wrong?' She hated the idea that he might have seen more than she did, and him in that awful state about Hallam.

'Not really.'

He didn't say anything more. Maddy looked hard at him when he wasn't looking at her and she thought, yes, he understood what it was like when you were badly treated. How hard it was to go on day to day as though nothing had happened. Too much had happened now and they were all suffering.

Maddy went back to her work, really upset. It was what he didn't say that worried her. Why would Ruth have left? She couldn't have, she had no reason to. She was probably shocked and tired, as they all were. But it was true that she had never before absented herself in any way; she was always around. Surely she knew that if she was troubled, she could come to Maddy. Never had Maddy felt so unable to manage. She wished she could go into her little room and lock the door and howl the place down.

Unfortunately, there was no lock on that door, and Abigail and Hilary were used to the door being not just ajar, but wide open. That was how Maddy had wanted to present herself – not shut off from them in any way, still a part of them. They were a team and she was not leading, she was just there.

Abigail was not to be put off.

'She's gone, hasn't she?' Abigail said as Maddy reached her office door.

'I don't know. Why would you think so?'

'We're all at sixes and sevens and I didn't think she looked very well yesterday, that's all. I hope she hasn't fallen over and hurt herself. If she went off and broke a leg and was lying there all night, I would never sleep.'

This was not helpful, but neither did Maddy want to be alone in her concern.

'Why would she go off?'

'To think about stuff.' Abigail waved a thin arm. Despite safety and good food, Abigail was still skinnier than anybody else. She was so quick, so on top of everything in some ways. 'I hope some flaming bloke hasn't tried to run off with her or do away with her.'

'Abigail—' Maddy protested.

'Did Mr Gilbraith say anything helpful?'

Maddy thought nobody had seen her go out, but Abigail had been on the streets too long not to know exactly what was going on around her. Maddy told her.

'He's all right, that way, he'll find out and she'll be all right,' and with that Abigail went back to her work and Maddy had to try and content her whirling mind.

Ruth did not come home that night. Sister Bee walked the house, so with one not being there and another being there too much, Maddy didn't sleep. She had hopes that Sister Bee would get better and Ruth would come home, but nothing had changed the following morning, except that she was tired and fractious. She tried not to take it out on any of them.

Jay came to her to make sure that Ruth had not come back and then he went off. He would go to Wolsingham and Frosterley and then up the bank at Stanhope where she had lived. Perhaps she had gone home.

'She did always worry that her mother might come back or her father might, I don't really know.'

'Don't worry, somebody is bound to have seen her.'

She had to be content with that and was grateful to him for

doing what he could. She was pleased to know that somebody was doing something. If you could do something, no matter what, it always seemed to help. In the meanwhile, she had been able to talk to Mr Gray after his clinic and tell him that she was even more concerned than she had been about Sister Bee. He nodded. They went outside to talk since there were a lot of people about, and there he said reassuringly, 'I have been thinking a lot about this. I know that Sister Bee says that she is not ill, and I'm not sure what I can do, but I think there is something very much the matter with her. I would hazard a guess that she has what the old medics called melancholia. I do know a little about mental health, with my wife having been so ill all these years. When we do get a hospital up and running here, I want it to deal with problems of the mind, as well as problems of the body. Sometimes they run concurrently.'

Maddy didn't quite get what he was on about, but she was in pursuit and glad to know that he had given it a great deal of thought.

'What is that?' she asked.

'Sometimes when people have to bear more than they can stand, their minds turn against them to make them stop, because it is too much for them. Usually this happens with very strong people, because they will not take on board that you must live a little for yourself; you cannot live exclusively for others. There is something in her past which she is not admitting, not coming to terms with, if you like. Although I worry about saying it, I think she might be better if she went back to Newcastle.'

'She was fine when she was there.'

'I remember you saying it,' he said. 'That could be part of the answer. She seems used up by the way that life has treated her and her mind wants her to die. She is destroying herself without realising it.'

Maddy stared.

'You mean she wants to die?'

'She is fighting not to, and that is why she cannot eat or sleep. She is taking on this huge battle every day. If she cannot be helped in time, I think she will die.'

'What can be done?' Maddy could hear the despair in her own voice and she felt it in her own heart.

'If she would talk to me, I might be able to help, but she will not at the moment.'

He went off, having done his clinic and seen the people he needed to see.

Ruth did not come back that night and neither did Jay. Maddy went across to the fell house more worried than ever now, because he had so obviously not found her.

She went back and that night again, Sister Bee walked the house. Maddy was so worn down with worry that she kept falling asleep, even aware of the nun's footsteps through the ceiling and walls and up and down the stairs. The poor woman was so agitated, Maddy knew.

After that, she kept an eye on Sister Bee all the time, but without letting her know. That was hard because Sister Bee was not stupid. To be fair, she did try to eat and was slightly more successful, but the sleepwalking went on and on.

She didn't go far, that was Maddy's consolation. She didn't seem to know where she was, but always followed the same pattern with the wanderings. Between worrying about Ruth, and trying to help the others during the day, Maddy felt like bursting into tears, except that she knew it wouldn't help.

*

Jay didn't want to go looking for Ruth; he felt resentful that she had run away. He didn't understand why and his life was already difficult enough without this. It was a cold bright day and for the first hour, he sat on Phyllis and fumed; after that he began to feel better. He felt as though it was doing him good to have yet another problem to try and sort out; at least he was away from the village. Why it had not occurred to him that it would be easier to be away for a short while, he did not know. He felt almost as though he was on holiday and then felt awful. Ruth would have gone back to Stanhope; at least, he hoped she had. Where else she might go he had no idea. He rode down the banks and into Wolsingham.

He thought that if he had to spend any more time in Wolsingham he would learn to hate the place. He was aware every second that Eve had gone. But he called in at several shops and business premises and asked if they had seen anything of a young girl with bright red hair and very white skin. They knew him so they did not suspect her of doing anything wrong; maybe they even knew that the girl had lived up in the village. Nobody would say anything to the police – they were a close lot – but nobody had seen or heard anything.

He called in at the farms and cottages between Wolsingham and Frosterley but turned up nothing, and between Frosterley and Stanhope nothing either. When he got to Stanhope, he went to a businessman he knew and asked where the farm was where she had lived.

He therefore rode out of Stanhope towards Eastgate and turned up Crawleyside bank. Then he knew exactly where the place was, and he was appalled when he saw it. He had not quite known that Ruth had come from such very reduced circumstances. It wasn't a farm, it was more like a farm building, and had around it no good land, only a few fields. What had been a garden had returned to the wild, and the place itself was empty, with its door hanging off and its windows smashed.

He moved inside. She could not possibly be there; at least, he hoped not. He hoped that she had not gone there with some mistaken idea that her father still lived or her mother had come back. He could see how she might, though he could not work out why she had been so unhappy that she had left. What had happened? It must be something that he knew nothing of.

Inside there was very little left. The furniture was broken into pieces, the table lying on its back on the floor. Somebody had lit a fire but it was a long time ago. He disliked the place so much that he barely lingered long enough to ensure that she was not there. He shouted her name several times and then he got back on to his horse and returned to Stanhope.

There he called in at the house of the carpenter he was on such good terms with and they encouraged him to spend the night. He liked them better than anyone else he could have named, so although he protested that he should go back, he stayed and was glad of the respite. He slept better than he had slept since Hallam had died. He was so glad of the good food and drink that had got him there and of the soft bed which he fell into. He had no dreams at all.

The following day Jay went back to Maddy's office. He could see that she was as worried as he was, and when he closed the door, she said to him, 'You didn't find her, did you?'

He shook his head and didn't look at her.

'I went everywhere I could think of that might help, and

nobody had seen her. I went up to the house where she had lived. It was a ruin. The windows have been smashed in, there's glass all over the floor and the doors are off their hinges. It's an awful place and her mother has not come back. Have you got any ideas as to anywhere else she might have gone?'

Maddy shook her head.

'But you thought there was something wrong?' she said.

'My judgement is all over the place. I was thinking about myself and Hallam so much and then when Eve – when Eve left, I couldn't trust any of my thinking; it was in such a mess. But I thought it was just that everything was getting to her. Why wouldn't it? But not sufficiently so to make Ruth run away.'

'Somebody might have taken her?'

'I have had various men out in the dale and at the villages up here making enquiries, so although it is possible someone could have taken her, it seems unlikely.'

'But why would she leave voluntarily?'

'I don't know. I've thought and thought about it and can't come up with anything plausible. I daren't alert the police. Other than what we've done, I think we might have to just wait and see what happens.'

'That's so hard to do.'

'I know,' he said.

Eve was a huge novelty while they ate. She could see the girls looking at her, so she kept her gaze on her plate. There was sufficient on it, bread and cheese, tepid cabbage and cold meat, but she could see that they had eked it out because everybody had less than she did. So although she was not hungry and wanted to gag with each bite, she forced it down.

There was little conversation and nobody seemed surprised. Afterwards all she wanted was to go to bed, though it was only mid-evening.

The girls sat down and began sewing.

'Do you do fine sewing, Miss Gray?' Mrs Esher asked.

'I – I don't sew at all.'

Everybody looked at her.

'Do you help in the village with poor people? Do you do charity work?'

'No, I – no, I don't.'

'Did your mother not teach you to sew?'

Here, being able to talk about her mother was some relief. She felt guilty at that, but it was true and real. 'My mother has been very ill since I was a small child. I barely remember her.' She did remember Mrs Florence trying to teach her to embroider pansies on a handkerchief, saying it would please her mother, but she hated doing it and kept running into the garden.

'I help in the garden.'

'We would have loved a garden,' Mrs Esher said. 'I was brought up in the country, you know, and we had a fine garden there. I still miss it. All we have here is the business of day to day, and a back yard and the pavement. A little more space would have been such a delight.'

'What is your home like, Miss Gray?' one of the girls asked. Eve wasn't quite sure which of them it was.

'It stands by the river and has big gardens around it. My mother's family have had a house on that site for upwards of a thousand years.'

'Oh, how wonderful,' Mrs Esher said. 'And will your mother get better? It must be very hard for you and your father.'

'She has a form of mental disease,' Eve said; that was what

her father had bravely taught her to say when people asked such questions, 'and cannot leave her room.'

After that there was a long silence and they all looked at each other.

Later when Eve went out to use the lavatory – the cabbage had not agreed with her, her stomach had given her what her father would have referred to as 'the gripes' and she was just hoping it wouldn't embarrass her again, having to run back outside into the darkness – she found Noel in the hallway.

'I've been watching for you,' he said, drawing her into the dining room, which still smelled slightly of the boiled cabbage they had eaten with their cold meat. 'I was wrong to bring you here. We have to get away again.'

She stared at him.

'What do you mean?'

'We have to leave. We cannot stay here and be married – my parents won't allow it.'

'But what about your family?'

He looked hard into her face.

'Eve, I've never been in love before—'

'Amy says you do it all the time.'

'Oh, Amy doesn't understand. This is different. She's just afraid to be left.'

'I think I would be.'

'You don't ever have to worry. You're beautiful and courageous,' he said, 'and you gave up everything for me and I'm going to give up everything for you.'

'You can't. Your father is ill, and you have all your sisters—'

'Don't you understand? As the only boy I have to do everything. I have to work hard and marry well and look after everybody. How can I do that?'

'By becoming a doctor and marrying Cynthia.'

'I am tired of her name. I've known her all my life. Why should I sacrifice my future for them?'

'Because they have nothing. You cannot just go and leave them in poverty.'

He looked defiantly at her and then said just as a small child would, 'You can't go back. You're a disgraced woman. We have no choice but to go on.'

'I have no money and neither have you.'

This seemed news to Noel.

'Doesn't that house belong to you?' he asked, frowning.

'What house?'

'The house you live in. Didn't you say that your mother's family gave it to you and not to your father when she started being ill? We could sell it. It must be worth a great deal of money.'

Eve stared at him.

'But my mother and father live there.'

'You will never see it or them again; you won't be allowed any life after this if you go back, don't you see? Your father is qualified, he could afford a small house with a surgery and dispensing place. He doesn't need a huge house like that. I could go as an apprentice until I'm qualified and then we could go anywhere we wanted. You're twenty-one next year, you said; you come into your inheritance.'

He was staring at her and when she didn't say anything, he tried to take her into his arms. She pushed him away.

'I can't do such a thing to my parents,' she said. 'What about my mother?'

'You have only me now. You will have to.'

'I certainly will not.'

'So you will go back to Wolsingham with your reputation in

tatters? Nobody will ever marry you. Nobody will ever want to know you. You have to come with me.'

She wanted to cry and had a hard time not doing so. She had given herself to this clown?

'Even now,' he said softly, 'you could be pregnant with our first child. Have you thought of that? I have and of how wonderful it will be.'

At that precise moment, Amy appeared in the doorway saying, 'Noel, my father is looking for you.'

He glared at her.

'Am I not allowed a minute's peace? We are talking here.'

'He said directly.'

None of the girls was pretty; three of them were short and dumpy like their mother, the other three were skinny and thin-faced. They hadn't a decent frock among them, Eve had thought earlier, as they all bundled into the bedroom with two candles between them. Amy said, 'You don't mind them being here, do you?'

'I didn't think any of you would want to talk to me.'

'Of course we do,' one of the others said. They all looked alike in one way: they wore huge grey-white nightgowns with their hair plaited so that it would not tangle. They were so open and friendly; it was their manner. They were well bred even though they had no money and no future. Their parents were good, decent people and she knew now that she could not betray them or their parents or hers.

'Will your father come for you?' She thought this was Belle. She had been badly named; she had chubby hands and arms, and small dark eyes and a big nose.

'I suppose so.'

'Did you leave him because he treated you badly?'

Eve shook her head.

'Are you poor and thought that we were rich?'

'No, I'm actually quite well off. Noel didn't say you were rich; I just assumed it somehow.'

By the light of two candles – there had been one for each bedroom – they all sat on the three beds. Was this what it was like having sisters? Eve couldn't help but think that this companionable getting together and talking when you went to bed must be something close. She envied them, she who had been given so much, and they who had nothing but cold meat, cabbage and cheese for dinner. They had one another to talk to, somebody to help them with their innermost thoughts and problems.

'We were quite well off at one time,' Amy said. 'I remember when we had new dresses and a carriage and used to go to the seaside for holidays and stay in a hotel. Now we never go anywhere.'

'I work in a shop,' Nancy said ruefully. 'The woman who owns it is awful to me. The old women come in and they are all knitting stuff, like those things you might use to open the oven door. I hate knitting.'

'I have to help Mother in the kitchen,' Fred said. 'I spend the whole day peeling vegetables and making soup and washing clothes and floors.'

'If your father is kind and you have plenty of money, you must really like Noel an awful lot to leave such a home,' Lena observed. They were all looking at Eve with warm pity, as though they didn't blame her but knew that she was wrong.

'Yes, I—' She was about to say 'I did' and then couldn't. Had she fallen out of love with him so quickly? She couldn't believe how selfish he was. Were all men selfish? Her father wasn't.

Thinking of her father made her feel guilty and worse. Whatever would he think when he had to take time away from his practice to come and fetch her?

She had never been so ashamed of herself, never thought she could be so mistaken in a man. A decent, hard-working man had asked her to marry him, and she had run away because his friend had died and they couldn't get married straight away.

It was a week before her father came to collect her and it was the longest week of her life. She had nothing to do; they had a limited supply of books and they were always busy. Noel kept trying to take hold of her every time they met in the darkness of the hall.

She couldn't sleep, she was not used to being so cold at night. She had little to sustain her because her stomach was not used to cabbage; she spent a lot of time in the outdoor privy. She did not feel as if she deserved tears and she tried to brazen it out with herself, while longing to be anywhere but here.

Every time she thought of going back to Wolsingham, she wanted to run, but there was nowhere to run to. The hours were like days. There was little conversation and no rest. The girls worked and she had no skills so she couldn't help. She tried to make herself as small as possible and be of no trouble, as though they might forget about her.

When her father came for her after a week, she couldn't look at him or find anything to say to him. They met on their own in the living room; God knew where the rest of the household had scattered to, that they should have such privacy.

She couldn't speak. She was ashamed of herself and aghast at what she had done. She wished she didn't make herself look at him. She could see how upset and disappointed he was and how very tired. She had made his life harder and it had been bad enough before this. But her father was always honest; it was one of the things she liked best about him.

'I am sorry,' he said. It was the last thing she had thought to hear. 'You have lived the life you had to because your mother was ill, and I was always out there paying the bills. It hasn't been easy for you. No wonder you were driven to this.'

Eve started to cry. It would have been easier had he shouted, or even struck her. She didn't think her father had ever struck or shouted at anyone. Why was she wilful? Finally, she managed, 'I thought I loved Noel. How could I be wrong twice over?'

'A great many people are wrong over and over again. How could we think that God planned couples?'

He looked into her face so kindly that Eve wanted to cry again.

'Didn't you love my mother?' she said.

'Very much, and still do. But she was so ill that she didn't understand how to love, and I was left with an infant and the responsibility of the practice.'

'And I have made it worse.'

'Nothing of the sort. I have, however, talked to Noel's father. He is very ill and he needs Noel to help the family. Do you understand?'

'Of course I do. If I had known that, I would never have run away with him.'

'So we will go home.'

'Oh, Papa, I am so very, very sorry. I will make it up to you if I have the chance. I never thought to cause you to have to come after me like this. I can't wait to get out of here and back to the place I thought I despised. I don't care if I never marry. I don't care for anything but that you will take me back. How could I do such a thing to you when I love you best of anyone in the world?'

He enfolded her against him and held her tight while she cried. In fact, all the way down there, he had been worried that she would run away once again and end up in poverty, and he would have to go to some awful, obscure place to take her back. He wished things differently, but he was selfish enough to be glad to have her back in his arms.

Noel was not bad, he was just ignorant and very young. But that didn't help now. Noel would go on and marry Cynthia, but Eve was ruined.

Thirty-One

Ruth had left because she couldn't stand herself. She didn't know that you took yourself with you. She would have given a great deal to have left herself in the village up on the tops and never seen that self or the village again. However hard you tried, you could not wipe the past; it was a part of who you were – and presumably the older you got, the more of a burden it was. Perhaps this was what old age was about, that you could not walk far without being so weighed down so that your whole body could bear no more.

She had set off without saying anything and all she took was the heel of a loaf from the kitchen and a bottle of water. The water was heavy, but she thought she needed it. After she walked for about three miles, some farmer stopped and offered her a lift so she got up on the cart and there she fell asleep. She didn't know why; she never slept during the day. But she had lost a lot of sleep lately and the rhythm of the horse and cart got to her. When she awoke, they were just outside Durham.

She thanked the farmer, and then she wandered into the middle of the place and saw the railway line. Somehow she made her way through without anybody noticing her and she got on the train. She reached Newcastle and nobody had asked for her ticket and there she got off.

It was bigger than she had thought. It was fourteen times as big as Stanhope, she thought, and quite scary, but she rather liked it. Her food and water had run out, but there was a drinking fountain in the station so she made the best of that. Now all she had to do was find food and shelter. Not too much then, Ruth, you idiot, she told herself as she set off away from the station.

For some reason on the road an old woman had given her a silver sixpence; she clutched this to her and saved it for when she was very hungry.

The town was huge. She made her way to the waterfront, the quayside. There were big ships docked and huge buildings. It was very busy with people coming and going from the shops, which must be to do with the shipping. She was nervous; she thought she might be attacked or have her money taken from her in such a place. But nobody seemed to notice her, so in the end she exchanged the silver sixpence for a cup of tea and a sandwich of she wasn't quite sure what. She got plenty of change from the woman behind the counter, and although there were lots of men about with various accents she didn't understand, drinking beer and talking, nobody took any notice of her.

This was how business operated. In some ways it was like Jay's new town: the men were important and busy and didn't notice women. She found a cap lying in a gutter and twisted her hair up under it so that her most noticeable feature was out of sight. She kept her eyes lowered. She also bought for a penny a pair of shabby trousers. She thought she probably looked like a boy, which was useful. There were lots of poor people in the town and children everywhere in ragged clothes, so skinny that she thought they must never have eaten a proper meal. The small children were begging for pennies and being brushed aside or ignored. In one unfortunate case a man kicked a small child, which knocked him over.

A bigger boy with him cursed the man and she winced at what she presumed was awful language. The man who had kicked the child merely walked on, but the lad put the small boy on to his feet and spoke softly to him. As Ruth watched, he put a coin into the child's dirty palm. Sudden sunlight glinted for a moment and then the boy's fingers closed around the penny; he ran off, apparently none the worse for the kick.

The bigger boy, eyeing her carefully, came over. She stood her ground. Her first instinct had been to run away, but firstly, she didn't know where she was, and secondly, she had nowhere to run to. He was older than she had thought, perhaps fifteen or sixteen.

'New?' he said.

Ruth couldn't think of what to say.

'You dinna look much like a lad, love.' His voice was scornful, but kind too.

Ruth heaved a sigh of relief and disappointment all at once.

'I had to try. I thought I might get into worse trouble with hair this colour.' She took off the cap and then put it back on again. He gazed.

'I can see.'

He set off down the street at an easy pace and there seemed to be nothing to do but go with him. She didn't trust him – she didn't trust anybody – but she had nothing else to do, and he didn't run, so he was obviously waiting for her.

Very soon they were in poor streets, buildings half pulled down. Many houses had no windows and no doors, and lots of people seemed to have nowhere to go or they would have been inside, over a fire. She regretted leaving the village now, but there was no chance that she could go back. She must go on and do her best. The streets were filthy, but after a while she stopped stepping aside because it didn't make any difference.

Finally, he turned in at a building and she hesitated. He stopped and looked back. He went on so she followed him.

It was dry and warmer in there. It was a big house, probably with several rooms, though she couldn't see very well. The windows were unbroken. The light fell softly on everything; it was a pretty day, even here. The sun was delicately making its way inside and providing patches of gold on the floor.

She was amazed at the number of children. Some of them were very small, hardly able to walk, and very dirty and thin. There was a big fireplace but no fire in it, as though they could afford nothing.

'Got to get summat to eat,' he said. 'That was me last penny.'

'I have some money.'

He looked at her. And then laughed and shook his head.

'Hang on to it,' he said. 'And no point you begging – you need to be a little kid for that, and even then it doesn't always work. Greedy bastards.'

'Can I come?' She dreaded being left here among strangers. The others seemed to be looking at her, yet every time she ventured to return the look, they either weren't or had moved their gaze; it was a kind of respect, as if it was the only privacy left to them.

'You'd just be in the way,' he said, and off he went.

When he had gone, she stood about, not knowing if it was polite to sit on the floor, or whether somebody might object. After a little while, a girl of about her own age, with thick, matted hair and a face either very brown or just plain dirty, came over. Her face didn't look very friendly. Ruth avoided her eyes.

'How do you know Nate?' she said.

'I don't.'

'He brought you here.'

'Well, I—'

'He's mine, you know.'

'Oh,' was all Ruth could mumble.

'He keeps me. I do things for him.'

Ruth had imagined they were several days from confidences like this. Here time moved more swiftly.

'You know about that stuff?'

She did, of course, and nodded. The girl moved away. Nate wasn't gone long but it felt like fifty years. He had bread inside his jacket. He broke it and distributed it evenly, and then magicked another loaf as well, so that everybody could eat. The bread was fresh and Ruth was hungry.

'You upset Poppy?' he said, nodding in the direction of where the other girl stood back.

'She thinks I'm after you,' Ruth said, feeling heartened by the bread and by the mug of water which he found and handed to her.

'It's just talk. She likes owning folk,' he said, shrugging.

Somehow after somebody offers you bread, you do trust them, Ruth thought, eating gratefully.

Things got worse with Sister Bee. Maddy wanted to call in Mr Gray again but she was not sure that Sister Bee would allow her to. She would be angry, which wouldn't help. But she was so tired during the day after walking most of the night that she couldn't eat, and she kept falling asleep every time she sat down. She retreated finally to her office and locked the door.

Maddy tried to get her to come out and help, but the trouble was that when she tried, she passed out. She passed out in the schoolroom and in the chapel again, and so Maddy could not persuade her to come out of her office.

She called for Mr Gray and he came. He tried to talk to her through the door, but she wouldn't listen. After two hours of failed persuasion, he was obliged to go off and deal with another urgent case.

For three days, Sister Bee did not leave her office. But on the fourth day when Maddy pleaded with her, she actually got up and opened the door.

The room stank. Sister Bee had always been so fastidious. She allowed Maddy to empty the chamber pot and that was all. The air in the office was foetid; she had not washed and the bed linen had not been changed. Maddy longed to open a window but Sister Bee shouted at her when she went across.

When Maddy came back, the chamberpot emptied and washed clean, Sister Bee locked her out again. Maddy left her a big jug of water, a glass and a sandwich.

Maddy thought of calling the doctor back but she had the horrible feeling that he might call Sister Bee mad, say that she had lost her wits. He knew about such things; his wife hadn't left her home in years. His wife he could shield, but he could not shield a nun who had gone mad. Maddy had awful thoughts about Sister Bee being carted off to some ghastly asylum.

She knew that some people would have said they were stupid to try to establish order in such a place, that it was no wonder Sister Bee could not cope. Many people had no religion, no education and until now, no decent living. Perhaps the enterprise had been meant to fail. This was either the beginning or the end, if Sister Bee was to be put away and beyond their help.

Maddy had never felt so tired; everything was going wrong. It was as though the children sensed this, and they became difficult, crying or running out of the schoolroom, or just not attending. She told the other two nuns as little as possible but they worried anyway, she knew. They didn't want this to fail after all their hard work.

She wanted to write to Mother and say that Sister Bee should go back to the convent, but she worried about that too. Failure was not an easy thing to admit. She could not bear the idea that they might have to pack up and go home.

Five nights after this, when Ruth had not come back and Maddy was beside herself with worry, she thought she could hear Sister Bee crying. It was very late.

She ventured softly to Sister Bee's door and yes, she had been right. Even through the stout wooden door she could hear a kind of relentless moaning. You couldn't be in any doubt that it was despair. Anybody who had ever felt like that could not mistake it.

She touched the handle and found it unlocked, so she let herself into the room. It was quite dark and all she could see was Sister Bee hunched up in bed, in such a hopeless fashion that Maddy was there at once. As Sister Bee took in her breath, Maddy said, 'It's only me.'

'I can't stand any more. Whatever am I to do? I can't live like this.'

Maddy sat down on the bed and took Sister Bee into her arms. She held the nun as she broke into a great storm of crying. She sobbed and sobbed against Maddy's shoulder. She was so skinny by now that she was nothing more than a collection of bones in

Maddy's arms. Maddy stroked her head and let the storm go on until at last, completely exhausted, Sister Bee quietened.

And then she said, 'I can see him sometimes, here in the night. I can see him everywhere. He haunts me.'

Maddy rocked her like she was a small child and Sister Bee stopped talking and just sat there. Maddy waited. She knew that if she stayed there and kept still that Sister Bee might confide in her. She could only hope. She thought it might do the other nun some good if she could unburden herself; she thought it might help. Eventually, when she was half convinced that Sister Bee had gone to sleep, Sister Bee moved just slightly in Maddy's arms and took a deep breath. Then she said, 'My mother didn't want me to marry Michael, but I cared about him so much.'

The words went into the darkness but were not lost, like something had become new and tangible in the room, as though the dawn might just be breaking somewhere beyond the window.

'He took my boy.' Her voice was like a breath of wind. 'I ran outside. It was St Cuthbert's Day. I have never forgotten it. I couldn't see for the wind and the rain. I called and called after Michael, said his name over and over, as though the saying of it might help. I ran and ran all over the village, all over the area, wondering where on earth he could be. I couldn't see, the rain and the wind were so bad, and yet I couldn't go back without knowing where he was and what had happened. It was a short, wet March day.

'We had quarrelled. He never wanted to be at home with us. He would stay out night after night, drinking with his friends, and come back drunk when it was almost daylight. When he finally came back that night, we quarrelled. Nothing was ever right for him, nothing was ever good enough. The meal was never on the table as it should have been the moment he walked into the house. His boots were not polished enough, and the house was not swept clean, as though he knew better, though he did not.

'The harder I tried, the more he demanded. He told me that I was not a good wife, nor a decent mother. He shouted it outside and I was so ashamed. I tried to remember that the other people in the village knew that he was a drunk and would not mind him, but I was also miserable because I had failed. His parents and my parents would hear him, and I burned in shame that they knew who I had married and how badly I had done. I cringed before him. I would have promised him anything, if he would just stop shouting and come inside and we could go to bed. The child was crying, and I had nothing left to give.

'I couldn't leave; you weren't allowed to do such a thing. Then I would have been not only a bad wife and mother, but an outcast for having brought such shame on my family. You had to endure what God had sent you. There was no going back when you had defied your parents. But there seemed no going forwards, either.

'I wanted to tell him that I didn't mind how often he got drunk, that I knew I was causing him to hate me. I didn't care how often he came home penniless after work; I cared for nothing but him and for our boy.

'I had not believed what my father said when he told me not to marry him. He had begged me not to because he and my mother felt that he was all wrong. He had given other women children, they said, in other places, but I did not believe it. I even laughed, I think, at one point. And I felt so powerful. I could change him. He was mine, and however many children he had fathered – which I doubted – and however many women he had left – which I also doubted – he would never leave me. It was a special love which had been ordained, sent by God.

'I was right for him and he was right for me. We were even happy for a while. He told me he loved me as he had loved no one else and I believed him. We were married; I thought that proved how he cared for me. He told me so when I lay beneath him and I thought the stars came out in the sky for us.

'And on St Cuthbert's Day, I stood there with the March rain all over my face, soaked through so that my dress and coat and boots stuck to me. The rain fell down on to my legs and into the boots, which had been so stout and were now so old that they were falling to bits.

'I stood there and waited and waited for him to come back with our boy. Then I fell to earth and slept, because I could stay awake no longer.

'My dreams brought him back to me; he was always waiting just outside the door. We could go home, the three of us, and everything would be all right.

'Somebody carried me home. Somebody saw me into my house, the empty room, where there was no man and no child. I told myself over and over that he would come back, that he had to come back. What would he do without me? And what would my boy do? I lay there until I couldn't stand it any longer and then I went for help.

'They told me that he had taken my boy away and that he had set sail with him for America and that I would never see either of them again. I tried telling myself that I was better off without him, that he would give our child a good life in a new land.

'We had talked about leaving. There was so little to eat here and so little to achieve. I had tried and tried to get him to take us away so many times before, but in the end he didn't give me a chance. He took away my boy and ran from me. He had left me here. But I knew that I could leave; why would I not? I could follow them and see my boy again.

'My parents gave me all they could to help me get away. And then the news came to the village. It was the hardest day of my life. I would never get there; I would never hold my boy again. Their ship had been lost.'

As she lay there in Maddy's arms, letting go of the story in little bits with her breath all over the place, Maddy saw for the first time that Bee finally believed it, after all this time. Her husband and child were dead, and they would never come back.

Dear Mother,

I have hesitated over this letter. I was going to write before but I was unsure what the problem was and I thought it might solve itself. I know that you wanted the four of us here together and imagined it might work. It does — or at least, it did. You know that from the various letters I have written to you over the past months. But I ought to have mentioned that Sister Bee has a medical problem.

I didn't know whether to contact you. I didn't want to go over her head or seem disobedient. But since I feel sure now that she has not written, I think I can say that she ought to go home to Newcastle, should that be at all practical.

Mr Gray agrees with me. I think the crisis has passed, but she needs care and understanding beyond what she can get here, and I know that she depends on your wisdom and your love. She needs to heal and to have all responsibility lifted from her. Now I am not telling you what to think. I only mean that I have had to judge the time and I think she should go as soon as possible.

I understand that this will be difficult for you, as she is very valuable, not just as a nun but as a leader. And in the beginning, we could not have done this without her. Gradually we have had to shoulder the extra burden of her illness. Mr Gray said I ought to tell you that she has what they used to call melancholia, a disease of the mind, as when your leg snaps and you can no longer walk on it. He did ask whether he should write to you but I thought it might be better coming from me.

She had a terrible trouble in her young life. She was married and had a child, and her husband went away to America, taking the child with him and leaving her behind. The ship went down and they were lost. I think we try to push such things to the back of our minds, but having grieved inadequately, or not at all, she needs to grieve now. She needs to be given time and rest and leisure so that her mind can build itself up again, and come to terms as best she might, so that she will be well enough to get beyond what happened to her and look again to the future.

With your permission, I thought I would bring her back to Newcastle. I do not think it would be kind to let her go by herself and among strangers. The other two nuns will cope with what there is to do here. We are well established by now and have lots of help in the village. So if you will write and let me know whether I am doing the correct thing, I would be truly grateful.

Yours in Christ,
Madeline.

Thirty-Two

When Eve and her father finally got back to Wolsingham and
he went off to see his neglected patients, Mrs Florence looked
severely at her. Eve couldn't look at her. She couldn't believe
what had happened.

'Do you understand what you've done?' Mrs Florence had
obviously been bottling this up. She let her anger out as she
approached Eve, who had retreated to the sitting room and
was shaking and ashamed and wanted to speak to no one. She
couldn't believe that Mrs Florence was berating her so hard, but
then Mrs Florence was really the mother that she lacked. It was
the first time Eve had acknowledged this.

'Your father had to employ someone to do his work while
he spent a week trying to sort you out. As if he didn't have
enough to endure. All these years he has had no wife to speak
of and has never complained. And your mother has been so
very ill.

'How could you do that to him? You were all he had, all he
hoped for. And he was so proud of you, and that you were to
marry a man he admired. Wasn't he a good parent to you? Wasn't
he kind? Being pleased that you should marry a man who is not
a gentleman and nothing like he is? A decent, hard-working man.

Did you really think that a doctor's son from London would marry you? How could he afford a wife?'

Eve ran up to her room and there her wedding dress hung on the outside of the wardrobe like a rebuke. She cried so much that she couldn't breathe. She stayed there for as long as she could, until Mrs Florence came up and told her that her tea was ready, so she had to go downstairs and sit down. She couldn't eat, in spite of Mrs Florence telling her to stop her nonsense and get on with it.

The most awful thing was that nothing had changed. Her father's house was exactly as it had always been. Why had she thought it might have changed in a few short days? The only thing that was different was that nobody came to call, and she dared not show her face beyond the garden. People would be talking in a small place like this, they must all know by now that she had run away with the apprentice.

Mrs Florence no longer talked to her or bothered with her. Even the women who came to do the washing and cleaning looked askance at her so that she avoided them. She had not known how much time Mrs Florence spent looking after her mother as well as the house, but often now she was nowhere to be seen until she came down from the attic. Eve had suddenly become more aware of a lot of things. It had taken such a calamity to make her grow up. She was more ashamed than she could ever have thought to be, and yet only Mrs Florence treated her as though she should be.

She had forgotten how beautiful her home was and how lucky she had been. She had everything any young woman wanted, except a lover she could marry and respect. She had tried too hard and had reaped a bitter harvest. Now the hours crawled past and she had nobody to talk to. She didn't sleep and couldn't eat and thought a great deal of what she had done. She had no friends. All she could do was read and try to keep out of everybody's way. She understood why her mother had gone mad. She was surprised everybody wasn't mad.

In the end, when there was no one in the house but themselves, she went into the kitchen where Mrs Florence was sewing over the fire and she said, 'Did my mother ever want to see me?'

Mrs Florence looked up in surprise.

'Don't you remember?'

'Not once.' And then she thought about it, and she did remember being very small and her mother being there for her. She almost smiled.

'She adored you. She used to dance you around the garden and sing to you, and read to you when you went to bed.'

'I wish I could remember it. I never see her.'

'I don't think she remembers anything but this feeling that she can't breathe unless she stays up there.'

'I wish something could be done.'

'I feel the same.' Mrs Florence looked at her properly for the first time since she had reached home. 'Can I get you something?'

'No.'

Eve turned to leave the kitchen and Mrs Florence got up and took Eve into her arms. She said, 'My poor girl,' and Eve could see at once that she didn't mean her mother.

'I tried too hard,' Eve breathed against Mrs Florence's shoulder.

'You did indeed. It's not much of a world for women, no matter who they are.'

'Did you think Mr Gilbraith right for me?'

'He's not a gentleman in the strictest sense, though I like him very well. And from what I gather, Mr Esher wasn't a gentleman either, though in a different way.'

'He certainly wasn't.' Eve sat down across the fire and told Mrs Florence the whole story, other than that they had slept in the same bed. Her story was punctuated comfortably with 'Oh, he didn't' and 'Oh, how could he have done that to his family?' It brought Eve no comfort and did not make her feel less guilty.

Afterwards Mrs Florence told Eve that she must try to eat. If she was ill, it would worry her father. Eve didn't eat that night. She went to bed and wept for her father and for Jay, and even for Noel, but mostly because she didn't remember her mother dancing her around the garden.

She could not forgive herself for lying with Noel and she was worried now. As a doctor's daughter, she knew what it was like for women who were pregnant. That would finish her off. If she was having Noel's child, she would kill herself; there could be no other way round it. Worst of all, she must wait to see whether her bleeding occurred at the right time. The hours crawled past and she was exhausted. She had to wait, she had to hold on and hope against hope that she was not having Noel's child. Because if she was, there could be no way forward.

To say that Maddy was surprised to see Eve Gray that morning would be accurate. She had heard that Eve was home, but after the knock on the door – which she didn't expect because her door was half open – she looked up from the papers on her desk. She gazed at the young woman who stood in the doorway. The knock was very slight, as though she didn't really want to be there, or was worried about imposing or disturbing somehow. Eve's looks were gone. She was skinny and as grey-faced as her name. Her hair had no lustre and she was missing a hat, as though she had so many things to occupy her that she did not think of such ordinary necessities.

'Do come in,' Maddy encouraged her and waved a hand at the chair at the far side of the desk.

'I'm sorry, I don't mean to impose.'

She looked like she was about to burst into tears. Maddy didn't need that so she got up and encouraged the young woman inside and closed the door. Maddy would not have recognised the confident young woman in the blue velvet riding outfit that she remembered so well; how beautiful this girl had been. Maddy had not known that the first feeling when she saw her would be pity.

'You're not imposing. Sit down, do.'

'Oh, Sister Madeline, I didn't mean to come here, I really didn't, but I have no one to turn to.' Her voice wobbled precariously.

'That is what we are here for. I'm so sorry things have been awful for you.'

'Awful for me?' Miss Gray looked at her as though she didn't deserve sympathy.

'Do sit down.' Her visitor was standing there as though she might run outside.

'I put my father through such a lot for something I shouldn't have done.'

'I don't think that's true.'

'Don't you?' Eve looked hopefully at her.

Maddy was surprising herself. She really had come on a lot since she became a nun, she thought now, and she was glad of it. Without such experience, how could she ever have sympathised with this young woman? And she truly did.

'I don't think I ought to have come to you,' Eve said. 'I know that Jay loved you once and asked you to marry him long before he asked me.'

'We were both very young at the time and I comfort myself that I don't think it would have worked.'

'I was worse. I liked him but I was ambitious. I just wanted to get out of here. I feel so bad about it now, but it wasn't just the dale and the small mean lives that people lead here. I wanted to get away from my father, and most of all, from my mother and her illness. I thought Jay could do that for me, I thought he was my escape route. How awful that sounds now.'

A pang of guilt shot through Maddy. She had the feeling he had been the same for her. But she had not chosen to go down that road and in the end, neither had Eve. She wondered now whether it was instinct in both of them. How odd.

'He cared more for Hallam than he did for me,' Eve said, and Maddy thought once again that Eve was right. She had realised it, whereas Maddy had not before now. Hallam had always been the most important person in Jay's life. Perhaps he always would be.

'You know I ran away with Mr Esher?'

Maddy nodded. Everybody had talked about the scandal of the doctor's daughter running off with the doctor's apprentice.

'I am ruined and have no one to talk to. I'm sorry to burden you, but I think I will go mad if I do not tell someone. You don't mind, do you?'

Maddy reassured her, watched the huge tears pour down the other woman's face and hoped that she could help. Eve was no longer looking at her, as though she wanted to tell her but couldn't face it. She drew off her gloves, just for something to do, Maddy thought. They were pretty – white leather and very expensive.

'The thing is—' She stopped here and Maddy thought how

often difficult situations began with 'the thing is—' Maddy held her breath.

She watched Eve take a deep breath and then plunge in.

'I admired Noel Esher. He was as unlike Jay as I could imagine, and I had blamed Jay for what had happened to us. So when Noel asked me to go back to London with him, I agreed. How stupid it sounds now, but I was desperate to get out of here and I thought he could offer me so much that I went with him.

'I was horrified when I got to London and saw that his family relied on him. His father doesn't look as though he has long to live and he has his mother and six sisters to support. They had betrothed him to his cousin, an heiress and apparently beautiful.

'I understood immediately that we could not be married. He did not. He wanted me to sell my house and put out my parents and run away on the proceeds until he could qualify as a doctor. It was a momentary thing; he was not looking at it realistically.'

She stopped there and Maddy waited while she wiped her face with a handkerchief from her coat pocket – though it didn't seem to make any progress, the tears were falling so fast.

'And then?' she prompted.

'Papa came and brought me home. I find it hard to despise Noel, and I thought I might have after he was so awful – not just to me, but to his family and his betrothed. And I had to come back here, where everybody knows what I did. But it's even worse than that.'

Maddy didn't immediately see how it could be worse, but she understood seconds later.

'I am worried that I might be carrying Noel's child. I know that I was evil in giving myself to him, but I thought we were in love and would be married. Sister Madeline, I am sorry to come to you with this. I can't imagine how shocked you must be – you, a nun – dealing with someone like me, but I don't know what else to do or who to talk to. How could I bring up a child here with everybody knowing? I couldn't. I know I shouldn't have given myself to him, but I didn't know how not to when we were so close together. And I thought I loved him so very much. Now I know better. I feel stupid and selfish and naïve. How could I face the burden of a child?'

She broke down and sobbed and Maddy leaned over and took her hands, which had by now given up her wet face.

'You don't know it for certain. Give yourself time. If you are having a child, your father will understand.'

'No. No, he won't. He will think I was a loose woman, that I cared nothing for who I was, nothing for who he is and how much respect he has built up here. What will I do?'

'You loved Mr Esher.'

Eve hesitated.

'I thought so at the time, but I feel he was just another escape route. We will never be together. I feel so stupid, as if I ought to have known. Somehow it was still all wrong for me. I feel as if I'm not the kind of person who could marry anybody. I tried so hard and look what happened.' She attempted a smile but couldn't quite do it.

'If you think there is to be a child and your father rejects it, which I don't think he will, you can come here. We will protect you and look after you and make sure that you and your child prosper.'

Eve sobbed out her hurts but Maddy had never felt so powerful. She could protect women like this, whom men had betrayed and not loved and not cared for. This was part of what she and the other nuns were about. They were there for those who could not manage by themselves.

When the tears finally stopped, Maddy went to the kitchen and asked Hilary to make some tea, just to give herself a little more time. Her visitor looked as though having blurted out so much, she might flee. Maddy had the feeling that if Eve was having a child, her father would send her away so that nobody knew. Afterwards, the child would be adopted. It was a solution but not a good one. She could hardly start praying that Eve did not have a child, but she wished and wished that something good would happen for the young woman.

They sat down and talked about silly things – at least, Maddy did – and when Eve had drunk her tea, she looked into the fire and she said, 'The worst thing of all was that I have been wrong twice now about men. Maybe I just can't love anyone. Noel turned out to be so immature.'

'But he's young,' Maddy said, feeling about ninety. 'He must feel so caught in his circumstances. Although he felt like that about you, he couldn't do anything about it. He just wasn't thinking. I think the death of those three men at the pit altered him and made him grow up very fast. He was so good down the pit, so caring and professional. Perhaps he hadn't come across something like that before.'

'He said you were very good.'

'I have God on my side,' Maddy said, smiling. 'Try not to worry.'

'Do you think I should tell my father?'

'I wouldn't. There's nothing to be told yet, as far as he is concerned. If you are having a child, you will know very soon.'

'I always tell him everything.'

'Not this time,' Maddy assured her. As Eve went, she watched the young woman go across to the horse and trap. She looked as though she had aged twenty years since the last time Maddy had seen her.

Thirty-Three

Back at the safe house – that was what they called it – one of the girls who lived there came in and said, 'I got taken on at the shop.'

Everybody crowded around her. She couldn't have been very old.

'It's just around the corner from here,' Nate explained to Ruth. 'They have everything. Sometimes they let us have stuff if it hasn't sold. Their daughter has up and gone with a man to Australia or somewhere, and they needed help, so we thought if we sent Bob here they might take her on.'

Other boys of Nate's age appeared that day. They had been on some kind of job and were able to provide food. Ruth was pleased that he was not the only lad who was helping. She expected Nate to ask her about the way that she had lived up to now, but he didn't ask much. It was part of the way that they lived, an unwritten code that you asked as little as you could stand. So she said nothing, but she was unhappy.

She had thought she could fade into the background here, but thinking as she was now about the foundling school brought back memories of the children and how much she had cared for them. She thought of how she missed especially

Pansy and Primrose and they would miss her. But she could not go back.

There were younger children here too, so instead of thinking about what she had left, she helped them. The older girls accepted her straight away; no doubt they were pleased with the help. It was only then that Ruth saw how much she had learned from the nuns.

She got the fire going and she instructed the boys to shop, not steal, since they had some money. When they came back, she made a huge pan of porridge. She put water on to boil and washed the children's faces and hands. She kept the fire going and sat them on her knee, and wiped away their tears and told them stories. She was glad to be able to help.

The thing they had really lacked here was direction and hope, and she was able to give them that. The boys came back with other things, such as clothes for the children. She didn't like to ask whether they had stolen them. One boy had been to the quayside market where old clothes were sold and had come back with great armfuls of blankets and woollen garments. Every time they went out, they brought things in. Part of it was to please her, she thought, but they had just needed somebody to lift them that little bit on to a different plane.

They needed money. She wondered how she would get proper help for them. In the meanwhile, there were now books, and she had taught them how to get the stove burning and keep it going. One lad had got a job working for a local coalman, which solved a huge problem. He had gone and asked and been taken on, he told her.

'Well done, Billy,' Ruth said.

Billy looked about the same age as Nate and although he was skinny, she thought he looked strong. He was so proud of what he had done. Better still, the lads brought the money to her that they made, because she knew what best to do with it. She lit fires in the other rooms so that the children could spread out and sit around. She wanted beds for them, but there was no point in them going upstairs to cold rooms. She got the lads to bring lots of blankets so that the youngest, most delicate children could lie on the floor in comfort.

The very small ones she fed. To her surprise, Poppy came to her and said roughly, 'I can do that.' So Ruth gave her the feeding of the children; she was good at it and pleased with herself, Ruth thought, by the look on her face.

After the first day, she could hear Poppy talking softly to them.

In the evenings, Ruth gathered them around her and told them what life in the dale was like. The good bits, obviously, all about sheep and cows. She told them about the nuns and the goat and how Sister Abigail had wanted to sell the golden candlesticks from the altar. She wasn't sure they understood this; they knew nothing about Jesus. So she began to tell them Bible stories, just as she had heard them.

'You keep thinking about something,' Nate said to her two days later. 'Is it where you came from?'

So she told him about the nuns – in particular about Sister Maddy – and how they had helped her.

'Isn't that what they are meant for?'

'Don't they help you here?'

'There are so many people that those who want to help can't cope. So we have to help ourselves. Why don't you go to her?'

'You want rid of me?'

'I don't understand how I couldn't do all you've done in just a few days, but I couldn't. It looked obvious when you did it, but before that there were so many problems I couldn't sort out.'

'The nuns taught me. And you had most things in place; look at Billy, he just needed a sort of kick, and the others too.'

'But you organised it. I can't do that.'

'You can't expect to do everything yourself,' Ruth said.

'I'm worried that you'll leave now,' Nate said.

She didn't want to go. She didn't know what she wanted, just that helping these people – who were ready to go on and help themselves, but needed just a little aid – was enough for now.

Later she and Nate went out and sat down on the edge of the dock. She had become almost comfortable here with him. He knew nearly everybody, and nobody bothered him and he bothered nobody. He would have been happy sitting there in the spring sunshine for a lot longer, she thought. She really liked him, not just as a lad, but possibly as the man he might become. Now that she was beginning to know him, she thought he had only two speeds, relaxed and running. She had never seen anybody move so fast when he needed to, nor keep so still when he didn't.

So they just went on sitting. She didn't know she was going to say it until she murmured, 'I killed four men.'

Nate looked out across the Tyne at Gateshead and then he sighed.

'Knocked them down, did you?' he said with some scorn. Ruth was amazed he didn't believe her.

'I killed my dad with a knife because he – he did things to me. The other three died down a pit.'

'You couldn't have killed anybody, you're too little.'

'I kept putting the knife into him until he stopped trying to hurt me.'

'Sounds like sense to me,' Nate said.

'But I shouldn't have killed him, and I did. For a while I kidded myself that I hadn't, but I think now more and more that I did.'

Nate said nothing to that.

'It was a sin. You go to hell for killing people,' she said.

Nate finally looked at her.

'If things were that simple, it would be different. Wasn't he trying to kill you?'

'No, just have his way with me. I was almost full term with his bairn.' It was the first time she had said this, and as the words came tumbling from her mouth, it seemed that a huge stone rolled away from her. It had not just been the child that was heavy, but the feelings about losing it. How awful, how she had not wanted it, and then had wished it was hers. But it had been his and he was so awful.

'Just?' Nate said. 'He "just" wanted his way? You were his child.'

She cried. She sat there on the edge of the dock and cried until she couldn't see anything.

Nate didn't do anything and he didn't say anything. The sun was way up in the sky and the seagulls were squawking. The seamen never took any notice of anybody, they were busy. She thought that she would never forget the sound of those seagulls as the burden in her mind eased. It was possibly the most wonderful sound that she had ever heard. And she loved the way that he just sat there with her while the sun glinted on the river.

'If you do go to hell,' Nate said after a long time, 'you're going to have a bloody big company, cos we'll all go after the flaming life we've had. God should do better by us.'

He made her smile; he was so down to earth, so practical. Her sight cleared. She watched the gulls; they were diving clean and straight into the water after fish.

'What about the other three?' Nate said. 'You couldn't have killed them all. What are you, some kind of killing machine?'

'It was an accident. They died down the pit when the roof fell in.'

'And you were holding the roof up?'

'No! No, I just . . .' She couldn't say it, she couldn't say it ever, but he went on looking and looking at her.

'It was my fault. This man, he was going to get married, and I didn't want him to and – it sounds daft now – I prayed to God that he wouldn't be able to. When the pit fell in, he had to stay and sort things out and she ran away with another feller.'

Nate sighed.

'You and God need to get your act sorted out,' he said finally.

That made her smile again – not externally, but more into her own body. He was making her feel better somehow.

'How could that possibly be right?' he said. 'If God was listening to anybody, he would put things right. He certainly wouldn't be listening to one little lost lass like you. You fancied this feller, then?'

She had never told anybody how she felt about Jay, but she could so easily now.

'I love him. He'll never want me because of what I am, and I just couldn't stand it anymore. I did that to him; I spoiled all his life.'

'No, you didn't. You couldn't have. You couldn't have caused any of that. You just weren't thinking properly, that's all.'

Nate was almost smiling at the sun on the river; little gleams of light danced on the water and he was apparently mesmerised.

She felt suddenly so very good, as though things were a lot better. Even though nothing had changed, everything had – how she felt had changed. He was right. It was not her fault, how could it have been? She was a very small cog in a very big wheel. Who had told her that? She didn't remember now, but it was true. Everybody was small.

'You don't get it, do you?' he said. 'Look at that sunbeam, how it alters the water. That's what God is. That's what he does and we get to see it. And look at the way that the breeze moves the water.'

Ruth gazed at it.

'The summer's coming,' Nate said. 'And we get to see it.'

Thirty-Four

The letter came back from Newcastle, and Mother was so positive and helpful, as she always was. Sister Bee was already better from being shown the letter. After that, she got better every day in her desire for the home she had loved best. Her eyes lit and she smiled and thanked Maddy. She was even able to get out of bed, though the others would not allow her to do anything.

'I'm worried anyroad,' Abigail said confidentially to Maddy when they were for once alone in the kitchen. Hilary had gone off to shoot rabbits with Mr Nattrass.

'He has pheasants,' Hilary had said, 'but he says they are so beautiful he can't shoot them. They taste very nice.' Mr Nattrass liked the glossy birds with their long tails and iridescent feathers, all green and brown, and so odd up there in the middle of no place, like some kind of far-eastern foreigners.

'About what?' Maddy said.

'About who we'll get to replace Sister Bee. It could be anybody; it could be that Sister Precious. Do you remember her?' They had called her that because she was very fussy and nobody ever got anything right for her. They had all hated working with her, even in the garden. Maddy had liked the garden unless Sister

Precious was there, because she questioned everything you did, even when you knew more than she did.

'She isn't there anymore. She went off to Darlington.'

'She might come back just to upset us. We're just getting settled here, we don't want some interfering cow—'

'Abigail!'

'Well, you know what I mean. Sister Bee might have had some crabby ideas, but at least she cared for us and for everybody here. Her heart was in the right place and she could be talked round. What if we get some nun who won't be talked round and has strict ideas? A lot of convents are like that, you know.'

'Which is why we aren't there.'

'I think praying all day is all very well if you feel closer to God, but there are things that need to be done,' Abigail said and Maddy thought she couldn't have put it better. She was also worried. There were a number of nuns back at the convent who Mother might think suitable and she went through them when she tried to sleep. She must do her duty, she kept telling herself, remember her vows and do her best. But it was very difficult, not knowing what sort of person they would end up with, when they had tried so hard and done so well.

Also she did not think Jay would take kindly to a nun telling him how to run his town and some of them were capable of it, she knew. That was one thing Sister Bee had backed away from, cleverly letting Maddy go to him. She must have been aware instinctively that they had some rapport between them, even though Maddy had very much disliked spending time with him at first.

The convent seemed smaller than Maddy remembered, but she was so pleased when Sister Bee got down from the cab and could not contain the beaming smile on her face. Newcastle had been a shock to Maddy, and to her horror, she remembered the ghastly house by the river where her father had left her in poverty, and she had not had the sense to marry Jay when he had asked her.

She didn't really think she had loved her father so very much, but perhaps she had. Perhaps you could not get beyond parenting and nurture. Her father ought to have been more generous, but then what father could have looked at Jay and thought he would make a good husband to an only child in such apparently elevated circumstances?

Nobody could ever have been good enough, and Jay was what they called an upstart, a gutter child. He had come from nowhere. The thing about people who came from nowhere was that you were never quite sure how far they would go. Jay had gone a very long way.

Mother welcomed them back and they were soon comfortably housed. Sister Bee was already so much better that you would think she had not been ill at all. Maddy would have excused this, but Mother said, 'I understand. It was a mistake for me to send her there, but I thought it was the right thing to do. One must admit when one is wrong and I was.'

'But who would you have sent?' Maddy said, thinking she might glean who was to be next to come back to the wilds of Durham with her.

Mother frowned.

'I don't know. I have thought about it a great deal, and I think it must be a special person to do such work. Somebody very strong. I know how hard it is in such places. You have done wonderful things there, all of you, but especially the three of you, considering how poorly Sister Bee has been. I can't believe that you have achieved so much.'

Maddy hadn't looked at it like that; she only saw what they had not achieved.

'Your letters told me so much,' Mother said.

She had not known that either.

'You told me about the school, the clinics and the butterfly house, and how good Mr Gilbraith has been. You took on the children, and kept them there in your orphanage and got the foundling school going – not just for the children you were housing, but for the entire village.

'You have done so very much more than I ever envisaged; I want you to know that. Your letters are dear to me. Your stories about the goat and about Sister Hilary shooting pigeons made me laugh to the point where I read out your letters over dinner to the other sisters. I didn't think you would mind. They cheered us enormously and I think they drove all of us to try to do better. We have achieved more because of what you did there.'

Maddy couldn't think of a single thing to say. She was inclined to weep but she tried not to, because Mother was always so kind. Everything she did she did for others, to bring everyone on to strive for better things, to do good so that other people would benefit. Mother was a brilliant business person and a fine leader.

'I should like you to spend the first of these few days telling the other sisters about your life, and then not do much else. Think of it as a retreat. You need time and a little outdoor life in the city, to wander beyond the convent walls and see how it is. How it is like what you left, and unlike what you left, and judge it then. You will be thinking of your mother and especially your father and of the house you lived in. I think if you walk a little and sleep and eat, then you will feel able to go back.'

Going back was not going to be easy, she thought. Ruth had left the village and they had lost Sister Bee and if they were given a difficult nun to lead them, it would cause a whole new spate of problems, she thought. She would have to talk to Jay and make sure he understood. She was determined to go forward and make the best of everything.

Already she missed Hilary and Abigail and the whole place: all the children and the life they had built there.

She kept running through the order of nuns and was horrified by the idea of taking back any of them to rule over Abigail and Hilary and herself. They were used to the city, and although they would know their duty – to do what Mother bid them but with a huge amount of licence – it could be worse than having Sister Bee ill. Then she was ashamed of herself; that was not Sister Bee's fault. It had been nobody's fault. Ease was not their goal.

After that, she took Mother's advice and ventured into the city. It felt so strange. After being in the new village, where everybody had work, where everybody had a house, she was appalled to see how poor the streets in the city were. She could see how hard Mother, and the nuns helping her, worked to combat the poverty and the bad housing and the dark alleyways.

She could not help thinking of the air up on the tops, so clear and free from the stench of unwashed bodies. So many people here wore rags during these sharp spring days. She began to long for the home she had made. She was surprised and then rather grateful that she had such a place to go back to.

She wandered all over the city. She went to her parents' graves, but unsurprisingly found nothing there to make her feel positive. She went into the prosperous housing areas and then down the main shopping area, but she was more drawn to the poor streets, though she could do nothing practical to help.

It was a very cold day and only those people who had to be were on the streets. Worse than that, it began to snow. It might be a blizzard in the new town. She wondered if Hilary and Abigail missed her; she could not believe how much she missed them. That was her home now, this was her parents' home. It made her feel glad that in a few more days she would be back there.

Thirty-Five

Eve thought she had never been so glad of anything as when her monthly bleeding arrived. She sat on the bed and cried. She was so grateful and so thankful that apparently she had got off lightly for what she had done. Because she couldn't talk to her father or Mrs Florence, she thought she would ride up to the village and tell Sister Madeline and thank her for the help. But when she got up to the village and was about to dismount outside the butterfly house, the first person she saw was Jay.

She wanted to get back on to her horse and ride away, but he had already seen her. So she got down from her horse and went over to where he was standing just outside the fell-side house. She tried not to see the house; it brought back so many awful memories. But she owed him this much. She also couldn't look straight at him, though she tried.

'Eve,' he said, rather stiffly, she thought. 'How are you?'

Then she made herself look at him and she thought he didn't look as bad as she had thought, maybe thinner and a little bit older. He was trying to smile so she tried too.

'I've been better,' she admitted. 'How about you?'

'The same. Will you come to the house?'

She hesitated and said nothing, but they started to walk

towards the house. When he shouted, a young man came out and took the horse from her.

Inside, he introduced her to his new housekeeper. The woman was much too polite to look surprised, Eve thought, that he was bringing in the woman who had jilted him and run away with another man.

They went into the sitting room. It was almost spring up here on the tops and for once it was a fine day. Eve didn't regret the house or him, though she did feel ashamed for what she had done. The place was more comfortably furnished than she had ever imagined it would be; there were lots of tables and easy chairs and even a piano. There was a big ginger cat lying by the fire asleep. That made her want to smile – despite everything it had become a home.

'Jay, I want to say that I am so very sorry.' She met his gaze again once the housekeeper had left the room.

'Don't be,' he said, and he sounded better, almost relaxed. 'You were right. It would have been a disaster.'

'I wasn't right to run away and leave you like that. It was an awful thing to do.'

'It would have been worse if we'd got to Paris and then you decided you didn't like me. I don't quite understand what you're doing back here. I knew your father went for you. So what went wrong?'

'Again, you mean?'

They sat down but she found the words coming out anyway. 'I thought I loved him, but then I discovered that he was very immature and selfish, and I wasn't much better. His family is poor; he is the only son and he has to marry for money. I don't have any, of course, but I had imagined castles in the air in both cases. How ridiculous. Nobody has that.'

'So what will you do?'

'I don't know. Dwindle into an old maid.' She brought herself up short on that word; she couldn't honestly claim even that anymore.

'Not much of a prospect.'

'Things could have been worse.'

He was looking so hard at her that for a few moments she thought he was going to ask if they could get married, despite what had happened and what he had said. But the thought went as fast as it had arrived. He would never do that, and she would never want him to.

'The problem is the same though, isn't it?'

'What do you mean?'

'You don't like it here, you needed to get away and you made two vain attempts.'

Eve winced. To hear it put as starkly as that hurt.

'Don't,' she said.

'But it's true. You need to be somewhere there is life for you. There is nobody like you here. Between industrial villages and dale families, you just don't fit. And you have always had problems at home, with your father not there most of the time and almost always distracted, and your mother ill for so many years. Perhaps you need to look at it differently.'

'How do you mean?'

'Well, I have some friends who live in Newcastle and they have daughters about your age. They're cultured people and well off. I just wondered if maybe that was part of the solution.'

She stared at him.

'For you to go and stay with them,' he said.

Eve couldn't believe her ears. He was offering to help, after all she had done. She couldn't stop looking at him. She thought that if she did, she might cry, and she had done so much crying lately that she would never get wrinkles. This of course was his business: he saw problems and then he found solutions to them.

'Nobody would have me after what I've done.'

'They don't care about such things, they're French.'

That made her laugh.

'It's true. Colette left her first husband and ran off with Michel, and when her first husband died, they were married. They had two children by then. They're very open-minded. They often go to Italy or Spain; they do a lot of travelling within Europe. But they come home sometimes and spend the summers here while the weather is good. Would you like me to write to them and see whether they can help?'

'I would have to ask Papa,' she said, breathless with excitement from the whole idea, but unable to believe it might happen.

'I could do that if you like.'

She couldn't breathe for sudden tears at the idea of getting another chance. She felt that she didn't deserve this.

'You must write to them first though, because they may not want me.'

'I'm sure they would love to have you.'

Eve gave a little sob and then felt very foolish.

When her father finally got home that evening, he looked even more tired than usual. She felt guilty because she had been most of the cause, but he smiled at her.

'Yes, I have been talking to Jay, and of course you may go if they invite you.'

Eve threw herself into his arms.

'Thank you so very much, Papa,' she said.

The following day Eve had a letter. It seemed so appropriate somehow, but it left her feeling mixed and odd. She was unsettled all over again.

London
Thursday

Dear Eve,

I am so terribly sorry for betraying your trust and your father's belief in me. I shall always love you. I know that sounds crass since I am to be married to the lovely Cynthia, courtesy of her family and mine. She is considered by both families to be a suitable girl; I feel I must do it. You were right, I am no hero. I'm so sorry that I caused you such problems. I really did and do love you and probably always will.

I would do almost anything to be with you, but I cannot. I'm sure you understand. But most of all, I must say how sorry I am that I behaved like a desperate idiot, talking of stupid things which could never be.

I would not really have asked you to sell your house, or upset your father or put your mother through anything more than what she already has to endure. That was just a momentary lapse. I was so keen for us to be together and I hadn't thought properly about it. Forgive me. I can only redeem myself by saying that the temporary madness was caused by how I felt for you. I have never felt like that for another human being and probably never will again. I was so desperate to have you for my wife. I think I will always feel as though we ought to be married. And that had I been older and qualified and in charge of my own life, it would have happened. I hope that you are no worse for having loved me. I am so very sorry for what I did to you and your family and not less to mine. If there should be problems concerned with what we did, you must let me know and I will try to put them right.

Yours as ever,

N.E.

He was to marry a suitable girl, what a ghastly idea. How were people ever to make progress if all their sons married suitable girls? But then he had no money and a big family and that was what happened. Eve could imagine Cynthia, beautiful and obedient, who would doubtless and hopefully bear him a great many sons. She would say the right things and be there for him, in Eve's father's words, for him to go home to.

At first she wanted to cry, and then she thought Noel spineless. Then she thought how good he was to have bothered to tell her what was happening, and how he was still thinking of her.

He also told her that he had really cared for her, and that if there had been a child, he would have tried to help. Though she didn't think she would ever have told him; he lacked imagination of how their marriage would ever have come back with such things against it. But when you fell in love, nothing else came within sight. Everything was pushed back so very far that it left you blind.

She could have been left here to measure out her days in coffee mornings and Bible classes and other people's children. The whole idea of it made her want to shudder. She hoped and hoped that Jay's friends would help her now; if not she could not imagine how she would live.

Dear Colette and Michel,
I am sorry I have not been in touch since Hallam's funeral, but I want
you to know that I was grateful to see you there.

I need a favour. I'm sure, though we didn't discuss it, you would
see that the young woman I was engaged to, Eve Gray, was not at
the funeral. Since the wedding was cancelled, you must know that we
are not married.

She ran away with the apprentice doctor, Mr Esher. I feel so guilty
over Eve. She needed an escape and when I couldn't supply it, she ran
away. I don't blame her. I was captivated by her looks, which I know is
ridiculous, but I kept putting off the wedding. Although I feel stupid
now, I didn't realise at the time that I didn't want to marry her, and
she didn't want to marry me. I was a way out for her and perhaps, in
another way, she was for me.

I couldn't even be angry; I knew it was my own fault. I was so
caught up in the village I am building that I forgot she wanted to go
to other places and see other things. I kept putting off the idea that
we would go abroad. And after Hallam died, I was so shocked that
I didn't reassure her as I should have done that we would be married
as soon as possible. I think that was when I realised that she would
never mean as much to me as Wesley Hallam did.

She has had a hard life in a lot of ways. She has no one to
talk to, her mother is strange and mad, and her father, a doctor,
is always too busy for her. Perhaps his work keeps him sane amid
his problems at home. She is very intelligent and needs to be with
people like herself.

She and Noel were not allowed to marry. He was the only son
and needed to marry money and Eve has none. Now she is back in
Wolsingham in disgrace, her father having travelled to London to
bring her home. She has no life here in this insular little world, which
is all the dale provides for people such as her. I feel that it is time for

her to be given the chance to see some of the rest of the world and how it operates.

I wondered if you feel you could ask her to come and stay with you. She is good company and very clever. You lead such interesting lives, quite unlike the way that things are done here, and know a great many people from different cultures and backgrounds. She is stifled here and doesn't know what she will do now. Goodness knows what she might gain, given the company of open-minded, educated people.

I am aware that you have done this before for other people, or I would not have asked you to help her now. Just a few weeks would make a huge difference. She would love to be able to read new authors, go to theatres and concerts such as you do, and spend her time in the city. It would at least give her a chance, away from the judgement of folk with archaic attitudes. If you could offer her another view of life, even just for a short time, I think she would benefit hugely. Let me know what you think, and if you agree, I will bring her to Newcastle.

I am sure you will consider this vulgar, but her father has put all his money back into the practice, which includes my village, so I will be happy to pay generously for all she needs. You will tell her nothing but some excuse which comes to mind at the time. In fact, you must tell her that her father is providing, should she need to know, which I think she will not. I shall tell him that he is not to do this; I hope he will accept it.

Yours affectionately,

JG

Jay knew from when he called in at the foundling school that Maddy had gone to take Sister Bee back to Newcastle. That they would be in Newcastle at the same time seemed odd to him, but Michel had written back immediately and told him to bring Eve to them; they would be glad to see her. Since he thought it best to get Eve away, they left as soon as her bags could be packed. He could see the relief on her face as she got away.

He thought he was pleased to go too, but he wasn't sure why. Perhaps he felt better about Eve because he was doing what he thought would be the right thing for her after he had made so many blunders. But he didn't know what he thought about seeing Maddy in Newcastle. Last time they had met there, he had asked her to marry him, had been very much in love. Since seeing her as a nun, he had thought so differently about her. But in Newcastle perhaps he would remember feelings which he had thought long fled. So it was with very mixed ideas that he went home.

Also he didn't need to remind himself that he didn't remember Newcastle without Hallam, so that was another hardship. But the look on Eve's face almost made up for it. She was so excited. He didn't think he had seen her like that since he first asked her to marry him. She was beautiful again.

Michel and Colette lived in Jesmond, in a very big house set in its own grounds. He had no idea whether Michel had inherited his money. Jay thought he had ancestry which went back a very long way, because Michel always assumed he was the most aristocratic person in the room. Hallam had always teased Michel and told him that he chose to set down roots in Newcastle because he was almost always the only aristocrat in the room. It had made Michel laugh. Hallam didn't like many people, but Colette and Michel had loved him. When Jay got there with Eve in tow, Colette had tears in her eyes. Later when he was alone with Michel, they talked about Hallam and recalled happy times.

They had two daughters of about Eve's age and usually took them to Italy in the spring. Michel promised they would take Eve if she would like to go. Jay told him that she would be entranced. Colette assured him that Eve would need a good many new clothes and all that first day Eve was shining with happiness. Jay almost forgave himself for the hurts he had inflicted on her.

'Such a beautiful girl,' Michel said as they sat in his library later, drinking brandy and smoking cigars. Jay rarely did such a thing, but he enjoyed the library fire and his friend's company. He knew that Michel and Colette wished he had not left to set up the new village, but had been too kind to say so.

Jay told him about meeting Maddy again and how she had become a nun. Michel shuddered and shook his head, but since his family was Catholic, Jay knew that he didn't mean it. It was just that he knew the story of Maddy's awful father and her poverty, and how unhappy she had made Jay when she wouldn't marry him.

'You must find someone who wants to marry you, my friend,' Michel said, only half in jest.

'I've given up,' Jay said. 'I don't care anymore.'

Michel looked down into his glass and then he said, 'We miss Wesley. Colette was always half in love with him. She thought he was – dangerous.'

'And I turned out to be the dangerous one.'

Michel shrugged.

'He would not have missed any of it. These things happen. We miss you both. You must come back to Newcastle more often. In the meanwhile, we are going to show little Miss Gray a wonderful time. My daughters have huge plans for her.'

Eve liked the house and the family, Jay could see. When they parted, she kissed him and thanked him. Jay hoped that she would find somebody or something which mattered to her, and that next time she came to the village, it would just be to visit, and she would be glad to be there because it would only be temporary. Some people never fit, he thought. He hoped she might find her future here, either with a man she might meet, or some other purpose.

Jay went back to the streets where he had grown up. He wasn't sure that it was a good idea; everywhere he looked he imagined Hallam. The streets hadn't changed for the better: there were still so many poor folk with nowhere to go. Maybe he should have done something here. Then he thought, no, it wasn't the right place. He had to set up something new, which he could manage; he wanted to give work to people and make money and for them to be as happy as they could be. Newcastle was too advanced for that, poverty spilling everywhere.

He went down to the quayside on Sunday and saw the market, clothes and blankets spread everywhere and people haggling. He turned towards the river and it seemed then to him that he imagined Hallam nearby. It was a very strange feeling. But the person was too young, not quite properly grown, even though he was almost six feet tall. Hallam had been very tall too. Jay turned again to the market and when he looked back, the idea vanished. There was nobody in sight who looked anything like Hallam. It was just that he wished he could see Hallam.

He glanced about him and there were a lot of people. Then in the distance he saw the same lad; he walked like Hallam, stood like him. Jay tried not to be too brisk; it was nothing but his stupid memory, his longings. He lost sight of the lad again but no, there he was, turning a corner, up into the next street away from the river. Jay went after him. Up the hill and then he was gone again. Jay turned, hearing something, and there he was: the lad, looking

Jay squarely in the eyes. Jay couldn't believe how much like Hallam he looked.

'So.' The lad stood very tall, confident, sure of himself. And he had to be, this was his town. It was almost amusing. And the more Jay looked, the more he was convinced that this lad must be Hallam's son. His poor heart rejoiced. Jay thought that he and Hallam had stood like that. This had been their town. 'You following me?'

'Yes. You remind me of somebody.'

'Is that right? Your mother, maybe?'

Jay shook his head and tried not to smile. 'Not exactly. A friend of mine.'

'I'm a bit young to be a friend of yours, unless you had summat else in mind, and believe me, it isn't going to get you any place so bugger off.'

'Hang on—'

The lad stood back but Jay was undeceived. He would be carrying a knife, you always did, and this lad would know very well how to use it. And judging by his eyes, he had done so before.

'Wesley Hallam,' Jay said.

'Ah yes, he was a legend.'

'He died a while back.'

'I didn't know.'

'And I'm Jay Gilbraith.'

'I heard about you too, but you shouldn't go following people around. You could get your throat slit, and you aren't young anymore, or fast, I'm thinking.'

'True. But you look like him.'

The lad's gaze was like flint.

'Well, that's just a likeness thing, isn't it? Lots of people belong here. It doesn't mean anything.'

'Do you have a father?'

'So my mother told me. I never met him. You think Hallam screwed my mother?'

'I don't know.'

'Well, I don't think so. I'm sure your mothers were whores, but mine wasn't, so not very likely.'

'I didn't mean to be insulting. Forgive me.'

Jay backed off. It was the sensible thing to do. The lad had caught him where he could be killed easily or wounded badly and pushed down an alley. There were plenty of them around there. As he did so, the boy merely strolled away, and that was when Jay caught a flash of red hair from around the corner.

He saw her, tiny and exquisite, laughing up into the lad's face and saying,

'Nate, where have you been?' The lad caught her up and together they ran away.

By the time Jay reached the corner, they had gone. People of that age, he thought, feeling old for the first time, were so fleet of foot they didn't think about it.

He followed all the streets, but it didn't matter. In that area, there were so many ways to get to places. He had once known them all, but now he was too slow and could find nothing.

He made his way back to Jesmond for dinner, but the following day he went to the convent to talk to Maddy.

Jay hadn't been anywhere near the convent before, though he knew its reputation for good works and teaching, and how many people they had helped. He was stopped by a very polite nun at the stone entrance, and after a little while of waiting, he was taken inside and into a small, rather friendly room with a fire and the smell of coffee. He had a wait of ten minutes before Maddy came into the room. She looked startled.

'I didn't know you were here,' she said, as though they had met yesterday.

He liked that about her. In his mind she was the Maddy of old, and her habit, her clothes, didn't make any difference. She was the first woman that he had loved; perhaps the only woman he had ever truly loved. He loved her lack of formality. They lived almost as closely together as some married people did, and she chose not to hide her affection for him. It came through now and she smiled at him. Her eyes lit as though they had a lot in common and secrets together. And they had a whole village, he thought.

'I don't mean to intrude,' was the only thing he could think to say.

'You're not intruding. Sit down. I didn't know you were in Newcastle.' They sat down and she said, 'Does it feel strange without Wesley?'

Everywhere felt strange without Wesley, but it was so kind and typical of her to ask.

'It feels strange without you as well, somehow. Sorry.' He kept saying things he didn't intend to say – she always had that effect on him.

'No, no, I understand. I've thought a lot about you as soon as I got here – well, even before. It's been a long time since we were in the city together.'

'How's Sister Bee?'

'Already a lot better.'

Jay told her about bringing Eve here and Maddy told him that she thought it was an excellent notion. After that, he leaned nearer, as though somebody might be listening – though why they would, he had no idea – and said, 'I've seen Ruth.'

Maddy didn't seem to take this in. She frowned. 'Here in Newcastle?' she said.

'Yes.'

'What would she be doing here?'

'I have no idea. That's why I came to see you.'

'As far as I know, she has no connections. She only knows the dale.'

'Well, she's keeping company with a lad that looks exactly like Wesley,' he said.

If Maddy could have looked any more keenly at him, he thought she would have done.

'Are you sure it was her?' Maddy said.

He smiled at her. She didn't dare to think that the girl who had run off had been found.

'Oh, come on,' he said, smiling even more widely at being able to reassure her. 'She's unmistakable. I only saw her for a few brief moments, but she said his name and she laughed. It was definitely Ruth.'

'Do you know where they went?'

He shook his head.

'Didn't you go after them?'

He looked quizzically at her. 'They were around the corner in seconds and ran away.'

'From you?'

'I'm not sure. Maybe they just go on like that. Young people do. Everything's too slow for them and I certainly was. I haven't been that quick since I was on the streets here myself.'

That made Maddy smile for a few seconds.

'Did she seem happy?'

Jay was pleased at Maddy's hungry face and how he was managing to fill it with light by what he said.

'Very. She called him by his name and laughed up into his face.'

'I would like to see her.'

'I would like to see them both, but I have no idea how we could go about it.'

'The bloke I was with—' Nate stopped there, not sure how to go on or whether to.

'What bloke?' Ruth asked.

He loved how she looked up at him with such loving trusting eyes. Nobody had ever looked at him like that and it made him want to dance and sing but if this was the bloke she cared for then his claim on her, fragile as it was, might be gone forever.

'Didn't you see him?'

'I didn't see anybody in particular.'

'He was Gilbraith.'

Ruth stared.

'You knew Gilbraith and Hallam? It was their village you went to and the nuns helped you there.'

'So did he. He did everything for me.'

Nate looked hard at her. 'It was him? The man you liked so much?'

'I love him.'

'He's old.'

'He's not that old.'

'He's middle-aged. He couldn't run after me.'

'Maybe he didn't choose to.'

'You liked a man that old?'

'I love him.'

'Oh my God,' Nate said, wanting to run away and unable to while she looked so earnestly into his eyes. 'Is it because he's rich?'

'Don't be stupid, Nathan.'

'And clever?'

'He rescued me.'

'Oh God, the knight in shining armour,' Nate said.

'Did he tell you where he's staying?'

'Oh, yes, I said to him, "By the way, I've got this lass around me that dead fancies you and she wants to find out where you are".'

'It was never like that.'

'It's very like that, lasses your age and blokes like him.'

'He would never do such a thing and I would like to remind you that I would have died if he hadn't found me.'

Nate found that he had had enough of this conversation and walked ahead.

'What?' she said, running after him and pulling at his sleeve.

He stopped. 'Do you want to marry him?' Nate stared straight at her until she looked to the side and for a short while there was silence. It felt to him like a long silence, but it wasn't really, it was just that he didn't want to hear what the answer might be.

'He would never do that.'

'What then?'

'Nothing. Oh, I see. You think he had me.'

'I think he might have done.'

'He didn't.' Her face was hard when she spoke and Nate was so glad of her sapphire eyes, glinting with temper. 'Nobody has ever touched me, not even you. Only my wretched father.'

'What do you mean, not even me?' He was beginning to feel hopeful in spite of everything.

'Well, you could have. We spend a lot of time together.'

'Maybe I just don't fancy you.'

'All right then,' she said, and she walked ahead of him, as though she didn't care, but he knew now that that wasn't so.

Nobody said anything for about ten minutes and then he came in front of her and said, 'I'm sorry, all right?'

She didn't reply.

'Ruth? I'm sorry.'

'As though you haven't touched anybody,' she said, almost spitting at him.

'I didn't say that.'

'Poppy?'

'Not Poppy. Not anybody recently.' Nate couldn't look at her. He wished he could have said no, but there had been times in his life when he had needed somebody close or they had needed him close or he needed the money and could find no other way of coming by it. He was ashamed of some of it, but he couldn't help being who he was. He was doing his best.

'Recently, how old are you?' she insisted.

'It's nothing to do with that. You do what you have to to get by. All right?'

She thought of her father and how awful it had been. Even now it made her feel sick.

'Women you didn't care for?'

Nate hesitated. 'Sometimes. Did you think you were the only one?'

Nobody said anything more, but they went on together and after a little while she caught hold of his fingers.

*

In the end, Jay hung around by the quayside, and on the first afternoon he saw the lad again. This time the boy had been waiting for him. Jay watched and saw that he didn't run away. He went over to him. The boy looked at him.

'Been watching for you,' he said, keen eyed and standing very tall. Jay admired his confidence and there again saw not just Wesley but himself in this lad. They were all so alike.

'Ruth wants to see me?' he guessed.

'Aye, she does. You can come with me.'

Jay walked with him at a steady pace as the streets grew poorer and poorer by the river. After about fifteen minutes or so, Nate led him into a building, a large place. There he saw the children by the fire; the smell of cooking was in the air. She was looking so different, so in charge, older somehow. The maturity in her face was such a surprise. She looked very happy like he had never seen her. She didn't quite meet his eyes at first, but when she did, he saw guilt and suffering too. And tears.

'Oh, Jay,' she said, and then she backed off slightly.

'We were so worried,' he told her softly. 'Sister Maddy is here. She brought Sister Bee back to the convent because she has been so poorly. She is so glad that you are here and that you are all right.'

'Shall I show you what we are doing?' She sounded so happy, so eager and so ready to let him see it all. 'It's like what you are doing, only more personal.'

She took him around and introduced him to the children. She told him about the plans that she and Nate had, about buying beds for the children, and more clothes, and how they were managing food. He told her that he would help.

'Does this mean that you aren't coming back then?' he said.

'Are you going back there with him?' Nate couldn't leave the subject alone; she could see right from the first. He was worried about it. More than that, he looked so wildly into her face that she was astonished. He couldn't even stand still while he was saying it; he walked about in sort of rings in agitation.

'Will you stand still?' she said.

He tried and then set off again. In the end, he ran outside, away from her. She followed him. Poppy was there and Edna, who was equally as good. Even though she hadn't been there long, she was a natural with children, and there was nothing she couldn't leave, so she went out after him. He hadn't gone far but he wouldn't look at her.

'He's rich and clever and not really that old,' Nate managed.

'Do you want me to stay here?'

That was when he turned, his face almost on fire with frustration.

'You what?' he said. 'Don't you know?'

'I don't know anything.'

'Yes, you do. I've never met anybody like you. I've never seen anybody take stuff and just alter it like you've got a magic wand. You have; you're magical in a funny sort of way. And so – so very beautiful, so very—' Nate stopped there. 'If you think it's the right thing to do, you should go back and we'll manage. We did manage before you got here.'

'Not very well.'

'No, not terribly well. But you've taught us a lot.'

'I ran away because I couldn't stay any longer after what I'd done to you,' she said to Jay now.

'To me?' Jay said in wonder.

'I thought it was my fault that you didn't get married. I told God to stop the wedding, and the men died and Miss Gray ran away—'

'Miss Gray is fine. She is here in Newcastle with some lovely people and they are taking her to Italy for the spring, and maybe summer too.'

'But you loved her?'

'Not really. I'm not very good at loving people; generally, yes, specifically, no.'

'I did kill my dad though.'

It was almost a question.

Jay sighed and then said, sort of all in a rush, 'Yes, you did. I thought if I told you outright, it might finish you off in those early days. You were so vulnerable. Not so now, though, eh? You look so different, so much older.'

'In charge, Nate calls it. I have started to get used to the idea that I really did kill him.'

'When it's kill or be killed, then you do.'

'I think it was. If you hadn't rescued me—'

'That was Phyllis,' he said.

She laughed. He thought how very beautiful she was when she laughed.

'The lovely Phyllis.'

'She's done me a lot of favours in my time, but I think that was the very best of them.'

She wasn't looking at him now.

'You made me love you,' she said softly, 'for what you did.'

Jay tried to be sensible and a little stern.

'Like you could have loved your dad, if he'd been a decent man.'

'I don't think so. I wanted us to be married. But I see now that it would have been a really stupid idea. I think we both know now that you aren't very good at such things. I suppose I would have put up with you for the house on the fell.'

Jay laughed with pleasure. He liked people who liked his house and he liked this girl so much that if she had been ten years older or he had been ten years younger he would have asked her to marry him, but she was right, it was a stupid idea and he didn't think he had anything to offer any woman and she deserved a great deal more.

'You really liked it?'

'I loved it. I think it's the most beautiful house in the whole world.'

Jay took her into his arms, and she closed her eyes against his shoulder.

'You didn't really kill anybody, Ruth. Those men risked their lives because that's what pitmen do, and your father was not the man he ought to have been. It was nothing to do with you. You've proved what a lovely person you are, and you should hang on to that.'

He let her go and she stood back, knocking the tears away with her sleeve like children did.

'Nate wants me to stay here with him and I think I will,' she said. 'He is so like Mr Hallam, isn't he?'

'Almost exactly, except that he seems to have a better temperament. Time will tell.'

'We're going to get married,' she said.

'Has he asked you?'

'No, but we are.'

'And you will bring him to the village so that I can get to know him?'

She nodded.

'I would like to see Sister Maddy,' she said.

Maddy was desperate to go home. She could no longer think of Newcastle as home. She longed for the sight of the school and of Hilary and Abigail and the children. But she was still worried about the idea of who would be put in charge. Mother had not said anything about which nun would be going back with her and she was worried about it. Whoever it was, it might make things even more difficult. They were used to the city. Although she tried to argue with herself that she too had not been out of the city before Mother had sent them up to the freezing wilds of Durham, and they had managed – well, three of them had – she could not be comfortable with any of it.

She was horrified by the idea of taking any of the nuns back with her. None of it would be easy. And then she was ashamed; ease was not their goal.

So when Mother called her into the office to talk to her, she was nervous. She dreaded being told that it was Sister Rhoda, who had the most irritating laugh in the world and did not seem capable of doing anything to which she was assigned – but she was very experienced and devout. Surely Mother would not burden her with Rhoda. Then there was Sister Vashti, who was born in the highlands and was obedient but sullen. Sister Martha never stopped talking and had an opinion of every other nun and didn't appear to like anybody.

As these thoughts flitted through her mind, Mother asked her to sit down. Then she said casually, 'So you and Mr Gilbraith have built a town together?'

It was so gently said that Maddy was already disturbed. She

knew Mother well and there was an important point coming. Did Mother think she had spent too much time with him? She decided to be frank.

'When I was twenty, he asked me to marry him. I was so devoted to my father that I refused. In some ways, I regret it; I am very fond of him. But I don't regret having joined the order. If I had married and been like other women, with a husband and children, just think how much I would have missed.' She decided to be completely truthful, because Mother always appreciated directness, so she added, 'I did think when I saw him again that perhaps I had made a mistake, but my father was a very difficult man and I don't think I want another man in my way. I've become very bossy.'

Mother smiled.

'But you work well together?'

'He lacks imagination with buildings.'

They talked and laughed about Abigail and the goat and Mr Nattrass and his pheasants. Mother's fine sense of humour must have rescued her from many a dull or difficult day, Maddy thought.

'Building is your special talent, in different kinds of ways,' Mother said. 'You are very talented people, which is why I sent you there. It sounds to me as though you are flourishing, learning to do a great many new things and accomplishing all manner of good works. I'm very proud of you all. So I'm going to ask you to do something even more difficult. Which I think if you had been less modest, you would have said you had been doing all along, because Sister Bee was not well from the start. But perhaps she needed to go there in order to reach this point in her life. You also did that for her, the three of you, and all the other people concerned. She needed to get that far and to admit that her grieving must begin, since she had never allowed it to happen before. She had been fighting against it all those years; no wonder she was so exhausted. It will take a long time before she is better, but being back here we will help her cope.

'I'm going to ask you to go back without giving you anyone else to assist. I can't spare anyone, and looking over the nuns here, I'm not sure you would be the better for having anyone else. I know you have a lot of help, and I know this is asking a great deal of you, but I think it is the right thing to do.'

Maddy was half pleased and half afraid, but she thought that Mother had made the right decision. She was ready to go back. There was just one thing that bothered her. She went into the chapel and prayed hard that Ruth would decide to come back with her. She didn't want to leave the girl behind. But she also told God that if it was the right thing and if Ruth was happy, then of course she must stay.

Now she changed her mind and panicked and didn't want to go back. Having been eager, but not knowing what would happen, she wished she could turn back time a couple of days, when she didn't have responsibility for anything, and it was all still in the balance.

It was the last night. The morning would bring real change. She stood outside the convent and just did some breathing. It was spring but not really. Here in the north it didn't seem to follow seasons as folk said it did in other places.

Jay took Maddy to see the safe house. Ruth came running across and Maddy beamed a smile at her. Ruth took her all around the place as she had done with Jay. She introduced her to Edna, who was very good with the children, and Poppy, saying that she was good with everything. Poppy smiled so much her face turned up. Most of the boys were out because most of them now had jobs of some kind. One was working in the market selling fruit and veg for a man they knew; Billy was a coalman.

Nate was not there.

'He said he would be,' Ruth said, looking past her at the door. 'But he hasn't met any nuns, so maybe he got scared.'

It was obvious to Maddy straight away that Nate had become very important over a short time. Suddenly Ruth's face brightened, and when Maddy turned, a tall young lad came in. He was a shock, though he shouldn't have been, because he did look exactly like Hallam. Jay wasn't looking at Maddy, but he didn't need to; there was enough feeling between them. She knew that this was either Hallam's nephew or his son, somebody very close. Maddy was pleased for all of them, but in particular for Ruth and also for Jay. This would make a huge difference. She must remember to thank God particularly in her prayers for this.

Nate was awkward. He had never spoken to a nun, she could see. But she smiled at him and asked him about the house as though Ruth had told her nothing. Ruth let him talk, but he talked about Ruth and the things she had done.

'You don't want her to go back with you?' he said while Ruth objected.

'Not if Ruth wants to stay here,' Maddy said, smiling at them both.

'I told you not to say that,' Ruth said.

'We could help,' Jay put in. 'I could put some money into this and other ventures you might have. You can come and see how we started a village, Nate, if you want to.'

Nate said he would and Ruth nodded, but Maddy was not sure they meant it. They would have to think, and in the end they were so very caught up in what they were doing that it might be enough for now. That was how Jay felt about his village. It was also how she felt about the foundling school; that it was hers — that she could go ahead and make decisions, and she would have Hilary and Abigail to help — but it was hers. Maybe everybody needed something like that.

Jay walked her back to the convent, and nobody said much. Somehow nobody needed to. They were going back the following day and she couldn't wait to get started.

Thirty-Six

Maddy had never thought she would be glad to get back to the village, but she became quite excited as soon as they set off. When they got as far as the school, Dobber and Bonny hurtled out to meet them and almost knocked her over.

Mr Nattrass whistled at the dogs to come back, but Maddy enjoyed the greeting.

Inside she was even happier with everything. It was clean and neat; there was the smell of stew and dumplings. Abigail was in the schoolroom with the children, but the lesson stopped straight away and soon Maddy was surrounded by children and a smiling Abigail. Hilary must have heard all the noise, because she came out of the kitchen wearing a huge apron, and told them with satisfaction that they were just in time to eat. It was perfect.

'So we get to run things?' was Hilary's contribution when they had eaten, and the fuss had died down. Jay had gone off to his house, keen to get on and find out what he had missed.

'Mother couldn't spare anybody else.'

'If Mother wasn't who she is, she would have been what you call a clever beggar,' Hilary said.

Maddy told them how happy Sister Bee had been to get back to the convent and how she already looked better. It had been the right thing to do. Abigail said she had worried.

'About us getting somebody I don't like. I know we are supposed to get on with things, but it's much easier without somebody like Sister Precious who thinks she knows everything.'

'We're a team,' Hilary said and Maddy liked that idea.

It was almost Easter. Maddy knew that as a nun she should prefer Easter to Christmas, but she didn't. Up here, Easter wasn't that much different from Christmas; if anything, the weather could be worse, and it was. She liked both the big festivals, but up here you usually got snow at Easter.

Mr Nattrass, being a sensible man, had brought all his ewes in lamb near his house. He had built a huge wooden shelter and it stopped him from having to pull them out of snow-drifts. Hilary said that she thought it was a very clever idea, but a lot of the farmers had a great many more sheep and it was impractical.

It snowed so hard for Easter Sunday that nobody could go anywhere beyond the village, and Maddy liked that. She liked what they called the hap up. It was an almost silent world and the little village was caught up in it, as many people imagined houses did at Christmas. She hated mild Christmases; it wasn't what it was all about up here in the north. Now they kept all the special offices for Easter, but it was Easter Sunday that she really loved.

Jay provided a feast that day for the whole of the village. He had stretched his resources to cover as many places as could take in a great number of people. The butterfly house and the fell house and the farmhouse were all ready for the villagers, who would go there after various church services and give thanks for the risen Christ, and that all was well in the world.

It wasn't usual, but Jay also provided various musicians to play all the old local tunes. He thought Hallam would have liked that. The snow just made things better.

After the meal Maddy and Jay, who were at the fell-side house, went outside. There Maddy found some snowdrops pushing through the whiteness; she saw the green leaves and the hope for the future, and she was glad. It would soon be the beginning of a new season. Spring was the most hopeful time of the year, she thought.

'I do think you ought to build us a proper church this summer,' she said. 'I know you do.'

'I mentioned it to you before?'

'At least a dozen times.'

'If I do that, I will have to build a church for the Protestants, and a chapel for the Methodists and there will be no end to it.'

'People need somewhere to worship.'

'They also need somewhere to live. When there are sufficient houses, I will think about churches.'

'The new Methodist minister wants a separate school.'

'He'll have to wait for it, then,' Jay said.

'I'm so glad I left Newcastle. It doesn't feel like home now.'

'I'm glad you said that. I wanted to feel like that too, but until now I have blamed myself about Wesley. I miss him.'

'I know. We always miss those people who have died and left us here. If you believe in heaven, you will see him again.'

'I believe in hell,' Jay said.

Maddy replied, 'Everybody does, even those who don't believe in heaven.'

The snow had stopped, the sky had cleared, and a million stars were out. Nothing in the blue-black sky could interrupt the shine of them, diamonds in velvet, light in the greatest darkness.

As they stood there, Dobber and Bonny and the Jack Russell came tumbling out of the house. Mr Nattrass was not far behind them but losing pace.

The dogs ran round and round under the stars and even Tiddles joined them. He sat beside Maddy as though they were old friends, and as cats do, he watched the dogs being really stupid, chasing their tails and one another and leaving great tracks in the snow and barking, destroying any mood which would have come out with the people.

Mr Nattrass put two fingers into his mouth and whistled so shrilly that all three dogs paused, stopped and came back to him. Maddy winced under the sound but the dogs ran to him, looking up at him, their tails wagging in joy. The moon was out, and Mr Nattrass fondled their ears and took them back inside.

Tiddles sat where he was.

'Tiddles,' Jay said, 'we are going in. After I have seen Sister Maddy to the school, I will be locking up the house. I know you like sleeping on Miss Proud's bed, so if you want to do that, you must come now.'

Tiddles therefore got up and followed them back to the school. Then he went with Jay to the house, but not too closely so that Jay should worry about him just a little. Jay looked back for him and Tiddles was pleased about it. And when they were all inside with the doors closed, the stars twinkled and the sky was so clear that a frost came down upon the land. There was shine all night over the fell and the sheep were cream against the blackness of the land. The only cries were of owls in the night, flitting between barns up there on the tops.

Acknowledgements

I would like to thank everybody at Quercus. Although it is my name on the front there are lots and lots of people involved in getting a book on to the shelves in libraries and shops and on the internet as an ebook. It's great having a force behind you, knowing that you are not really sitting there on your own, that people are labouring in London and at computers and it is indeed a team game from the cover designers and the printers to the folk who keep the publishing house as beautiful and welcoming as it is.

In particular I would like to thank my agent, Judith Murdoch, who spent a lot of time trying to get this novel to the stage where she thought my wonderful editor, Emily Yau, might find it acceptable. Emily did brilliant work and I am very grateful to her for her fantastic input.

Also Sharona Selby, who did the final edits, is such bliss to have around, inspired and trustworthy. Thanks to you all.

The Quarryman's Wife

When hope is lost, can she rebuild her home?

After her daughter Arabella passes away, leaving a poor, motherless child in her wake, Nell Almond doesn't think her life can get any worse. But then tragedy strikes a second time and she finds herself widowed, with her husband's quarry to manage.

But it's baby Frederick, her grandson, who troubles her most. Being cared for by one of the local families, he lives in hand-me-down clothes in a cramped and unrefined home.

Nell desperately wants him to return to his rightful place, as heir to the quarry, but should she put all her hopes in one child?

Quercus

The
Coal Miner's
Wife

Torn between love and duty . . .

When Vinia walked down the aisle she knew it was a marriage
of practicality: as the owner of the local pit, Joe could provide
her with a life of status. But her heart lies with another . . .

With gypsy blood in his veins and an intense passion
in his soul, Dryden has always held a torch for Vinia.
And with the death of his wife, he vows to make
good on the lost years when they were apart.

**Will Vinia find a new chance of happiness
or be forever destined to a loveless marriage?**

Quercus

Orphan Boy

He has no home to call his own.

Born to a mother who died in childbirth,
and to a father who could never truly love him,
Niall McAndrew grows up a solitary child, without a
home to call his own. His only friend is Bridget, a young
girl forced prematurely into womanhood. Niall has
brains, spirit and ambition, as well as devastating good
looks. He soon begins to make his own way in business,
and becomes famous throughout the Newcastle area
by befriending the wealthy and powerful mine-owner
Aulay Redpath and his beautiful daughter Caitlin.

**But Niall's loveless childhood has left its mark.
Can he ever find the personal happiness he yearns for?**

Quercus